An Exceptional Corpse

A Rolls-Royce careers off a mountain road on the Derbyshire moors, killing the driver, millionaire Sheffield businessman Richard Sutton, pillar of the community and the force behind a huge local industrial development. Freelance journalist Mike McLean is the first reporter on the scene and recognizes the man.

A post-mortem reveals a high blood-alcohol content and the police dismiss the crash as another drink-drive accident, but McLean starts to wonder when he discovers Sutton was a strict teetotaller. There was also a suspicious fire at the businessman's office on the night he died. Was there a connection? And why was Sutton's secretary so scared?

Before he can question the girl she is found dead in the canal and McLean himself is beaten up and warned off. Stubbornly, he persists in his inquiries, while still finding time to hold off Inland Revenue queries about his own dodgy tax affairs, annoy the police and attempt to bed his alluring accountant, Maria.

Gradually, he uncovers a trail of fraud, murder and blackmail which takes him from the derelict East End of Sheffield to the bleak hills of the Peak District and a desperate stand on the Iron Age fortress of Carl Wark.

PAUL ADAM

An Exceptional Corpse

THE CRIME CLUB

An Imprint of HarperCollins *Publishers*

First published in Great Britain in 1993
by The Crime Club, an imprint of
HarperCollins Publishers, 77–85 Fulham Palace Road,
Hammersmith, London W6 8JB

9 8 7 6 5 4 3 2 1

Paul Adam asserts the moral right to be identified
as the author of this work.

A catalogue record for this book is
available from the British Library

ISBN 0 00 232427 X

Photoset in Linotron Baskerville by
Rowland Phototypesetting Ltd
Bury St Edmunds, Suffolk
Printed and bound in Great Britain by
HarperCollins Book Manufacturing, Glasgow

CHAPTER 1

I noticed the lights reflected in the night sky above the hillside long before I rounded the corner and saw the scene of the accident. Two fire tenders, an ambulance and a police car were parked half way across the road. The rotating beacons on their rooftops cast a garish blue sheen over the moorland. I pulled in behind them and picked up my camera. As I got out of the car, the wind hit me with the force of a slamming door. The two cops were already waiting for me on the grass verge beside the road.

'No spectators, pal,' one of them said, shaking his head. 'Move along.'

They both wore luminous green waistcoats over their waterproofs and had cigarettes cupped in their hands against the wind. Their pale faces had a sickly hue in the gaudy light of the beacons. I pulled out my dog-eared NUJ card and showed it.

'Mind if I take a look?'

One of the cops shone a flashlight on the card. 'You with the *News*?'

'Freelance.' We were almost shouting to make ourselves heard above the howl of the gale.

They glanced at each other, men anxious to get back to the warmth of their patrol car. The second cop shrugged and took a quick drag on his cigarette.

'Just don't get in the way of the crews.'

I walked past the fire tenders and looked down the slope. It was an eerie scene. The car had left the road on a sharp bend and careered some seventy or eighty yards down the hillside before crumpling like a concertina in a deep gulley. The firemen had rigged a couple of powerful floodlights and were cutting away one of the doors to release the passengers. To one side, the two-man ambulance crew waited patiently with a stretcher and what looked like body bags.

The light glinted on frosted tufts of heather and a few stunted trees, twisted and bent by the weather. The grass cracked like porcelain beneath my feet but there was no ice on the road. To my right, in the distance, was the silhouette of Stanage Edge; behind me the dark, sinister bulk of Higger Tor, and down beyond the spurs of the valley, the village of Hathersage. The wind was blowing hard from the Dark Peak to the north-west, a damp, acid wind full of the stench of the peat bogs. It was not a night to be out on the moors. It was a night to be at home tucked up in bed with your wife. Or someone else's wife.

I zipped up my jacket and climbed down the hillside. A sheep, disturbed by the activity, scampered across my path into the shelter of a drystone wall. It was piercingly cold.

The car was a grey Rolls-Royce, almost new, but now just a crushed tin can. The bonnet was squeezed back nearly to the windscreen and I knew no one in the front seats could have survived an impact like that. The fire and ambulance crews knew too, I could sense it from their lack of urgency. They were cutting free dead bodies, not the injured.

I asked the fire chief if he minded my taking some photographs. He shook his head and I quickly ran off a roll of film. Then I backed off out of the way and stood by the ambulancemen, a dour-looking pair from the South Yorkshire service. We were inside the Peak District National Park here but still in Sheffield, not Derbyshire. They didn't look too pleased to be out in the middle of nowhere at this time of night.

'How many inside?' I asked them.

'Just one.'

'Dead?'

'Either that or he's a bloody good actor.'

I glanced at the car. The side window was shattered and through the opening I could see a man slumped over the wheel. His neck was twisted round horribly and his pale face stared out at me. I felt a faint, macabre chill of recognition.

'Know who he is?'

'He didn't say. Jesus, it's freezing out here. Why don't they hurry up?'

'Long job?' I asked. I wasn't getting anywhere but I always try.

'Depends how many bits there are to clean up.'

'Bits?'

'Of him.' He jerked his head at the dead man. 'Smash like that, he's probably mincemeat below the waist.'

'I wish they'd bloody told us,' his partner said. 'We could have brought the Thermos and the sandwiches.'

Caring sort of people, ambulancemen. I started back up the hill. Another car had arrived at the top and a trench-coated figure was clambering cautiously down towards me, one hand holding his hat on, the other stretched out for balance. I could see his features quite clearly in the flood-lights. A fleshy face, deep-set eyes, more than a hint of a double chin. Cropped hair, a flared, prominent nose and, beneath it, a black moustache, sleek as a garden slug in the morning dew.

I knew already who he was, but if I hadn't, I could have guessed. If you broke him open he'd have had cop written right through the middle like a stick of seaside rock. He was a detective-sergeant from the South Yorkshire CID called Chris Strange. I wondered what he was doing out here at eleven o'clock on a November night for a straightforward road traffic accident.

'What the hell are you doing here, McLean?' he asked abruptly as he reached me. The police never like it when the press gets somewhere before them.

'Just looking.'

'Who told you about this?'

'One of your lot.'

'Headquarters?'

I nodded.

'I'll skin the bastard. Who was it?'

'I forget now.'

None of this was strictly accurate. I'd actually been tipped off by a friend at ambulance control but I never tell the truth to the police: unprofessional conduct in a journalist.

'You touched anything?' he demanded.

'Like what?'

'Like the bloody car.'

'I'm not here for souvenirs, Chris. You think I'd nick the wing mirrors or something?'

'Well, keep out of my hair. And no pictures. You go anywhere near that car and I'll have you for obstruction.'

'Whatever you say.'

I didn't think it a good moment to tell him I'd already taken all the pictures I wanted.

He slithered on down the hill, no doubt going to let the firemen know who was really in charge, while I went back up the road. The two traffic policemen were out of their car again, trying to look as if they had something to do, the unmistakable sign of men whose superior officer has just shown up. Their cigarettes had gone, and they'd straightened out their waterproofs. I felt quite sorry for them.

I swopped a few remarks about the weather with them, then asked what happened.

One of them shrugged. 'Drove straight over the edge, didn't he.'

'Skidded?'

'Looks like it. There's tyre marks on the road.'

'I didn't see any.'

'Further up.' He jerked his thumb back up the road.

'Know why?'

'Can't tell.'

'Any idea when?'

'We got a call half an hour or so ago. Passing motorist saw the wreckage.'

'Anyone see the crash?'

'Couldn't say.'

I nodded and looked away. I waited a few seconds before asking casually: 'What's the driver's name?'

They were young, but not that green. 'Dunno,' one of them said.

Not true, of course. The first thing they'd have done when they arrived on the scene was radio in the registration number and get the owner's name and address. I rephrased the question.

'Who's it registered to, then?'

They hesitated a fraction. 'Can't say, mate.'

I checked the slope. The firemen had released the driver and were helping the ambulancemen put him into a body bag. His legs dangled loose, his head lolling back lifelessly. He was limp as a Bonfire Night guy. Strange was half way up, coming back.

'Sergeant Strange said it was all right to release it. It's too late for the morning papers and the Press Office will only give it to me in a few hours anyway.'

'Next of kin have to be informed first.'

'The Sergeant's taking care of that now. Why do you think he's here? Rolls-Royce, must be an important bloke.' It was pure guesswork, but plausible enough to sound convincing.

Strange was nearly on us.

'Come on lads, do me a favour. The Sergeant says it's OK. Then we can all get off this ruddy moor.'

'Sutton,' one of the coppers said. 'Richard Sutton. Address in Hathersage.'

The way he said it, I knew it meant nothing to him. But it meant something to me. That's why I'd recognized his face. And probably why Strange had left his cosy office and come out here into this windswept wilderness.

'You still here?' Strange said belligerently, more accusation than question. He was panting from the effort of climbing the hill. He turned to the constables: 'Next of kin have to be told.'

'We thought you were doing that, Sarge,' one of them said.

'Did you now? And what made you think that?'

'Well . . .'

'You've got the address, haven't you? Get over there as

soon as you're finished here. Someone will have to identify the body.'

'Yes, Sarge.'

'Must be off,' I said. 'Thanks for your help.'

'You haven't told this nosey sod anything, I hope,' Strange said.

One of the constables opened his mouth but thought better of it. 'No, Sarge.'

I started to go. The two constables glared at me and I knew I'd made myself a couple of enemies in the South Yorkshire police force. What the hell. Two more wouldn't make any difference.

I drove back into town and parked in a side street near the offices of the *Evening News*, the local daily. I knew quite a lot about Richard Sutton, but I needed the kind of detailed information I would only find in newspaper files. I took a torch from the glove compartment and walked to the works entrance of the paper. The staff had long since gone home but the building was kept open until midnight, guarded by that English equivalent of the KGB, the Corps of Commissionaires.

I stuck a cautious head round the corner and peered into the entrance. The doors were open but beyond them, in a glass-walled cubicle, was the commissionaire, on this particular night an ex-Infantry NCO named Arthur. I knew him well. Years ago, before I turned freelance, I worked for the *News* and I'd had brushes with all the commissionaires. I knew Arthur would never let me inside to look in the cuttings library. He had the old soldier's attitude to rules and regulations, particularly as applied to someone like me whom he'd always treated as an unruly squaddie.

I went back to the front of the building. Even at this late hour, the city centre was far from deserted: there were several groups of young men and women heading for the nightclubs. The men were in shirt sleeves, the women in thin blouses and skimpy skirts, all of them freezing in the name of fashion.

I waited until I saw two kids coming towards me, twelve- or thirteen-year-olds trying to act eighteen. Cockatoo haircuts you could paint ceilings with, stick legs with boots on the end, five sizes too big. A right pair of apprentice thugs. Trying hard, but a way to go yet. I stopped them.

'Now then, how'd you like to earn yourselves a couple of quid?'

They looked me over, cool, but skint enough to be interested.

'Doing what?'

'Come down here. See those dustbins over there?' I pointed to the back of the *News* building where there was a row of large industrial bins. 'I want you to push them over and run for it.'

They considered this proposition. 'Is that all?'

'Yes.'

I wished now I hadn't offered them money. They were the types who'd push over dustbins for nothing.

'What for?' one of them asked.

'Never mind. You want to do it?'

'For a fiver.'

'Get off. A quid each.'

'Two.'

'OK.'

Kids of today. I suppose this is what they call the Enterprise Culture. The Tories would be proud of them. I took out two pound coins and gave them one each.

'You'll get the other half when you've done it.'

We went down the side of the building and I waited in the shadows while they walked round past the works entrance. This was all basic commissionaire psychology. Commissionaires have two distinctive personality traits: officiousness and nosiness. To outwit them you have to play on their weakness for minding other people's business.

There was an almighty crash from around the corner. Then several more. Moments later Arthur came running out yelling, 'I'll have your guts, you little buggers,' and while he was off chasing the kids, I nipped inside past his cubicle. I hadn't paid the other two quid I owed, of course, but that was a lesson to the two junior hoodlums. Never trust a man who asks you to push over dustbins late at night.

I went upstairs to the newsroom. At one end was the library, a partitioned-off area full of rusty filing cabinets. The *News* is fully computerized, but to check the files you still have to look through tatty envelopes of yellowing cuttings.

I took out the file on Richard Sutton and shone the torch over the contents. He was in the news a lot, at least in Sheffield. There were dozens of cuttings, too many to go over now, so I stuck the envelopes in my pocket and added, as an afterthought, the picture file containing his photographs.

Getting back out of the building without being caught by Arthur was more of a problem, but the solution came to me as I walked downstairs through all the fire doors. I went into the machine room past all the silent presses, and out through a door marked Emergency Exit. In front of me was another door, locked but with a key in a glass panel on the wall which said, 'In Case of Emergency, Break Glass.' I'd always wanted to do this. I lifted my foot and smashed the glass with my heel. The alarm went off immediately. I opened the door with the key, walked down the alley and out into the night.

I was dying for a cup of tea and something to eat but the cupboards in my kitchen were bare save for an old mouldy crust of bread, hard as pumice stone. The worktop was littered with empty aluminium take-away containers and the place stank of two-day-old chicken tikka masala.

I rummaged in the flip-top bin and found a used teabag, dusted it off and put it in the pot. The crust of bread I scraped to remove the most obvious growths of penicillin and stuck under the grill.

Then, mug of tea in one hand, toast in the other, I went into the sitting-room and cleared a space in the mess of old newspapers, dirty crockery and half-read paperbacks. In the process I accidentally knocked over a cup of cold coffee which must have been lurking under the debris for days. The liquid flooded out on to what was left of the carpet. I mopped it up with a newspaper, sat down in the armchair and flicked through the cuttings on Richard Percival Sutton, now deceased.

He was, or rather had been, a remarkable man. An electronic engineer by training, he had made his first fortune in computer components, later consolidating it by branching out into the manufacture of the computers themselves. From there he had moved into property, light engineering and chemicals, building a company with a current stock market valuation of close on two hundred million pounds.

Outside the financial community he had not been particularly well known on a national level, but he had been a figure of some stature in Sheffield, not least because he had brought thousands of jobs to the decaying East End to replace those lost in the steel industry.

I had spoken to him several times and once done a profile on him for a Sunday colour supplement. I remembered him as a quiet, earnest, retiring sort of man, more like an academic than a businessman. And that, indeed, had been one of his strengths. He was not really a businessman, he was a man of ideas who had always been shrewd enough to employ good managers to run his businesses for him.

I had liked him. He had none of the arrogance of the self-made millionaire. He had been brought up a Quaker and supported numerous charities, he had an attractive humility and a generous nature. And now he was dead. Crushed in a senseless car crash on Hathersage Moor.

I took out some of the photographs, typical newspaper stuff. Stiff, formal poses. Sutton in a dinner jacket at a reception. Sutton donating a cheque to a local charity, sometimes on his own, sometimes with his wife by his side. An attractive blonde much younger than him.

The most recent picture showed them on a building site

watching a dapper little fellow in pinstripes lay a foundation stone in the mud. I remembered the occasion, I'd been there. Sutton was in the process of building what he called an Integrated Recycling Plant in the Don Valley, a huge industrial complex for recycling paper, glass, metal and other waste from all over the region. It was costing £50 million, partly funded by EC loans and government grants. That's why the foundation stone was being laid by David Wilberforce, junior minister at the Department of Trade and Industry.

I looked more closely at Sutton. He was a tall, wiry man in his early fifties, slightly stooped and thinning on top, but even in photographs there was something in his face which made him stand out. Yet all I could see now were those hollow eyes staring at me through the window of his car, eyes fixed in the blank stillness of death.

I finished my tea and toast with a grimace. The tea tasted vaguely of onions and the toast was like warmed-up hardboard. I checked my watch. Just after midnight. I picked up the 'phone and rang the home number of Miles Coburn, the News Editor of the *Evening News*. He took a while to answer and sounded none too happy when he did. I told him who it was. He sounded even less happy.

'I've got tomorrow's splash for you,' I said when he'd finished his what-the-hell-time-of-night-is-this? routine.

'Oh aye?' He was sceptical.

'Richard Sutton was killed this evening.'

There was a pause. '*The* Richard Sutton?'

'Car crash, killed outright. I've got photos.'

'Hang on a minute.'

I could picture him scrabbling for his cigarettes and lighter. His brain didn't work without a Silk Cut in his mouth. I heard the click of a lighter and the first wheezy drag on the cigarette.

Eventually he said: 'You sure?'

'Saw the body. The police confirmed the ID.'

'Any of our boys there?'

'No, that's why I'm ringing.'

Some poor *News* reporter who should have been doing the calls, but probably went to the pub instead, would get the bollocking of his life for missing this one.

'When was this?'

'An hour ago. You want the pictures?'

'Maybe.' He was stalling, calculating whether he could get a staff man out to the scene for some pictures of their own. It pains him to give money to a freelance.

'You won't find anything, Miles,' I said to help him out. 'I've got the fire crew cutting him out, the crumpled Rolls-Royce, the lot.'

'Was he driving?'

'Yes.'

'Passengers?'

'Just him. I could do you a good obit for the inside pages if you like.'

'I've got reporters for stuff like that.'

'I'll bring the prints in first thing, then.'

'No promises.'

'They're good, Miles.'

'OK. By the way, where did it happen?'

'I thought you had reporters for stuff like that?' I said, and hung up.

I went into the old boxroom off the hall I'd converted into a darkroom and developed my film. They'd take the prints all right. Coburn would ring the police to check what I'd told him, find out where the accident occurred and then send a photographer out just in case. The Rolls would still be there of course—they wouldn't tow it away until morning—but there'd be nothing else that was worth a picture. Not when they could use mine.

The obituary was more uncertain, but I sat down at the typewriter and wrote one anyway. Sutton was an important man in the city. The *News* would want to give him a big spread, but I was pretty sure the bunch of stiffs they employ wouldn't be able to write much on him without the files. And I had those.

I'd finished the obit and was in bed by two. I felt pretty bad about nicking the files. But not so bad it stopped me sleeping.

CHAPTER 2

I was in the *News* office at seven next morning. I got a coffee from the vending machine to remind myself how bad it was and strolled over to the Newsdesk. Miles Coburn was on the phone, morning papers in front of him, a lit cigarette stuck in the corner of his mouth.

I pulled up a chair and sat down, waiting for him to finish. Miles was one of the few things that had remained unchanged since my days on the *News*. He was older, of course, but he didn't really look it. He had always had grey hair and a gnarled complexion. His cheeks were redder, the burst blood vessels more prominent, but apart from that he was pretty much the same as ever. He still smoked fifty a day, still had two pints at lunch-time, more if someone else was buying, and even at seven in the morning, you could still smell his armpits from fifty paces.

The newsroom, on the other hand, had been transformed. Gone were the battered metal desks and old Adler typewriters that punched so many holes in your copy it looked like Braille. Gone were the metal spikes on the Newsdesk and subs table on which so many of my early stories had been impaled, and gone were most of the old hacks who had taught me what little I know of the job.

New technology had sterilized it all. VDUs had replaced the typewriters, the desks were uniform grey executive models. Even the worn green linoleum, pockmarked with cigarette burns, had been removed, replaced by carpeting and false flooring to conceal the computer cables.

The very atmosphere had changed, in a physical as well as a metaphorical sense. In my day there had been temperature variations which bore some relation to the weather

outside. In winter it was damp and draughty, in summer
so hot your crotch dripped and all the reporters left damp
patches on their seats. Now it was air-conditioned, kept at
a uniformly cool temperature which no doubt suited the
computers but meant everyone else had to wear pullovers
throughout the year. Newspaper management have always
thought more about machinery than people.

I glanced around the room. Apart from Miles, I recognized very few of the journalists. Half of them looked as if
they were fresh out of college. It made me feel very old.
The place where I had once sat was now occupied by a
callow youth in a pink and white striped shirt and silk tie.
He looked like a trainee stockbroker.

Miles put down the telephone and bawled orders at a
reporter across the room. He thinks stress is good for subor-
dinates and keeps the newsroom in a constant state of panic.

'You don't look well, Miles,' I said, when he'd finished
playing at News Editors.

'Thanks. That really cheers me up.'

'You should give up smoking.'

'I want medical advice, I'll go to a doctor. You brought
those pictures?'

I threw the photographs across his desk. He looked
through them. I'd brought him the four best prints and
they'd all captured the stark horror of the car smash.

'Want them?'

He grunted and lit another cigarette from the stub of the
one he was finishing. It was technically a no smoking area
but an exception was made for Miles who simply couldn't
function without a regular intake of nicotine. I studied his
wrinkled face. His eyes were bloodshot and his skin had a
pasty texture like uncooked dough. He really didn't look
well.

'OK,' he said grudgingly. 'These two.' He picked out a
couple and put them to one side.

'And the obit?'

'You write one?' he asked and I knew I'd made a sale. I
took it out of my pocket and handed it to him.

'You not getting one of your own?'

'Some stupid bastard's lost the files,' he said.

I clicked my tongue. 'Terrible.'

He read it through. 'You seem to know a lot about Sutton.'

'I've got a comprehensive filing system. Very efficient.'

'Invoice us, usual rate,' he said and tossed the obituary into his out-tray.

I left the building, this time through the proper exit, and strolled down to police headquarters on Snig Hill. I signed in at the front desk, clipped on a visitor's badge and went through the barrier. The Press Office is right near the entrance to make sure reporters don't go wandering round the building opening the wrong doors. I didn't linger. Police stations make me uneasy: the smell of too many coppers, or maybe I've a guilty conscience.

I used to come here all the time when I did the crime beat for the *News*, but now I only call in for the daily briefing. I don't miss the crime job. There was always too much knocking on doors to interview pensioners who'd been robbed, too much talking to tearful victims, the burgled, the beaten up, the swindled. Too much drinking with coppers, pretending to laugh at their jokes. You get a warped sense of humanity on the crime beat. You acquire a certain respect for the police, but you also get to know too much about them and knowledge, as in all walks of life, ultimately leads to disillusionment.

The Press Officer, Gordon Crieff, was behind his desk at the far end of the narrow, claustrophobic room. He was a civilian, not a police officer, a laconic Scot with a malicious sense of humour. On the walls, in the midst of a selection of 'Wanted' posters for real criminals, he'd put spoof photo-fits of the journalists he had to deal with each day. I was one of them but I always made a point of pretending I hadn't noticed.

Crieff was a rarity in a press officer: he didn't have favourites to whom he gave exclusives. He never gave out information selectively. He was absolutely impartial and briefed all journalists, no matter whether he liked them or not, in the same way. A big man with a middle-age spread, he'd worked in Glasgow for many years and found Sheffield very dull. Not enough multiple killings and sectarian wars for his liking.

'First in?' I said, sitting down in one of the rock hard plastic chairs that seemed to have been moulded to fit the spine of a hunchback and no one else.

'The *News* has been down. Wantae coffee?'

'Sure.'

He poured me a polystyrene cup from a filter machine on the filing cabinet, then tossed me a wad of photocopied telexes, stapled together. The daily press releases.

'Anything interesting?'

He shrugged. 'Usual crap. Fatal RTA on the moors. But I hear ye've got that one already.'

'Who told you that?'

'Chris Strange.'

'You've spoken to him?'

'Aye. He disnae like ye very much, laddie.'

'Yeah, I've kind of got that impression.' I took a sip of coffee. It tasted more of polystyrene than coffee.

'Nosey bastard, he says.'

'Perceptive bloke. What was he doing out there?'

'Nothing better tae do.'

'Is that official? South Yorkshire's underworked police force.'

Crieff pulled out the bottom drawer of his desk and stuck his feet in it, one of his little quirks.

'The traffic boys radioed in the ID. You know Strange, he'll do anything tae mix with the rich and famous.'

'Even when they're dead?'

'It's the only time he meets them.'

That's what I like about Crieff. He's supposed to be a PR man for the police, massaging their tarnished image, but a lot of the stuff he tells the press has the opposite effect.

I flicked through the daily releases. There's rarely anything of interest to me, but I always look just in case. Mostly it's minor burglaries, criminal damage and the odd assault, all grist to the local newspaper mill but useless to the nationals which is where I do most of my business.

There was a telex about Richard Sutton's crash but nothing in it I didn't already know. I skimmed the rest. A couple more traffic accidents, no fatalities; a mugging in Castle Square subway, almost a nightly occurrence these days, and a whole catalogue of video and jewellery thefts from houses.

The last item was a fire in an office block near the city centre. The address looked oddly familiar: 184 Green Lane. I couldn't place it. No matter, it probably wasn't important. I shrugged and put the releases in my jacket pocket.

'I told you,' Crieff said. 'Just the usual crap.'

'Anyone know why he crashed yet?' I said.

'Who?'

'Richard Sutton.'

'Why d'ye think? Pissed out of his brain. Off the record of course.'

'Who says? You can't have a post-mortem report yet.'

'Accident report. Entirely unofficial. And I dinnae tell you if anyone asks.'

'Whose accident report?'

'The patrol car that got there first.'

'It's not in the release?'

'Internal consumption only. I'm giving you the background. Not for use before the inquest, you understand?'

Crieff pulled a plastic sandwich box out of his briefcase and opened it. He produced a thick cheese and tomato roll and bit into it. Tomato juice ran down his chin. He wiped it off with a hairy hand and chewed contentedly.

'This is supposed tae be lunch,' he said. 'But I always eat it well before nine o'clock.'

'So what do you do for lunch?'

'Go tae the canteen, of course. My wife canna understand how I'm putting on weight. She thinks I only have a sandwich a day.' He stroked his paunch lovingly and took another bite.

'What does it say in the report?'

He finished his mouthful. 'The two laddies who got there first took a look inside the car. They said it reeked of booze. There was a bottle of whisky smashed on the floor inside. They could see the label on it.'

'So? That doesn't mean Sutton was drunk. What makes you think he drank the whisky?'

'They tried tae administer emergency first aid. His mouth stank of it. He'd been drinking all right. Probably been to some business piss-up.'

'Anyone witness the crash?'

'Nae one we've found so far. Not many people out on those moors at that time of night. It sounded a bad one.'

'His car looked like a crushed bean tin. I think they pulled him out in pieces.'

Crieff winced. 'Please, not while I'm eating.'

'It's bloody sad really, to go like that. He was an exceptional man.'

'Aye,' said Crieff. 'And now he's an exceptional corpse.'

I went for breakfast at the Oasis Café near the bus station. Or what used to be the bus station. It's called the Transport Interchange now but nobody's fooled; it's still the bus station. The council's tarted it up, knocked down the old shelters and put up some flash new ones with red and blue trimmings, dug up the tarmac and replaced it with mosaics of coloured bricks, but it's still basically the same. It's still full of people moaning that the 53 to Low Edges is twenty minutes late, winos kipping out on the benches and pigeons that shit on your head as you walk underneath.

A tramp came up to me outside the café.

'Could you lend us a few pence to come inside for a drink, sir?' I'm a bit of a soft touch for tramps. They're the only people who call me sir.

'I don't think they serve meths here,' I said.

'For a cup of tea.'

I looked him over. 'OK. So long as you sit downwind of me.'

The distinctive atmosphere hit me as soon as I opened

the door. The windows of the Oasis were always steamed up, no matter what the season, and it had an almost tropical humidity, composed largely of evaporated chip fat. The floor and formica-topped tables seemed to secrete grease and they emptied the ashtrays every three months with a JCB.

I lined up at the counter and ordered a tea and some toast. The woman behind the counter temporarily inter-rupted her conversation with the cashier to splash tea in the general direction of my saucer.

'I wouldn't mind it in a cup next time,' I said.

'Bugger off, cheeky sod,' she replied. South Yorkshire wit, you can't beat it.

'And a tea for him, too,' I added, nodding at the tramp.

The tramp helped himself to a Danish pastry and took a bite out of it so I'd have to pay for that too. Bunch of chancers, tramps.

I saw Harry Raymond sitting at a window table and went over.

'Join you?'

He looked up morosely and nodded. I sat down. Harry was eating one of the Oasis's 'Coronary Specials': fried bread, chips, black pudding, bacon, eggs and a side plate of butter with a little bit of bread.

'Haven't seen you in here for a while,' Harry said.

'I can't take too much health food.'

'You well?'

'Fine. You?'

Harry paused and I knew he was going to tell me.

'Well, me sinuses aren't too good. All this damp weather we've bin 'aving. Gets to me chest too.' He gave a little cough to emphasize his point.

'You're the worst hypochondriac I've ever met, Harry.'

He looked up indignantly from his plate of hot grease. His eyes were watery, his jowls sagging beneath hollow cheeks. He looked like an anorexic bloodhound.

'I'm a sick man, I'll have you know. The doctor says he's never come across a patient like me.'

'I bet he hasn't.'

'If it weren't for the fact I'm an independent businessman I'd be on a sick pension by now.'

I changed the subject before he outlined his full medical history to me. Yet again.

'How *is* your business by the way?' Harry had a lock-smith's shop down near the market.

'Boring.'

A girl brought my toast over and dumped it on the table. I took a bite and about half a pound of butter oozed down my throat.

'You're not thinking of packing it in, are you?' I said.

'No. But I miss the old days. I could work nights then. Now I have to stop in and watch telly with the wife.'

I could sympathize, I'd met his wife.

When Harry talked about working nights, he was referring to his days, so to speak, as a burglar. He looked like a down-at-heel, very ordinary clerk: the kind of lifeless bureaucrat you find taking housing inquiries at the front desk of the Town Hall. But he had a bizarre past.

I first met him six or seven years ago in the Crown Court. I was waiting for another case to come up when Harry was brought into the dock on a series of burglary charges which, even then, were five years old. The case was thrown out, but not before I'd listened to a fascinating tale of escape and imprisonment.

Harry had been arrested years before for a number of petty burglaries, but had jumped bail and gone to South Africa. On arrival he'd been picked up by the Cape Town police who locked him in their cells. Harry escaped. He went to Johannesburg and was locked up by the immi-gration authorities. He escaped. He went to Durban and was caught again. This time they sent him to a maximum security prison and, being the civilized people they are, put him in irons like a galley slave. Harry escaped.

He then headed north and over the next few years com-mitted minor offences and was locked up in practically every state between South Africa and England. On every occasion he escaped. Then, returning to Sheffield, he made one of those banal mistakes that so often betray criminals. He went into his old local for a pint and was caught by the same bobby who'd arrested him years earlier.

I interviewed Harry after his case was dismissed on a technicality and kept in loose touch with him thereafter. He tried to go straight but with his record no employer would touch him. Homeless and broke, he joined the Moonies for free board and lodging but they asked him to leave after three weeks because he was a corrupting influence; the only person in history to be thrown out of the Moonies.

After a long time on the dole he got on the government Enterprise Allowance Scheme but needed £1,000 capital to set up as a locksmith, utilizing his incomparable knowledge of locks and alarms. The banks were no help, so in the end I lent him the money. He paid me back long ago but I still take an interest in how he's doing.

'Sometimes I'm tempted,' Harry continued. 'Those big 'ouses out at Fulwood would be piss easy to do. People should look after their 'omes a bit better, they deserve to be done over.'

'A lot of them are.'

'Aye, but who by? Kids barely out of nappies. It's a disgrace. They're taking the living away from the real professionals, men what's got wives and babies to support. It used to be a vocation, burglary, now any Tom, Dick or 'arry thinks they can do it.'

'They're only learning,' I said.

Harry almost choked on his fried bread. 'Learning! That's not the way to learn. Smashing windows to get in, then vandalizing the house, pissing on the furniture. Where's the skill there? In my day they never knew you'd been in. We left everything shipshape. We had pride in us work.'

'Never mind, Harry. Write a letter to the paper.'

'Anyway, I couldn't go back to it now. Not with the arthritis in me knees. When I think 'ow I used to shin up drainpipes.' He shook his head gloomily. 'I'm a broken man, broken.'

I finished my tea and checked my watch. Eight-thirty, not too early to ring. I got up and patted him on the shoulder.

'I've got to go, Harry.'

'Come down the shop one afternoon. We'll have a drink together.'

'I'll do my best.'

As I went out I heard Harry ordering another plate of chips. For a broken man he certainly ate a lot.

I found a call-box in Fitzallan Square and rang Richard Sutton's home 'phone number. A woman answered, but not his wife. Probably a servant of some sort; they were wealthy enough to have a household staff. I told her I was the *Financial Times*, much more likely to meet with a favourable response than the truth. She put Mrs Sutton on.

There aren't many ethics in this game, but as a matter of principle I never doorstep the bereaved. I always ask for an interview first. Mrs Sutton sounded very calm for a woman who'd lost her husband ten hours earlier. She agreed to see me. I arranged to go out to the house at nine-thirty.

It was a fine morning for a drive, crisp but sunny. I took the main A625 south west out of the city and climbed into the Peak District. The hilltops were streaked with sunlight and when I turned the corner above Hathersage, the whole shimmering beauty of the Hope Valley opened out before me. At least, shimmering as far as the chimney of the Hope Valley cement works; after that a sort of murky grey glower.

Hathersage nestled on the north side and I could see the church whose main claim to fame is the grave of Little John in its churchyard. The grave lies under an old yew tree and is about ten feet long. Occasionally I think about sneaking out there at night and digging it up to see if there are really bones inside it, but I know I'll never do it. I prefer to keep some illusions intact.

I drove in through the gates of the Suttons' house, an

impressive looking pile with a sweeping gravel forecourt and a turret on one end. It looked Victorian to me, built for solidity rather than elegance. An ugly stone portico guarded the front door and ivy trailed over the red brickwork. There was a grey and yellow Suzuki four-wheel drive in front of the garage, a converted stable block by the look of it. I immediately put Mrs Sutton down as the type who goes to Sainsbury's in a jeep.

The door was answered by a maid in a white apron. My first maid; you don't encounter them often in Sheffield. She took me down a long corridor to the back of the house and showed me into a huge room overlooking the garden. Sitting-room I'd have called it. The maid called it the Drawing-Room.

It was furnished quite simply. A polished wood floor overlaid with Chinese rugs. Delicate antique tables and one or two tasteful ornaments. A three-piece suite in a pale flowery material and enough open space for a game of croquet. A lot of money had gone into it but not much personality: the whole room bore the hallmark of an interior designer, not the people who lived in it. It was not a room you'd want to curl up in with a good book. Or a lover.

Jacqueline Sutton was sitting on the settee. She didn't look as if she did much curling up, with a book or anything else. She was leafing through a newspaper, turning the pages carefully by the corners to avoid getting ink on her fingers. It was the *Daily Telegraph*, I noted. Figured. I revised my opinion of her at once. She wasn't the type who would go to Sainsbury's in a Suzuki. She'd probably never heard of Sainsbury's.

I'd seen photographs of her in the *News* files but they didn't do her justice. In the pictures she had the lifeless good looks of a fashion model, the chocolate-box perfection we have come to accept as beauty. But in the flesh there was more to her. A warmth in the eyes, a sensuality and intelligence in the face which were somehow more noticeable than her beauty.

She was composed without being cool, and had an air

of sex-but-not-for-the-taking which most men would find alluring. Her shoulder-length hair was the colour of a Van Gogh cornfield, her complexion flawless and she was wearing sheer stockings and plain black mourning, expensively tailored. She looked as if it had taken her about a fortnight to get dressed.

'Mr McLean.' She stood up languidly and offered me a limp hand, the way women do when they don't want to chip their nails.

'It's good of you to see me, Mrs Sutton.'

'Would you like some coffee?'

'If it's no trouble.'

'For two, please, Louise,' she said to the maid, who went out and quietly shut the door behind her.

Mrs Sutton offered me a seat and I sat down facing the garden. They had a terrace, an all-weather tennis court and an outdoor swimming pool, now drained for the winter and full of drifting leaves and puddles of rainwater. The flowerbeds were obviously the work of a professional and the lawn looked as if it should have had peacocks strutting across it. Maybe they were in the kitchen having breakfast.

'Did you have a good journey?' she asked.

'Yes, thanks.'

'It's a lovely morning.'

Jesus, I thought. This woman's husband was killed last night and she's making cocktail-party small talk with me.

'Several other reporters have rung. You're the first who's actually come out.'

'I don't like the telephone.'

'You don't work for the *Financial Times* though, do you?'

That threw me. Must have been the windcheater gave me away.

'I string for them,' I said, which was only slightly untrue. I'd done work for them in the past.

'They don't have a staff man round here,' I explained as her green eyes probed me with an uncomfortable insight. I felt like a shifty double-glazing salesman caught pocketing the silver.

'So you're freelance?'

'Yes.'

She tightened her mouth and nodded. 'And will they print what I tell you?'

'They usually do. Your husband was nationally well-known in the business community.'

She softened a bit at that, absorbing some of her husband's renown and taking it for her own. Common enough in the relatives of famous people.

'I was sorry about his death,' I said. It sounded meaningless, but I meant it.

'It was a great shock.'

'He'll be missed. Do you mind if I ask you a few questions about him?'

She shook her head. Her lips trembled with a breath of emotion. She was self-possessed but the underlying strain was clear and no amount of make-up could hide the red eyes and puffy skin beneath them. She'd been weeping.

I felt a callous intruder on a very private grief but I went ahead and asked her the trite, embarrassing questions reporters always ask after a death. The how-do-you-feel, what-about-the-children, cry-on-my-shoulder questions that have the same predictable answers each time. I've done it on countless occasions, always feeling it was unnecessary and insensitive, yet sometimes sensing it was a cathartic, beneficial release for the bereaved.

The wives of well-known men are often quite desperate to talk about their loss. Part of it is vanity, but mostly it's the illusion that by talking they can somehow give their husbands substance after death. Yet even then I find it a shallow, degrading ordeal. There are many ways of measuring grief, but only journalists think they can do it in column centimetres.

The maid brought the coffee in on a carved mahogany tray, oriental in design, and went out. It was a relief for both of us. Mrs Sutton uncrossed her legs and poured coffee from the pot into delicate china cups.

'Milk or cream?'

'Milk, please.'

'Sugar?'

'Two.'

She handed me the cup and poured her own. She took it black without sugar. I felt guilty at my own indulgence. I sipped it. It was strong with an edge of bitterness.

'Nice coffee.'

'Colombian,' she said.

'It's good.'

I studied her discreetly over my cup. She was not an easy woman to read. She'd answered my questions quite willingly, but not without difficulty. Once or twice she'd stopped and swallowed hard, fighting back the tears. I'd asked if she wanted to stop but she'd shaken her head and continued talking. It was as if forcing herself to talk about her dead husband helped suppress the grief.

She took a couple of sips of her coffee and tried a quick smile. It didn't come off but I admired her for trying.

'Richard used to sit there,' she said. 'In that chair. He'd read the papers and have coffee with me on a Sunday morning. It was practically the only time we had together.'

'Did you not see much of each other?'

'Richard was always out.'

'Working?'

'Most of the time. He had other interests too. Chamber of Commerce, charities. He devoted a lot of time to charitable causes.'

'He did a lot of good work for this city.'

She nodded. 'When he wasn't working he was always at some function or other.'

'Was he at one last night?'

'No. He was working late at the office.'

'That can't have been easy for you. If he was never here.'

'I didn't mind the functions. I often went to them with him. At least I could be with him then.' She paused. 'The funny thing is, he didn't enjoy most of them at all. He hated small talk and black tie evenings. Yet he always went out of a sense of duty. He gave money for the same reason.'

'Duty?'

'And perhaps guilt. Guilt that he had so much. He felt he had to give some of it away.'

She turned her head and stared pensively out of the window. A gardener in wellingtons and fingerless gloves was pushing a wheelbarrow along the path by the lawn. I could hear the distant squeaking of the barrow's rusty axle.

'You know, I never thought he would go this way,' Mrs Sutton said after a while. 'In a car crash, I mean. I thought it would be overwork. Heart attack, a stroke, that kind of thing. I can't believe it was a road accident. He was always such a careful driver.'

'What will happen to the company now?' I asked.

'It will continue as usual.'

'Even without him?'

'Richard wasn't a day-to-day manager. The executives he appointed are competent enough to keep it running.'

'What about the plant in the East End?'

'The recycling project? That will not be affected. The financing is all in place and building work has begun. If I do nothing else I'll make sure that's completed. It meant a great deal to Richard.'

'In what way?'

'Well, I don't want to sound hypocritical. No one believes rich men have principles. But Richard did. He wanted to do something about the way we waste so much. He wasn't a great campaigner or anything but, well, he wanted to do something.

'He felt a recycling plant was the answer, making a business out of it so people would actually have a motivation to do it. It was going to be his . . .' She choked and lowered her head but I had already seen the tears welling up.

'It was going to be . . . his memorial,' she said indistinctly. She was dabbing at her eyes with a lacy handkerchief.

'I'm sorry,' she said, apologizing not for her grief but for letting me see it. I only realized fully then how desperately she'd been holding back her emotions.

'I shouldn't have intruded,' I said.

She brushed her hair back with a hand and sniffed. The tears had trickled down her cheeks leaving streaks in her make-up. 'That's all right. You're only doing your job.'

'I'd better go.' I put down my coffee cup and stood up.

She came to the door of the room with me, her composure returning.

'I'm glad to be of help,' she said. She held out a hand and I took it.

'Thank you for seeing me.'

I opened the door and went out into the passage. When I glanced back into the room, Jacqueline Sutton had already turned away to hide her face. Her shoulders shook with pent-up, silent sobs.

CHAPTER 3

A feeling of intense self-disgust came over me on the drive back into the city. I thought about Jacqueline Sutton, a woman already distraught with grief whose torment I had increased by prising open her heart and picking at the scars.

I wondered why I'd done it. Why I ever did it. Yet the habit was too ingrained to change. Facts were never enough for a newspaper, there always had to be a human reaction. A quote, a cry, a scream, a tear. And it was my job to supply them, to tap into other people's pain and extract a sample for the entertainment of the whole world.

I felt unclean. I wanted to take a shower to wash away the dirt, but showers wash only the outside. The grime inside always stays.

I drove across the city to my flat in Burngreave. There was sunlight high above but none of it penetrated into the grey-shrouded streets. The wind scratched at my face as I went up the steps to the front door. The lock had been smashed again. I pushed open the door and went into the hall. There was a pile of mail on the mat. I sorted through it to extract the letters addressed to me. Most looked like bills or junk mail; I never get letters I actually want to read. I went upstairs. Through the walls I could hear the woman in the ground-floor flat yelling at her kids. A child whimpered faintly in the background.

The light on my telephone answering machine was glowing red when I went into my own flat. I played it back. I'd had three calls. The first two were from magazine editors, politely reminding me I had missed the deadlines on two features I'd been commissioned to write and requesting me, not so politely, to get my finger out and produce them. The third was from my accountant, asking me to call in and see her urgently. That was ominous. I have never yet got any good news from my accountant.

I went into the kitchen. It still smelt of curry. The flip-top bin was overflowing with rubbish. If I left it much longer it would walk downstairs to the dustbin of its own accord. I pulled out the bulging plastic liner, tugged open the sash window and carefully dropped the plastic bag down into the back yard. Someone else could deal with it.

Then I opened the fridge. I was out of coffee and tea but needed a drink. There was a half-empty bottle of German *pils* in the door of the fridge. It had been there a couple of days but smelt all right. I took a swig. It was flat, but still drinkable. Just.

I looked out of the window. It was not a pretty view. A timber yard ran all the way along the back and beyond it the rows of slate-roofed terraced houses stretched down the hillside. Palls of smoke hung over the valley.

I'd lived there too long. It was depressing to come home to such an ugly view, such a squalid flat. There was mould on the kitchen walls, dirt everywhere, and after five years I still hadn't found any curtains for the window.

A sudden pang of nostalgia came over me. Was it the after-effects of Richard Sutton's opulent mansion or simply a momentary twinge of regret? I thought how different things had been during my marriage. The house we'd shared, the trouble Alison had taken to decorate and furnish it. I'd lost it all in the divorce, but what I missed was not so much the house as the female imagination which had made it a home.

My thoughts were interrupted by the telephone ringing. I went into the sitting-room and picked it up. It was one of the magazine editors who'd rung earlier. I told him, untruthfully, that his feature was written and would be in the post today. He didn't believe me but it got me off the hook for a day or two. Then I rang the other editor and told him the same thing.

Next I scribbled some notes and phoned the nationals to flog them a few paragraphs on Richard Sutton's death. A couple showed some interest in the pictures and I said I'd wire them prints later.

My last call was to Martin Furness, deputy City editor of one of the quality Sundays. We used to work together when we were both trainees and I knew he'd take more than a couple of paragraphs on this one. Sutton was worth more than that on a City page. He agreed to four hundred words, then we swapped ten minutes of gossip: who'd got new jobs, what they were earning and who they were sleeping with—sex and money, the only subjects my Fleet Street friends were interested in.

I wrote the article and 'phoned it over to the copytakers before settling down at the typewriter and starting the two overdue magazine features, a couple of very tedious trade articles. One on waste disposal, one on loft insulation. I'd done all the research for them already but it was still a bind to have to write them.

By mid-afternoon they were finished and sealed in envelopes waiting to be posted. I lifted up my jacket to look for the book of stamps I kept in my wallet. As I did so, a bulky object fell out of one of the pockets. It was the wad of photocopied telexes from the police press office.

I picked them up. The back sheet tore off, leaving a corner still attached to the staple. I ran my eyes over it, about to screw it up and throw it into the waste paper basket. Something caught my attention. It was the telex about the office fire near the city centre the previous evening. The address was definitely familiar: 184 Green Lane. Why did I know it? I'd come across it recently but couldn't remember in what context.

I took a street map down off the shelves and looked it up. Green Lane was down near the River Don. I tried to think why I knew the name. It was not a part of the city I went to very often. There was nothing much there as far as I could recall. But it meant something to me all the same.

Then it came suddenly with a faint prickle of excitement. The address was familiar because I'd seen it *very* recently. Last night, in fact.

I took out the cuttings file on Richard Sutton I'd borrowed from the *News* offices and checked a couple of articles. The head office of his holding company was at No. 184 Green Lane.

Long ago, when I was just beginning, I met a boozy old Fleet Street hand on a job who took me for a drink to pump me for information he was too lazy to find for himself. An old dodge, I do it myself now: find some keen young reporter anxious to show how smart he is and pick his brains. In between double whiskies, this old hand said to me: 'There are only three rules on Fleet Street, lad. Never miss a story and never drive a bigger car than your editor.' 'What's the third?' I asked. 'Never believe in coincidences.'

And I didn't.

Having posted the articles and wired my photographs to London, I called in on my accountant. I believe in getting bad news over quickly.

Her secretary, Muriel, eyed me with suspicion when I walked into the outer office. She always looks as if she's convinced I'm going to nick the fixtures and fittings.

'Is Maria in?' I said.

'Miss Wells is engaged,' Muriel replied stiffly, emphasizing the 'Miss Wells' to reprimand me for being familiar.

'She wanted to see me.'

'She has a full diary this afternoon. Did you make an appointment?' She knew I hadn't, of course.

'I'm sure she'll squeeze me in,' I said. I sat down on a chair in one corner of the office. 'Any chance of a cup of tea?'

'Certainly not,' said Muriel. 'And don't put your feet on the coffee table.'

I removed my feet.

Muriel watched me.

I watched Muriel.

'Don't mind me,' I said.

Muriel narrowed her eyes at me and got on with her work. She was a big woman in her fifties, very head-mistressy, with cascading chins, a blotched wallpaper complexion and a chest like a Widnes prop forward. She wore large clip-on earrings and pearls, had a ramrod posture and smelt faintly of mothballs. She was the type of woman who starched her thoughts as well as her corsets. She scared me.

After a while she pressed the intercom switch on the desk and Maria's soft voice came over.

'Yes, Muriel?'

'Mr McLean is here to see you, Miss Wells.' She said it in the tone of voice she'd use for introducing a convicted axe murderer.

Maria sighed over the intercom. 'Send him in.'

'You've a meeting in ten minutes, Miss Wells. And Mr Sullivan at four.'

'Yes, I haven't forgotten.'

Muriel clicked off the intercom and said: 'You can go in.'

I raised a finger in a salute. 'Thanks, Muriel. I'll buy you a drink some time.'

'Over my dead body,' Muriel said.

I went into the inner office. Maria was sitting behind a large, battered desk, littered with mounds of paper. Her office management's a little sloppy but she's the best accountant I've ever met. She'd have to be, of course, to sort out my affairs.

'Busy?' I asked.

'Yes.'

I walked across to the desk, my feet sinking into the deep shag pile.

'I think your carpet needs mowing,' I said and sat down in the chair opposite her.

Maria took off her reading glasses and fixed me with her smokey blue eyes. She had black, wavy hair framing high Slavic cheekbones, full lips and lightly tanned skin. She was wearing a severe businesswoman's blouse but then a big fluffy pink jumper over it which made her look cuddly as well as professional. She was far too attractive to be an accountant.

'I don't think Muriel likes me,' I said.

'She doesn't. She thinks I should get rid of you as a client.'

'Really? And are you going to?'

'I'd miss the headaches.'

I pulled a face. 'You left a message asking me to call in.'

'Yes.'

Maria stood up and walked across the office to a filing cabinet. I watched her. She had a good figure, slim legs. Definitely too attractive to be an accountant.

She brought a file back to her desk and sat down again.

'I've had a letter. From the Inland Revenue.'

My heart sank. The worst kind. 'I don't suppose they're giving me a rebate, are they?'

She opened the file. 'You want to read the letter?'

'I can't understand their English. What does it say?'

'They're querying your last set of business accounts.'

'They did that last time.'

'I know. And the time before.'

'Do you think they're picking on me?'

She pushed back her chair and crossed her legs. 'It looks a bit like it, doesn't it?'

She didn't sound very sympathetic, given that she's supposed to be on my side.

'Victimization. Isn't that an offence?'

'Not for the Inland Revenue. It's normal practice for them.'

'Why do they keep picking on me? Why don't they go after the big boys who get away with millions?'

'You're easier to catch.'

I didn't like the sound of that. 'Does that mean they'll succeed this time?'

'That depends.'

'On what?'

She shrugged. 'All kinds of things. Your books, your bank account, the tax inspector's mood on the day he makes his decision.'

'His *mood?*'

'They're only human, Michael.'

'Well, we'll give them the benefit of the doubt.'

'They have a lot of discretion in what they do. They can be lenient or they can throw the book at you.'

'Haven't they run out of books by now? You know I'm honest, so what's their problem?'

'Well, you've got to admit your earnings fluctuate rather a lot. Usually downwards,' she added unnecessarily.

'So what do we do?'

'I need your books and all your invoices and receipts. Then I'll talk to you again.'

'Why don't we do it over dinner tonight?'

'I never mix business with pleasure.'

'Well, we don't have to do too much business.'

She gave me a dry look. I ask her out now and again but I never get anywhere. Even when she accepts. She was hesitating.

'I'll pick you up at eight,' I said quickly before she could think of an excuse.

'What if I'm staying in to wash my hair?'

'I'll come round and hold your shampoo.' I stood up. 'I'll book a table at The Frog.'

'Michael, I'm your accountant. You can't possibly afford The Frog.'

'I know. You're paying.'

*

The offices of RPS Trading plc, Richard Sutton's holding company, were in a nondescript concrete block near the river. The area had a run-down feel to it. Shabby buildings and decrepit warehouses gave way to ancient engineering and cutlery firms. Through open windows all down the street I could hear the thud of drop forges. Occasionally the ground shook beneath my feet. Above, on the barren hillside was the dry ski slope at Parkwood Springs, juxtaposing the new booming leisure industry with the fading steel crafts of the past.

I looked up at the offices from outside. The windows of the top storey, the fourth, were broken, the frames and what I could see of the interior, blackened by smoke. There were cars parked outside and various people wandering in and out. I recognized one of them: a Scenes of Crime Officer, one of the civilian forensic experts employed by the police. He was heading for the entrance, carrying a black leather case. I tagged along behind him.

Inside the foyer a uniformed WPC was leaning on a counter chatting to the receptionist. She glanced round as we entered. I kept close to the SOCO in front of me.

He nodded at the WPC and she acknowledged him. I waved a hand casually and said, 'Hi', then followed the SOCO to the lift, acting as if I belonged. No one attempted to stop me.

'Top floor?' I said to the SOCO when we were inside the lift. He nodded.

'Terrible business, this fire. Any idea what happened?' I said conversationally, trying to tempt him into an indiscretion, but he just shrugged and ignored me. Cagey bastards, SOCOs.

We got out on the top floor and I let the SOCO disappear down a corridor before making a move. I wasn't absolutely sure why I was there. Mostly curiosity, I suppose, but also perhaps a touch of suspicion. A man is killed in a car crash and the same night his office catches fire. Two accidents in the space of a couple of hours. Sounded very careless.

The floor was in chaos. There were people everywhere, moving files and papers, salvaging bits of furniture, sorting through the mess. The place stank of smoke and the carpets were soaked with water and charred debris. The fire seemed to have been confined to one side only for the offices at the back of the building appeared untouched by flames or smoke. Their doors were open and I could see several people trying to work.

The SOCOs were in one of the front offices, methodically searching the floor, putting things in plastic bags and taking photographs. I kept out of their way.

I checked a few doors and stopped at one with Richard Sutton's name on it. It was wide open. Inside, a girl in her mid-twenties was sitting listlessly behind a word processor staring into space. Her eyes were red and swollen. Behind her another open door led into a large corner suite, presumably Sutton's office. I caught a glimpse of a white leather settee and the corner of a black executive desk. Apart from the pervasive smell, there was no sign that the fire had reached this part of the building.

I smiled at the girl. She attempted one in return but it didn't get beyond the corners of her mouth. I guessed she was Sutton's secretary. I knew she'd been crying.

'Quite a mess,' I said.

She nodded weakly.

'But you're all right here.'

'The fire didn't get this far.'

'Why was that?'

'I'm not sure. I think the fire brigade put it out before it spread.'

I perched on the edge of her desk. 'I'm not disturbing you, am I?'

'No, it's not very easy to concentrate with all these people around.'

'Is this Mr Sutton's office?'

'Yes, but he's not . . . I'm afraid he . . .' She swallowed and her eyes watered.

'I know,' I said to spare her the pain. Poor kid. Only

young. And probably very loyal to her boss. Sutton had been the kind of man to inspire both loyalty and affection in his staff. I thought suddenly about Jacqueline Sutton too. I wondered if when I died there would be two women like them who would weep for me.

The girl wiped her eyes with a soggy tissue. 'Are you with the police?'

I was tempted, but it was too risky. 'Reporter,' I admitted. 'Mike McLean.'

'Debbie Nolan,' she said. 'I'm . . . I mean I was, Mr Sutton's secretary. Have you come about him?'

I shook my head. 'I wanted to ask about the fire.'

'I'm not sure I can help you.'

'Any idea what started it?'

'No. The police have been here asking questions. They're still across the corridor if you want to speak to them.'

'Presumably the building was empty at the time?'

'Oh yes. It was after hours.'

'Anything valuable lost?'

'Debbie!' A man's voice, sharp, tainted with anger. He was standing in the doorway of Sutton's office. He must have been in there all along, hidden from view.

'Have you finished those letters yet?'

'I'm sorry, Mr Sinclair. I got distracted.'

She started tapping the keys of the word processor. The man frowned at me behind his rimless glasses. He was short and plump with thin moist lips like two slivers of raw kidney.

'Can I help you?' he asked frostily.

I introduced myself. 'Just asking about the fire.'

'We have no comment to make to the press,' he said. 'How did you get in?'

'Any estimate yet of how much damage was done?'

'We have no comment to make. Would you leave, please.'

'Any question of arson?'

'If you don't leave now, I'll ask the police to eject you.'

'We'd enjoy that,' a voice said behind me.

I turned. Detective-Sergeant Chris Strange was in the

doorway, his back propped on one side of the opening, his beer gut on the other.

'Hello, Chris. Just the man I want to see.'

'Out.'

'I only need a couple of quotes.'

'I'll give you a couple of quotes all right, but they won't be for publication. Out.'

'A few questions, that's all.'

'You want one of my lads to show you the door?'

'No, thanks, I saw it on the way in.'

Strange put his head into the corridor and barked, 'Clayton'. A copper the size of a small mausoleum appeared behind him.

'OK, I'm going.'

I retreated gracefully. I know when to take a hint.

But I didn't retreat very far. I went to a café in town and had a pot of tea and a ham sandwich. Then I bought an *Evening News* and read about Richard Sutton.

His death was on the front page, accompanied by one of my photos. No by-line on the picture, of course, nor on the obituary on page three, but then I hadn't expected one. All the news I write now is anonymous. The subs had butchered my copy, mucking about with the sentences to make me look illiterate. Even after all these years that still gets to me. It's like being done over by muggers.

At five o'clock I picked up the car and drove back to the RPS Trading offices. I parked up the street where I could see the front door and waited for home time. It was already dark. The sodium lights cast yellow puddles on the road. A scrawny cat strolled insolently into view and disappeared down a passage towards the river.

Debbie Nolan came out just after half past five and turned away from me. She was alone. I started the car and drove after her. I pulled in and opened the passenger door.

'Offer you a lift?'

She glanced across, hostile, the natural reaction of a woman accosted in the street. Then she recogized me. Hesitated. Shook her head quickly and walked on.

I drove after her and pulled in again.

'Come on, get in.'

'Please, go away.'

Surely she didn't think I was trying to pick her up?

'What's the matter?'

'I can't talk to you.'

'I'm only offering a lift.'

She looked back up the street. Did I imagine it or was that anxiety I saw in her face?

'Get in.'

She hesitated again, then seemed to make a decision. She climbed into the passenger seat and folded her arms tightly over her handbag.

'You going home?' She nodded. 'Where do you live?'

'I shouldn't be here.'

'I'm not going to attack you. Where to?'

A tiny pause. 'Out Attercliffe way.'

'Give me directions.'

I turned on to West Bar and headed towards town.

'You didn't get into trouble for talking to me, did you?'

Debbie said nothing. I stole a glance at her. Her face was shadowy but now and then it caught the light. She was pretty, but it was the prettiness of youth rather than any inherent beauty. In the office earlier she'd struck me as an open, warm-hearted girl. The chatty, gossipy type. Her sudden surliness seemed out of character.

'Who was the guy in the glasses?'

'He said I wasn't to talk to any reporters.'

'I won't tell if you don't.'

'What do you want anyway?'

'Nothing. I don't want to make things difficult for you at work.'

I concentrated on driving. You learn to sense when silence will produce more than probing with questions. We crawled through the rush-hour traffic, trapped between lines of cars and belching buses. Debbie stared out of the side window, still and distant.

'You liked him, didn't you?' I said eventually.

She turned to look at me. 'Who?'

'Richard Sutton.'

She considered this, probably calculating whether it was safe to talk about him.

'Yes, he was a wonderful man.'

'Good to work for?'

She looked across at me. I could sense her wariness. We turned into The Wicker. 'Where to now?' I asked.

'Attercliffe Road.'

Then she said: 'Yes, he was good to work for. I admired him. He was rich but he didn't do everything for money. He gave a lot away.'

I made no comment. There was an element of truth in what she was saying. Sutton probably had been more altruistic than most, but only within certain limits. I've never yet met a businessman who did anything unless there was something in it for him.

'Were you his secretary long?'

'Eighteen months.'

'Is the man in glasses your new boss?'

'God, I hope not.' The first flash of real honesty. She seemed to relax a little.

I grinned at her. 'You don't like him?'

'Not much.'

'Are you going to stay on?'

'I don't know. It won't be the same now.'

'You must have got pretty close to Mr Sutton?'

She didn't like that one. Hostility surfaced again.

'What's that supposed to mean?' she said, a touch angrily.

'Not what you think. Secretaries get to know their bosses well, working all day together, maybe the odd drink afterwards. That's all I meant.'

'Mr Sutton didn't drink.'

'OK, so . . .' I stopped. 'You mean he didn't drink with you?'

'He didn't drink with anyone. He was teetotal.'

I put my foot on the brake, slowing down so I could turn to look at her.

'You sure?'

'He never touched it. What's so funny about that? He was one of them . . . what d'you call them? Like a religion.'

Of course. I remembered suddenly from the profile I'd written on him. 'He was brought up a Quaker.'

'That's right. Alcohol was forbidden in the office, even at Christmas.'

The headlights coming towards me were just a blur now. I'd slowed to a crawl, my mind on other things. A car behind tooted its horn, jarring me back. I pressed the accelerator and caught up with the traffic ahead.

'Turn right here,' Debbie said.

I turned off. We were going towards the canal now. The streets were narrow, poorly lit.

'You live down here?' She nodded. 'Bit rough, isn't it?'

'It's cheap.'

'You rent somewhere?'

'Shared house. Just the other side of the canal.'

'How much damage did the fire do?' I slipped it in, hoping she might be off guard, but her mouth clamped shut.

'You can drop me here.'

I pulled into the side of the road.

'Please don't bother me again, I've nothing else to say,' she said coldly as she got out.

I watched her open the front door of a small red-brick terrace house and disappear inside. I wondered if I was imagining it, but she seemed frightened.

CHAPTER 4

The Frog was an unpretentious place, tucked away near the cathedral between a solicitor's office and an estate agent's. It looked more like a French transport café than a restaurant, right down to the red-checked tablecloths and Ricard ashtrays, but the food was outstanding. Not to mention expensive. I ate there only infrequently but knew the proprietor, Olivier Reboul, quite well. He was a dumpy, amiable man who claimed to be a native of Bordeaux but was actually a miner's son from Wath-upon-Dearne, real name Ollie Robinson.

His experience of France and French cuisine extended little further than a few day trips to Boulogne to buy cheap beer, but he had been running The Frog successfully for several years, largely because he was smart enough to employ a real Frenchman in his kitchen. The food was genuine *haute cuisine*, combined with a South Yorkshireman's idea of quantity, so that a meal at The Frog left you not only tantalized by delicious flavours but stuffed to the point of bursting.

I'd put on my only suit, and a white shirt and tie, but was still conscious of looking a mess. Maria wore a pale blue woollen dress which matched her eyes. Her dark hair glistened and her only jewellery was a couple of small diamond studs in her ears.

Ollie escorted us to our table and made a great Gallic show of helping Maria sit down.

'But madame eez looking very beautiful tonight,' he said, overdoing the cod accent. 'Monsieur eez a very lucky man to 'ave such a charming companion.'

'Give it a rest, Ollie,' I said. 'And get us a couple of drinks.'

'But of course, monsieur. An apéritif perhaps? Your usual, madame?'

'Please,' Maria said.

'And monsieur?'

'Just a mineral water.'

He scuttled off to the bar and came back with the drinks and two menus for us to peruse. Maria had what looked like a martini.

'How does he know what you drink?' I asked.

'I used to come here quite a lot,' Maria said. She took a sip of her drink and murmured: 'Mmn. No one makes an apéritif quite like the French.'

'You know he's not really French.'

'Who? Monsieur Reboul?'

'Ollie.'

'Of course. I just go along with the act.'

'You shouldn't. It only encourages him.'

She smiled. 'I think he's rather sweet. He sounds just like Maurice Chevalier.'

'You should hear him sing,' I said.

We browsed through the menus. When I'd made my choice, I turned my attention to the other diners. At lunch-times The Frog was full of lawyers and businessmen entertaining clients on expenses. In the evenings it was full of the same people entertaining rather more dubious guests.

I recognized a couple of middle-aged men with young women I knew were not their wives. One of them was getting up from his table to leave. He was a pompous local councillor called Brian Godsall, chairman of one of the city council committees. He hadn't seen me yet, he was so busy pawing the buxom young woman at his side.

I waited for him to come past our table and pretended to notice him.

'Brian, hello. What a surprise.'

He stopped dead and smiled weakly.

'Oh, hello, Mike.'

'Had a good dinner?'

'Yes, thank you.'

He glanced nervously at his companion. She looked about twenty-five and was wearing a low-cut, off-the-shoulder dress which revealed rather more of her character than her blank, somewhat vacuous face. I didn't think they'd been discussing council business together.

'I hope the poll-tax payers aren't footing the bill for your meal,' I said.

'What? Oh . . .' He gave a lame little laugh. 'No, no, of course not. Well, I must be off. Nice meeting you.'

'See you around. If anything interesting comes up, let me know.'

'Anything . . . ?'

'Council business.'

'Ah yes. Of course.' He ushered his companion past our table, anxious to leave.

'And Brian,' I said as he turned to follow her. 'Give my regards to your wife.'

I watched them leave, then looked back at Maria to find her watching me, half amused, half disapproving.

'That wasn't very nice.'

'What wasn't?'

'You know what I mean. Who was that poor man?'

'City councillor. Chair of one of the committees.'

'You did all that deliberately, didn't you? He was clearly embarrassed.'

'Serves him right for cheating on his wife. And doing it so publicly.'

Maria's gaze was very shrewd. 'But I don't think that's why you did it.'

'Isn't it?'

'You're going to use the knowledge against him somehow, aren't you?'

It was scary how perceptive she was. I shrugged. 'Probably.'

'For what? To get information about council business?'

I didn't say anything.

'You wouldn't tell his wife, would you?'

'Of course not. But he doesn't know that. The fear that I might is what will persuade him to be helpful the next time I ring for some confidential information.'

'Michael, that is appalling. Don't you think it's unethical?'

'This is politics, Maria. Ethics play no part in it. Anything I can use to put pressure on people like him to find out what's going on is legitimate as far as I'm concerned. You think they'd tell me voluntarily?'

'Wouldn't they?'

'Come on. It's their job to conceal things. It's my job to catch them. You ever been to a council committee meeting?'

'No.'

'It's like the Muppets, only not as funny. A rag-bag collection of misfits, megalomaniacs and self-publicists motivated by vanity and ambition. A psychiatrist's dream. You think they really want us to know what they're doing? As soon as anything interesting or controversial comes up they pass a resolution to exclude the press and public. I want to know what happens after they throw me out and I want you to know too.'

'And how far will you go to find out?'

'Don't feel sorry for politicians, Maria. They write all the rules in their own favour. Democracy is always stacked against the interests of the common people. Someone has to try to redress the balance. I'll go as far as it takes.'

'Even doing things dishonestly or illegally?'

I grinned. 'Those are the most fun.'

Ollie interrupted discreetly just then to take our orders. We told him our starters and he scribbled on his notepad.

'And 'as madame chosen 'er main course yet?' he said to Maria, continuing his impression of a bad actor auditioning for the role of a French waiter in a television sitcom.

'I think I'll have the *plat du jour*, please.'

'An excellent choice. And monsieur?'

'The veal, I think.'

'Of course. And ze wine?'

'What do you think?' I asked Maria.

'I don't know. The house white?'

'Ze 'ouse wine eez of course excellent,' Ollie said. 'Eet would suit most people.' He glanced at me to let me know this meant me. 'But perhaps madame would prefer something a touch more unusual.'

'The house white will do,' Maria said, refusing to participate in any wine snobbery.

Ollie bowed, took the menus and disappeared into the kitchen.

'I think he likes you,' I said.

Maria smiled. 'I'm an old customer. Though I haven't been in for a while.'

'You entertain clients here?'

'Occasionally. Good food can work wonders in business.'

'Maybe we could invite the tax inspector for dinner and get me off the hook.'

'Tax inspectors are not so easily corrupted, I'm afraid.'

'How do you know?'

'I've tried it before.'

'They must be stupid. I'd let you corrupt me any day.'

'On your showing this evening, I don't think there's anything I could teach you.' She finished her martini. 'Have you dug out your invoices for me yet?'

'Not exactly. They need a bit of sorting.'

She eyed me steadily. 'I hope you're not going to do what you did last year.'

'What was that?'

'Give me a shoebox full of receipts and bank statements and expect me to put them in some sort of order.'

'You're very good at it.'

'You're supposed to keep up-to-date books, Michael. Like normal self-employed people.'

'I've been a bit short of time.'

She shook her head and sighed. 'I don't know why I do your accounts, you know. You're more trouble than you're worth.'

'It's your social conscience,' I said. 'Having people like me on your books makes you feel better about all the money you earn from your rich clients.'

'Is that so?'

'Doing your bit to help life's unfortunates in the fight against the dark forces of the Inland Revenue.'

'Well, I do seem to have a lot of lame duck clients.' She looked at me pointedly. 'Some more lame than others. But I think it would be nearer the truth to say I simply can't get rid of you.'

'You want me to take my business elsewhere?'

'The accountancy community in this city is very small. If I foisted you on someone else's back, I'd never be forgiven.'

The wine arrived. Ollie went through the motions of showing me the label and letting me taste the wine, knowing

full well that I couldn't tell the difference between Château
Lafite and Castrol GTX. I gave my approval and he filled
our glasses before returning to the kitchen and bringing out
our starters.

I had some exotic concoction of chicken in pastry envelopes, Maria had a homemade terrine with about twenty
quid's worth of truffles on top. I asked Ollie if he had any
HP Sauce. He lowered his voice so the other customers
wouldn't hear and said, 'Piss off,' in his best Wath accent.
I grinned and bit into one of my envelopes. A creamy sauce,
laced with garlic and herbs and something alcoholic, crept
over my tongue and assaulted my tastebuds when they
weren't looking. A small grunt of pleasure escaped through
my lips.

'Good?' Maria asked.

I nodded. 'Yours?'

'Very.'

She picked off a slice of truffle with her fingers and slipped
it into her mouth. There was something sensuous about the
way she did it.

'Where do you suppose he gets these truffles?' she said.
'They're fresh. Can you find truffles in this country?'

'I don't know. Maybe Ollie's got his own pig he takes
truffle-hunting at weekends.'

It wouldn't have surprised me if he had. Ollie was a
fraud in many ways but he never cheated on his customers.
Everything was freshly prepared and of the highest quality.
It was the only way he could get away with the extortionate
prices.

'You busy at the moment?' Maria asked.

'I'm always busy,' I said. Standard freelancer's bluff:
never admit to being short of work.

'Doing what?'

I left out the features on waste disposal and loft insulation
and told her about Richard Sutton.

'Oh yes, I saw it in this evening's paper,' she said.

'Those were my pictures.'

'A bit gory.'

'Car crashes *are* gory.'

'It was a Rolls, wasn't it? You don't think of cars like that crumpling up.'

'It rolled a long way down a hill.'

'What happened, icy road?'

I shook my head. 'I don't think anyone really knows. The police think he was drunk.'

'Stupid.'

'But the interesting thing is, his secretary says he was teetotal.'

'He can't have been.'

I mopped up the last of my sauce with a fragment of filo pastry and popped it into my mouth, savouring the distinctive blend of flavours for the last time. I know nothing about Cordon Bleu cooking, but I'm pretty good at Cordon Bleu eating. I refilled Maria's glass with wine as she finished her terrine and dabbed her lips with a napkin. She was elegant even wiping her mouth.

'That was ve-ry good,' she said, exhaling slowly. 'I wonder how Ollie keeps his chef?'

'Pays well.'

'Not compared to London or Paris, surely.'

'Maybe he's got something on him.'

'Blackmail, you mean? I can't see Ollie as a blackmailer.'

'You've obviously never met many restaurateurs,' I said.

Maria smiled. She had very white teeth but one of the top ones was slightly crooked. A vainer person would have had it straightened. I liked the fact she hadn't.

'Chefs are ambitious people,' she continued. 'You'd have thought someone as good as this would have moved on by now.'

'Maybe he likes Sheffield. Some people do.'

'Is that why you're still here?'

I hesitated, then shrugged. 'It's my home.'

'And you've never wanted to move?'

'To London, you mean?'

'I suppose so. Wouldn't it be more interesting for someone in your line?'

'I don't know anything about London. And I've no contacts, the freelancer's lifeblood.'

'You wouldn't necessarily have to freelance, would you?
What about one of the nationals?'

I snorted. 'A staff job?'

'Yes.'

'I've done that before. You any idea what it's like to go
into an office every day and be told what to do by some
complete arsehole?'

'We all get that. But you move up the ladder and eventually it's you telling others what to do.'

'You think that's a worthwhile ambition? To become the
arsehole who gives the orders?'

'You don't have to be an arsehole, Michael.'

'You do in newspapers,' I said.

The main courses arrived. I had slices of veal cooked in
a mustard sauce. On the table in front of me were small
tureens of mange-tout peas, sauté potatoes and grilled
Provençal tomatoes. Maria had breast of chicken in an
Armagnac sauce. We said nothing for some time as we took
the edge off our hunger.

Then I asked her: 'And you? How come you're still here?'

'It's my home, too.'

'But not originally.'

'No. I trained here after university and just never left.'

'Have you wanted to?'

'Not really.'

'You got family here?'

She shook her head. 'Only my ex. And he's hardly family
any more.'

I knew she was divorced but this was the first time she'd
ever mentioned her former husband.

'You still see him?'

'No.'

'Why'd you get divorced?'

She looked at me very directly and I thought I'd pried
too far.

'Sorry. None of my business.'

'He was unfaithful,' she said simply. 'One of those men who can't stop screwing around.'

There was no bitterness in her voice, just a calm resolution. I nodded sympathetically, studying her face in the light from the candle on the table. She was a beautiful woman. I couldn't understand why any man would want more than her.

'He didn't look like a womanizer,' she said. 'Most people thought he was a straight, earnest, rather boring sort of man, but he had a compulsion to pick up other women.'

I didn't want to hear any more. I didn't want to be the one to open up the wound inside her.

'I shouldn't have asked.'

'It doesn't matter. It was all a long time ago.' She smiled. 'What's your excuse?'

'For being divorced?' She nodded. 'I'm impossible to live with some of the time.'

'Only some of the time?'

'Watch it.'

'You still friends with her?'

'Sort of. She's remarried.'

'How long did it last?'

'Three years.'

'Incompatible?'

I shrugged. 'I suppose so. We fought all the time. Lots of wonderful rows. But lots of wonderful makings-up too. Sometimes it seemed we only had the rows in order to get to the makings-up. When the rows continued but the makings-up didn't, it was time to part.'

'I'm sorry.'

She held my eyes for a moment, sharing the disillusion of love. Then she changed the subject and we consoled ourselves with The Frog's sweet trolley.

It was ten-thirty by the time the bill arrived. Ollie put it down in front of me and I passed it across to Maria. I'm not shy about that kind of thing. She paid it without a murmur and I pocketed the receipt when it came.

'Tax deductible,' I said.

'Entertaining is not deductible,' she said disapprovingly.
'I'll put it under miscellaneous expenditure.'
I helped her on with her coat and we walked to the door.
'I hope you don't do this all the time, Michael.'
'Everybody does it.'
'Not everybody is being investigated by the tax man.'
'I've got to give him something to investigate, haven't I?'
We drove through rain to Maria's house in Ranmoor, a
four-bedroomed detached place with a view over the Porter
Valley. Miles out of my league.
She made some coffee while I leaned on the worktop in
her kitchen. It was a comfortable room with few modern
touches. No formica tops, no ceramic tiles, no fitted cup-
boards concealing ironing boards or fridges. Wood pre-
dominated: mis-matched chairs, a stained oak table, a pine
chest. One wall was taken up almost entirely by photographs and postcards pinned to a large cork board.
It was an old-fashioned kitchen, but on one of the work-
tops was a variety of electrical gadgets; food processor,
liquidizer, blender, toaster, all practically new. The blender
didn't even have a plug on it.
'You do much cooking?'
'No.'
'Doesn't look like it.'
'I use convenience food.'
'So why all this lot?'
'I was given them as presents by grateful clients. All men,
of course. They think that because I'm a woman I must
like cooking.'
'Don't worry, I'll never buy you a food processor.'
'You never buy me anything.'
She had a point. 'I took you to dinner, didn't I?'
'*I* paid, remember.'
'Well, it's the thought that counts.'
I examined a curious metal machine with a handle and
holes along the bottom. 'What's this do?'
'It's a pasta machine.'
'Jesus. For the woman who has everything.'

'You put dough in the top and it comes out in strips.'

'Easier to buy a packet of spaghetti.'

'That's what I think.' She handed me a cup of coffee. 'Let's go through.'

We went into her sitting-room. Like the kitchen, it was full of her personality: warm, untidy, cluttered. There were piles of books on tables, magazines strewn over thick rugs, an assortment of battered armchairs and pictures and prints on every available inch of wallspace. In many ways it was like my own flat, yet while mine felt sordid, hers felt homely.

She put on a compact disc. String quartet music I didn't recognize.

'Borodin,' she said.

I sipped the coffee. 'Colombian.'

'You know your coffee.'

She sat down on the settee and kicked off her shoes. I kept my eyes off her legs as she curled them underneath her. She was too subtle for that.

'I had some this morning,' I said. 'Richard Sutton's wife drinks it.'

She didn't understand me at first.

'You mean you talked to her?'

'Out in Hathersage.'

'The morning after her husband was killed.'

I could see the distaste in her expression.

'She agreed. I didn't stick my foot in her door.'

'How can you do that?'

'She wanted to talk, Maria. Her husband was an important man.'

She shook her head. 'I don't know why people want to read that sort of thing.'

'Human interest.'

'Human voyeurism more like.'

'It's news.'

'Come on, Michael. Her husband's death is news. How his wife reacts is just pure invasion of privacy.'

'I didn't invade her privacy. She invited me in and gave me Colombian coffee.'

'All I can say is she must be a very strange woman.'

'Believe it or not, some people like talking to the press.'

'And did you learn much?'

'Not really. She was pretty upset.'

'What did you expect? Her husband was killed last night. Do you always go round knocking on doors the morning after?'

She made me feel ashamed. I cared what she thought.

'Sutton's death is a major news event in this city,' I said, trying to excuse myself.

'But his wife's grief isn't.'

'It's part of it.'

'Only to a journalist. No one else wants to know. It's an intrusion. Like all those pictures on television when someone's been killed. The funeral, the mourning relatives, the hordes of photographers snapping away. I don't want to see it.'

'But we have to report it. You can't omit the consequences of someone's death. It's important.'

'To whom?'

'To the people who knew the dead person, to the general estimation of what his loss means and to the public record. Without the consequences, the reactions, it's not a true picture of what happened. That's why I talked to Jacqueline Sutton. And why she talked to me. She wants her husband to be remembered.'

'In a newspaper article? It'll be old news tomorrow.'

'It's still more than most of us will get.'

Maria put down her mug of coffee and adjusted one of the cushions behind her back.

'To most people it's just another drink-driving accident,' she said.

'But different. He didn't normally drink.'

'You don't know that for sure.'

'He was brought up a Quaker. His secretary says he never touched alcohol.'

'He could have boozed on the side.'

'Sutton wasn't that type.'

'All men are that type.'

'Closet drinkers?'

'Closet deceivers.'

Her ex again. This time the edge of bitterness was there.

'We're not all like that,' I said gently.

'Did you never deceive your wife, then? Did you never lie to her?'

'Sure I did. I lied. And she lied to me. Marriage would be impossible without small deceptions.'

Maria wrinkled her nose. 'I prefer honesty.'

'Do you? Even when the truth hurts? Was there never a time when your husband told you the truth and you wished he hadn't?'

She looked away at that, her eyes clouding over with memories I could only guess at.

'I sometimes lied to her,' I said. 'But I never deceived her in the way you mean. Not all men are unfaithful, you know. That was one of my failings.'

Her eyes flickered back to mine. 'What do you mean?'

I shrugged. 'I think she resented my constancy. After she'd taken a lover of her own, that is. Her guilt would have been alleviated if I'd cheated too. As it was, I gave her no grounds for divorce. No adultery, no cruelty, no desertion. She never forgave that.'

Maria didn't say anything but there was softness in her face.

I said: 'I don't believe Richard Sutton was a closet drinker. I met him a couple of times. He seemed a remarkably sober man, in all respects. From what I can gather, he doesn't appear to have had any real vices.'

Maria smiled mockingly. 'Not everyone has as many as you.'

I grinned. 'You haven't seen half of them. Yet.'

'I can hardly wait.'

'What do you think would make a teetotaller get suddenly drunk?'

'I don't know. Some kind of stress, perhaps. He was a

rich, successful man. Rich, successful men sometimes crack up.'

'I wouldn't know much about that,' I said.

Maria laughed. The skin around her eyes crinkled like parchment. I wanted to see her laugh more.

'What about business problems?' I said.

'Did he have business problems?'

'His office caught fire last night.'

'So?'

'I just think it's a strange coincidence.'

'You mean it might not have been an accident?'

'Perhaps.'

'What do the police think?'

'I haven't asked.'

'You're not suggesting Sutton set fire to his own office, are you?'

'Stranger things have happened.'

'Was this before or after he got drunk? Why would he do that?'

'I know, it sounds unlikely.'

'You have to have a very devious mind in your line of work, don't you?'

'I try.'

She finished her coffee and looked at her watch. 'I ought to go to bed.'

I stood up and went out into the hall. The rain was drumming on the windows.

'I enjoyed tonight,' I said.

She smiled. 'Me too.'

I let her open the door.

'It's throwing it down,' she said.

'I could always stay the night instead.' I didn't look at her directly but I could feel her gaze. 'We could sit up and discuss my profit and loss account, if you like.'

'I haven't heard that one before.'

She was looking at me with a mixture of amusement and gentle tolerance. The way mothers look at their kids when they're clowning around in sandpits.

'You could tell me all about my Schedule D allowances,' I said.

'You're not very good at this, are you?' she said.

'I don't get enough practice.'

She pulled the door open further. 'Come back when you've got a bit better.'

'But, Maria, I'll get soaked out there.'

She rummaged in a box under a row of coats.

'Have an umbrella,' she said sweetly.

I found myself on the wrong side of the door in the pouring rain. I hate accountants.

CHAPTER 5

The inquest on Richard Sutton opened two days later. It was not the full hearing—that would take several months to schedule—but a preliminary formality to allow his body to be released for burial or cremation.

I got to the Medico-Legal Centre in Watery Street early and sat on the press bench in a deserted courtroom, reading the newspaper. The centre was specially built to accommodate the Coroner's Court, offices and the city mortuary. Unlike most public buildings, it was actually comfortable to be in. The floor was carpeted, the seats padded and it had air conditioning and microphones for witnesses. There aren't any others like it in the country, apparently, and it's given rise to a certain amount of civic pride. In most towns they're proud of their architecture or their football teams: in Sheffield they're proud of the morgue.

Shortly before the inquest was due to begin, the public gallery started filling up. A group of young men and women took seats near the back and I guessed they were some of Sutton's employees, a guess which was confirmed when Debbie Nolan came in with another young woman and joined them. She glanced at me but made no acknowledgement.

The door at the front of the courtroom opened and Bob
Davis, the Coroner's Officer, came in. He was accompanied
by Jacqueline Sutton and the man with the glasses, Sinclair,
from RPS Trading. Jacqueline Sutton was still wearing
mourning clothes but it was a different outfit from the one
I'd seen at her house. This time it was a black crushed silk
dress with a high neckline. A diamond brooch was pinned
to the left breast and round her neck was a slim band of
braided silver. Even in mourning she looked stunning.

Sinclair took her arm and led her proprietorially to the
row of seats in the well of the court, facing the Coroner's
bench. She detached herself from his clutch, as if she didn't
want to be touched, and sat down staring straight ahead.
I had a good view of her in profile. She was her usual poised
self but her face was tense and drawn. I saw her Adam's
apple bulge as she swallowed. Her hands gripped the black
clutchbag in her lap.

A young lad from the *Evening News* joined me on the
press bench and took out his notebook. I made a couple of
comments but he didn't seem interested in conversation so
I folded my newspaper and studied the rest of the public
gallery.

It was pretty full for an inquest but I doubted if any of
the spectators were disinterested members of the public.
People don't walk in off the street to watch an inquest. They
nearly always have some connection with the deceased.

A middle-aged man in a gabardine coat raised a hand to
me and I nodded a greeting, surprised to see him. It was
Stuart Sutherland, my ex-wife's husband. I wondered why
he was there, then worked it out. Sutherland was chairman
of a cutlery firm and a pillar of the Chamber of Commerce.
He'd probably known Richard Sutton quite well through
his business.

More interesting to me was a man at the side of the
gallery. I hadn't seen him come in but I noticed him now.
He was in his early forties, wearing a charcoal suit and
pearl silk tie. He had straw blond hair, the smooth winter
tan of the wealthy, hollow cheeks and an aquiline nose

which gave him a faintly Arabic appearance although his deep-set eyes were icy blue. He looked out of place in the drab surroundings. I wondered who he was.

As I watched, Jacqueline Sutton turned round and looked at the man. He gave a small nod but the cool aloofness of his expression did not change. Jacqueline looked at him for a second longer, then turned back to face the front of the court.

The door opened again and Bob Davis came back in.

'Court stand,' he ordered as the Coroner, Dr William Ridgeway, came in behind him.

We stood up momentarily as Ridgeway bowed to us and took his seat on the bench. He took a pair of half-moon glasses from his top pocket and peered at the documents in front of him. He cleared his throat and began speaking in a soft, almost inaudible voice tinged with the intonation of the Welsh valleys.

'This is the inquest into the death of Richard Percival Sutton, aged fifty-four, of High Close House, Hathersage, Derbyshire.'

He stopped, looked up and leaned forwards towards Jacqueline Sutton. With his small head and long, scrawny neck he looked like a tortoise peeking out of its shell to sniff the air.

'You are Mrs Sutton?'

'Yes.' Her voice was soft but firm.

'Before I go any further, I should just like to say how sorry I am about your husband. Nothing I say can bring him back, of course, but you have my deepest condolences.'

I've heard the Coroner say that dozens of times and it always surprises me how sincere he sounds. Maybe he means it.

Jacqueline Sutton said: 'Thank you.'

The Coroner shuffled his papers and turned to Bob Davis. 'Constable Davis.'

Bob stood up and went to the witness stand, actually just a small table with a mike on it. He picked up a Bible and swore himself in, then gave his name, rank and number.

His evidence lasted all of twenty seconds. He confirmed that Jacqueline Sutton had two days earlier identified to him the body of her husband, Richard Percival Sutton, aged fifty-four. Then he stood down and went back to his seat at the side of the court.

The Coroner called Police Constable Trevor Barnes, one of the two traffic cops I'd met on the night Sutton was killed.

'Could you describe what you found at the scene of the accident,' Dr Ridgeway said.

'May I refer to my notes, sir?'

'Of course.'

The constable took out his notebook and flipped it open. He gave the make and registration number of the Rolls-Royce and the location of the crash. Then said:

'The vehicle was approximately eighty yards down the hillside, the right way up but severely damaged.'

Severely damaged? That was an interesting way to describe a heap of pulped metal.

'Did you see any indication as to why the car left the road?' the Coroner inquired.

'There were skid marks near the scene of the accident, sir. The car had apparently gone straight off on a bend, taking with it a wire fence at the side of the road.'

'What were the weather conditions on the night in question?'

'It was a clear night, sir. Visibility was good, there was no fog and no ice on the road.'

'And the deceased, Mr Sutton, did you examine him?'

'Yes, sir. My colleague, PC Edwards, and I went down to the car. Mr Sutton was still behind the wheel. We attempted to revive him but he was already dead.'

'What time was this, Constable?'

Barnes checked his notebook. 'We arrived at the scene at approximately ten forty-five p.m., sir, after a passing motorist reported seeing the wreckage. The ambulance and fire brigade came about ten minutes later.'

'Thank you, Officer. You may stand down.'

The constable walked back to his seat past the press bench. I nodded at him. He glared back. Coppers are like elephants; they never forget.

The Coroner picked up a sheet of paper and read it out. It was the medical report from one Dr Elizabeth Addison, a pathologist at the Royal Hallamshire Hospital, who had done the post-mortem examination on Richard Sutton. She wasn't in court but would probably be present when the full inquest was heard.

The Coroner read out the report. It didn't make easy listening, particularly for Jacqueline Sutton. She looked down and closed her eyes as Dr Ridgeway described the injuries her husband had sustained. I felt intensely sorry for her.

Then Dr Ridgeway read out the results of the blood test. The alcohol reading was two-hundred milligrams per hundred millilitres of blood. The legal limit, I knew, was eighty milligrams. There was no doubt about it. Richard Sutton had been drunk when he died.

Jacqueline Sutton let out a small gasp when the figures were read out. She shook her head in disbelief. Sinclair clasped her hand for a brief instant. The lad from the *News* next to me was scribbling furiously. He'd got his angle.

The Coroner reached the end of the report and the pathologist's conclusion as to the cause of death. Quite simply, multiple injuries due to a road traffic accident.

Dr Ridgeway put the sheet on the file in front of him and leaned across towards Jacqueline Sutton again.

'I have given the necessary authorization for your husband's body to be released for . . . I understand you wish him to be cremated.'

Mrs Sutton nodded lifelessly. She appeared to be in a state of shock.

'I'm afraid I cannot issue a death certificate until after the full inquest, which I hope to hold as soon as possible. But I will give you a letter for your husband's bank or solicitor which may assist you in obtaining the necessary funds from his estate to pay the funeral expenses.'

He forced a smile of sympathy and pushed back his chair.
Bob Davis stood up and said, 'Court stand,' again. The
Coroner went out through the side door. The whole thing
had taken less than fifteen minutes.

I stayed in my seat while everyone filed out. Stuart
Sutherland stopped by the press bench on his way from the
public gallery. We shook hands.

'Hello, Stuart.'

'How are you, Michael?'

'Fine. You?'

'The same.'

'And Alison?' Alison was my ex.

'Very well.'

Stuart was in his late forties with greying hair, easy
manners and a restless energy which pulsed through his
wiry body. He was never still and when you talked to him
you always got the impression he was itching to be somewhere else.

'I didn't expect to see you here,' I said.

'Richard was a friend of mine. Are these things always
like that, so short, business-like?'

I nodded. 'The full inquest will be longer, but not much.'

'I'd expected more. Why was it necessary, in any case?'

'They always have them in road traffic accidents.'

'Putting his wife through a public ordeal like that. Is she
going to have to do it again?'

'Yes.'

'I suppose all that stuff about the alcohol's going to end
up in the papers.'

'It has to, Stuart.'

He pressed his lips tight and shook his head. 'Dreadful
business. Jackie is going to be very upset. I'd better go and
see how she is.' He shook my hand. 'Call in some time.'

'Say hello to Alison for me,' I said, but Stuart was already
half way to the exit.

I looked back through my notes. The scrawled, spidery
outlines made me wish, not for the first time, that I'd paid
more attention in shorthand classes when I was a trainee.

Half the words were unreadable and it was only because they were fresh in my memory that I could transcribe them at all.

I checked the quotes from the Coroner, writing the long-hand translations in above the shorthand outlines. They had to be accurate. I could get away with making up quotes on most stories, but not a legal hearing like an inquest. That was courting disaster.

One indecipherable scribble in the medical evidence eluded me. It began with a letter 'c', but I couldn't work out what it was. I mused over it for a moment without getting any further, then decided to ask Bob Davis for a hand.

Collecting up the notebook and pen and rolling up my newspaper, I went out of the courtroom.

In the ante-room outside, Stuart Sutherland was talking to Jacqueline Sutton, Sinclair and the blond man in the charcoal suit. Jacqueline Sutton saw me come out. She broke away and walked over to me.

'Hello,' I said.

Mrs Sutton nodded without saying anything. Then she hesitated, unsure of herself.

'I hope you don't mind . . .' she began. She kept her voice so low I had to lean towards her to hear what she was saying.

'. . . but if you're free, I wonder if you'd do something for me.'

I waited. 'What is it?'

'Would you come to the house this afternoon? Any time that's convenient, three, four o'clock. I'd be grateful.'

The words came out in a hurry as if she'd approached me on impulse. I sensed she didn't want to talk now.

'Yes, if you want me to.'

'Thank you.'

She didn't look at me. Her eyes were on the clutchbag in her hands. Her fingers were interwoven round the bag in a tight clasp. The strain was showing.

She turned and walked away abruptly. Sinclair touched

her on the shoulder, his face concerned. She shook her head and said something I couldn't catch. Then the four of them went out through the door and downstairs to the exit.

I crossed the landing, knocked on the door of Bob Davis's office and went in. He was behind his desk, writing notes in a cardboard file.

'Got a minute, Bob?'

He didn't look up. 'Thirty seconds, the Coroner wants to see me about another case.'

'More bodies?'

'It's always more bodies.'

I had a good view of his bald pate, a smooth, shiny dome of pale skin. I wondered offhand why bald people don't get dandruff. Does it blow away or do they just not moult?

Bob was one of the few coppers I liked. He had a relaxed, good-natured attitude and never seemed to think his uniform gave him the right to throw his weight around. He'd been Coroner's Officer for as long as I could remember but the work hadn't jaded him. I once asked him how he stood it, spending all his working life with corpses. 'Regular hours and the clients never answer back,' he replied.

'What do you want?' he asked now.

'Can I have a quick look at the Sutton file? My short-hand's a bit rusty, I just wanted to check a couple of things.'

'You should pay more attention.' He pulled a brown folder across the desk. 'And another thing, do you have to read the paper in court?'

'I don't do it during the sitting.'

'But the relatives see you before the Coroner comes in. It's upsetting.'

'OK, I'll remember.'

'What d'you want to check?'

'The post-mortem.'

'Which bit?'

'Can I read it?'

'It's a court document. You should have listened to what the Coroner said.'

'Come on, Bob, just a quick look.'

He shook his head firmly. 'Sorry. You want to check spellings of names, addresses, that kind of thing, that's OK. But I can't let you read through the whole thing.'

'Why not? It was read out in court.'

'Then you should have taken notes.'

The door opened and a young woman poked her head in.

'The Coroner is ready now, Mr Davis,' she said.

'I'll be right there, Sandra.'

He stood up.

'I'd like to help, Mike, but it's not on. I'm not bending the rules for anyone.'

'OK. Thanks anyway.'

I went out of his office, across the ante-room and through the swing door at the top of the stairs. I caught the door before it closed fully and peered back through the narrow crack.

Bob came out of his office carrying a folder and went down the corridor. I waited for him to disappear, then sneaked out and went back into his office. I checked the connecting office. It was empty.

The file on Richard Sutton was still on Bob's desk. I opened it and took out the post-mortem report. There was no time to read it thoroughly so I photocopied it on the machine in the corner of the office instead.

As I was putting it back in the file, another idea came to me. There were only a few other documents in the folder. Why not? It wouldn't take long. I weighed up the odds on getting caught and took a chance. I photocopied them all. I just can't resist it when I get my hands on a confidential file.

Then, the copies stashed safely in my inside jacket pocket, I went downstairs. Crossing the foyer, I was stopped by the girl at the reception desk near the front door.

'Excuse me. Are you Mr McLean?'

I turned. 'Yes.'

'There's a message here for you.'

I went to the counter and she handed me a piece of paper folded into a square. I opened it. It said simply:

'Please come and see me tonight.'

It was signed by Debbie Nolan.

I rubbed my chin pensively. First Jacqueline Sutton asks to see me. Now Debbie Nolan. My, I *was* getting popular. It was a totally new sensation for me. But one I could get to like.

I drove into town and went to Archie's wine bar for a coffee. At night it's a horrific place, full of blow-dried men in white suits and women showing their knickers, but in daylight it's bearable. The creeps only come out after dark.

I ordered a cappuccino from a waitress in a white shirt and red braces. The braces were tucked round the sides of her breasts to stop them chafing her nipples.

While I was waiting for the coffee I went to the payphone next to the bar and rang Gordon Crieff at the police press office.

'Gordon, a couple of days ago there was a fire. Green Lane. You remember?'

'Aye.'

'Got anything more on it?'

'Like what?'

'Like what caused it.'

'Hold on, will ye.'

There was a delay before he came back on the line.

'I've nothing on the cause yet. Stuff's probably with forensic still. Ye could ask CID.'

'Who reported it?'

'The night watchman at the engineering works up the road.'

'What time?'

I heard the rustle of sheets of paper. 'About ten past nine.'

'Any estimate of the damage yet?'

'Too early tae say.'

'What was lost?'

'Nothing very interesting,' Crieff said. 'Just office stuff. A few chairs, desks, carpeting, filing cabinets, stationery, that kind of thing.'

'Was it arson?'

'I canna say, laddie. That's all I've got at the moment.'

'Thanks, Gordon.'

I rang off and went back to my table as the cappuccino arrived; 90p for a bit of froth and a sprinkling of Cadbury's drinking chocolate. But if you will go to a poseur's place you have to drink what they drink.

I stirred the foam on the coffee and started to read the sheets I'd photocopied in Bob Davis's office, the post-mortem report first.

It was written in pathologist's jargon, full of medical terms and words like 'contusion' instead of bruise. Maybe 'contusion' was the word I couldn't read in my notes? I checked the shorthand. It wasn't contusion. I read on and found it. It was 'contrecoup'. No wonder I couldn't read the outline, it wasn't even English. 'Evidence of contrecoup on the back of the brain,' the report said. What the hell was contrecoup?

I read my notes again. I had enough to go on without that particular bit of the post-mortem. Sutton had died of multiple injuries: broken legs, crushed spleen, fractured thigh joints, chest wounds and a blow to the front of the head. I could leave out the 'contrecoup' without affecting the accuracy of my story.

The rest of the photocopied file I read out of sheer curiosity. Part of me was simply checking I hadn't missed anything important at the inquest. But another part was hoping to find something more interesting. Maybe something the police had withheld, a suspicious circumstance, a vital detail, anything that might have given me more of a story. There was nothing. Apart from the identity of the victim, it was just a pretty ordinary road traffic accident.

There were statements from the two traffic coppers who'd got to the scene of the crash first and various other official documents, including a copy of a police report on the vehicle itself.

This itemized the damage to the Rolls-Royce and continued with a mechanic's assessment of the roadworthiness of the car before the crash. Given the state of the vehicle when it was examined, this particular section of the report contained a lot of provisos, but the conclusion was as certain as it could be. There had been no mechanical fault in the car, brakes, steering, suspension or anything else, which might have caused the crash.

In addition, there was a list of the contents of the car: several maps, a torch, cassettes, a chamois leather, toolkit, a can of WD40 to help it start in winter—surely a libellous accessory in a Rolls-Royce—some de-icer, a windscreen scraper and a bottle of Opium perfume, presumably Jacqueline's, she was the type who would have emergency stocks of perfume all over the place.

There was also a smashed bottle of Bell's whisky. This was the bottle Gordon Crieff had mentioned when he told me Sutton had been drunk. I tried to imagine what had happened that evening. What had made Sutton, the teetotaller, buy a bottle of whisky, take it to his car and drink it?

But there was something else about the list of contents which bothered me. For some reason it didn't look right. I had a feeling it wasn't complete. It wasn't what was on it that seemed wrong; it was what was missing. I stared at the words for five minutes but couldn't work out why exactly I was troubled. Perhaps it was just my imagination.

I ordered another cappuccino and spent the next hour writing a few paragraphs on the inquest and phoning them over to the nationals, the Press Association and Yorkshire TV and the BBC in Leeds.

By the time I'd finished it was lunch-time, the perfect time to catch a policeman when he's at his most vulnerable: with a pint in his hand.

I went down to the Two Chuffs near police headquarters. This was a real spit and sawdust pub which looked as if it could no longer afford the sawdust and was getting by on just the spit. No one knew why it was called the Two Chuffs but I'd hazard a guess it was after the landlord and his wife who were the rudest, most bigoted mine hosts I'd ever encountered.

I went inside and braced myself against the lung-clogging barrage of tobacco smoke. It was half full, mostly with policemen and reporters from the *News*. The coppers go there because they like to mix with the low life; the journalists go because they *are* the low life.

I looked around. I recognized most of the reporters and subs, a bunch of bleary-eyed wrecks pickling themselves in gin. Some had been brain dead for years but it didn't affect their work. Brain death was almost a qualification for the job. You're only supposed to need a reading age of 12 to read the *News* but what most people don't realize is that you only need a reading age of 12 to *write* it. I've never subscribed to the theory that if you put a bunch of monkeys in a cage with a typewriter, they'll eventually produce the complete works of Shakespeare. But they'd manage to cobble together a story for the *News* all right. Probably faster than the reporters who work on it.

Chris Strange was round the side of the bar clutching a pint of Ward's bitter in a podgy fist. It hadn't taken much detective work to find him, he was always there at lunch-time.

I pushed through to join him.

'Buy you a drink, Chris?'

He scowled at me. 'What do you want, McLean?'

'I knew you'd be pleased to see me.'

'Don't bet on it.'

I squeezed into the bar next to him, not without difficulty. Strange was only just above regulation height but way over regulation width. He had a beer gut on him the size of a dromedary's hump but, unlike a camel, could only go without a drink for about an hour and a half maximum. He was an old-fashioned cop, but not too old-fashioned. The real traditionalists knock suspects about a bit in the interview room, then make up the evidence. Strange would just make up the evidence, which I suppose is progress.

'What do you want?' he repeated.

'I saw you at the bar. I thought you might want some company.'

'If I did, she'd be better-looking than you.'

'You working on anything at the moment?'

'McLean, you wouldn't be trying to grease some information out of me, would you?'

'Just oiling the wheels of police-press relations. What're you having?'

'You realize I'm a responsible police officer who cannot be bought by the offer of a drink? I'll have a pint.'

I've never known a copper turn down a free drink, it's not in their nature. I ordered the beer while Strange took out a packet of cigarettes and stuck one in his mouth.

'You'd given up smoking last time I saw you,' I said.

'I still need them when I'm under stress.'

'Are you under stress now?'

'I wasn't till you arrived. What're you after?'

'I hope you've recovered from your night on the moors.'

'You haven't come here to ask about my health.'

'What were you doing out there anyway? Traffic accidents aren't usually in your line.'

'I'm a broadminded sort of bloke. Is that all?'

'RPS Trading,' I said.

He inhaled on his cigarette and gave me a deadpan look.

'Green Lane,' I prompted.

'Yeah?'

'You going to make this hard for me?'

'I'll make it impossible if I have to.'

'I thought you guys were supposed to be cooperating with the press.'

'You can't believe everything you read in the paper.'

'You involved in the case?'

'Gordon Crieff send you over here?'

'It was all my own idea.'

'What makes you think I know anything about it?'

'You get all the serious cases. Arson's pretty serious.'

Strange sighed deeply. 'How come you're such a pain in the arse, McLean?'

'I take classes in it.'

'Why can't you be like all these blokes in here?' He jerked his head at a table of *News* reporters. 'Put your brain on hold for a while.'

He finished his pint and started on the one I'd bought him without a pause.

'You should get an intravenous drip,' I said. 'Save you having to lift all those heavy glasses.'

He wiped the froth off his Mexican bandit moustache. His jacket bulged over his biceps. All plainclothes cops wear tight jackets. They must have some special store where they buy undersized suits.

'Who says it was arson?'

'Just a guess.'

'It was a small office fire, that's all.'

'You can make it off the record if you like. What did Scenes of Crime find?'

'I'm not telling you that.'

'OK. But you're confirming it wasn't an accident. That's why you were out on the moors the other night, isn't it?'

'This more guesswork?'

'The fire was reported at nine o'clock. Two hours later you're out in the heather dodging sheep and looking over a body in a wrecked car. The body just happens to be that of the man whose office caught fire.'

'Coincidence.'

'I believe in fairies too.'

'Maybe I needed some fresh air and exercise.'

I glanced at his paunch. 'Well, I can believe that. But that's not why you were out there. Was it arson?'

He took his time. It breaks his heart to volunteer information.

'Yes,' he said finally.

'That wasn't hard, was it? You round up the usual suspects yet?'

'We've got nothing to go on.'

'That's never stopped you in the past.'

'Don't be too smart, McLean. I'm doing you a favour.'

'Any idea why anyone wanted to burn down the offices?'

'No.'

'Or who?'

'We make any progress, you'll be the first to know.'

'How about Sutton himself?'

Strange took his cigarette out of his mouth and flicked ash on to the floor.

'What makes you think he might have done it?'

'It must have crossed your mind. Isn't that the first thing you check with an arson? Inside job, insurance fraud, all that kind of thing. And Sutton was working late that night.'

Strange's eyes flickered with interest. He tried to hide it, but it was there all right.

'How d'you know that?'

'His wife told me.'

'His secretary said he left at six.'

'She see him go?'

'She walked out of the building with him.'

'He could have gone back later,' I said.

'The locks were smashed in.'

'So?'

'Sutton had keys to the place.'

'Maybe he wanted it to look like an outside job.'

'Aren't you making this a bit complicated?'

'You think it's simple?' I took a sip of my own drink. Strange was stubbing his cigarette out in an empty glass on the bar. Flakes of ash mixed with the dregs of beer in the bottom of the glass.

Don Soper, the landlord of the pub, paused in the pint he was pulling and leaned over from the Ward's pump. 'Now then, pillock. Don't stub your fucking fag ends out in the glasses.' He was restraining himself; usually he's rude to people.

Strange said mildly: 'What else do I use?'

'The bleeding ashtray, chuff.'

'You see one?'

'That's because you fucking coppers nick 'em all.' Soper continued pulling his pint. Strange looked back at me, totally unconcerned.

'Crieff told me there wasn't much damage,' I said. 'In the fire.'

'There wasn't.'

'Desks, chairs, carpets, he said. Anything else?'

Strange drained his glass. 'How much information do you get for a pint of beer?' He turned away.

'You going?'

'Back to the office for a rest.'

'Buy you another some time,' I said.

'No, thanks,' Strange said. 'It's too exhausting.'

He pushed his way through the crowd. No stamina, cops, that's their trouble.

I thought about what Strange had told me. And he hadn't told me as much as he knew; cops never do. None of it made much sense on the surface, but I've been around enough to know the surface is the last place to look for sense. It's the undercurrents that matter. Only right now the water was so cloudy I couldn't see the undercurrents.

One thing was sure, though. Someone hadn't set fire to Richard Sutton's offices just to destroy the carpet and a few bits of furniture.

CHAPTER 6

Jacqueline Sutton was sitting on the same flowery settee when the maid showed me into the room overlooking the garden. She rose to meet me and held out a hand.

'Mr McLean, thank you for coming. Would you like some tea?' Ever the perfect hostess.

'Thank you.'

She nodded to the maid. 'We'll take it immediately, Louise.'

'Yes, madam.'

Mrs Sutton sat back down and gestured with her hand. 'Please, join me here.'

I sat down at the other end of the settee and half turned towards her. She was looking better than the first time we'd met. The shadows under her eyes had begun to fade, the redness was less noticeable, but the air of sorrow was still there. It would be a long time before that disappeared.

She didn't say anything so I broke the ice.

'You must have found this morning distressing.'

She thought before she replied. 'Yes, it was rather. I'd never been to an inquest before. I suppose you've been to lots.'

'Quite a few.'

'I found it, well, a little impersonal. It was hard to believe someone had really died. I don't mean I forgot for even a second that Richard was gone. It's just that it seemed such a brief, indifferent formality for something as serious as a death.'

'They're not easy for bereaved relatives.'

'The Coroner was very sympathetic. And the Coroner's Officer . . .'

'Bob Davis.'

'Yes. He was kind. He said there would have to be another inquest.'

'There will.'

'Why is that?'

'It always happens. They open and then adjourn. I think in some places they wait and just hold the one, but that can take months. At least this way you have the funeral relatively soon.'

'It's next Tuesday. At the crematorium at Hutcliffe Wood. That's what Richard wanted. Something very simple. He was a Quaker, you know. He didn't practise but he was brought up as one. Ackworth and all that. The Quaker boarding-school,' she added by way of explanation.

She seemed on edge. It wasn't surprising considering what she'd been through over the past few days. I wondered when she'd get to the point and say why she'd asked me to come out to see her.

The maid brought in the tea on a tray. China cups and saucers, a silver milk jug and sugar bowl, a pot covered by a knitted cosy. Then plates and one of those peculiar, Christmas tree-like stacks of tiny shelves you get in expensive hotels. This one was silver and had three decks bearing, from the bottom upwards, triangular ham and cucumber sandwiches with the crusts cut off, buttered scones and slices of fruit cake. My system found it hard to adapt to such civilized living.

Mrs Sutton poured the tea through a silver strainer and handed it to me.

'It's Earl Grey. I hope you don't mind.'

I shook my head, trying to create the impression I never drank anything but.

'Help yourself to sandwiches or whatever.'

'Thank you.'

I put one of the sandwiches on my plate and perched it on my knee. The sandwich was small enough to eat in one go. In fact, by the standards of my normal two-inch doorsteps, it was about a quarter of a mouthful, but I controlled myself and nibbled one of the corners in a genteel fashion. Mrs Sutton had a very thin slice of fruitcake.

'What will happen at the full inquest?' she asked.

'Pretty much the same as today. The pathologist will be there to answer questions, and any other relevant witnesses too.'

'What kind of witnesses?'

'Well, like the police officer who was first on the scene. Or anyone else they find who might be of help. Perhaps someone who saw the crash.'

She paused, her teacup half way to her mouth.

'*Did* anyone see it?'

'Not that I know of. But there might be someone. The police will be looking. An eyewitness might be able to shed some light on how it all happened.'

'And then the Coroner gives his verdict?' I nodded. 'Will there be a jury?'

'No. Juries are a rarity. Especially in straightforward road accidents.'

I saw her expression and regretted the remark immediately.

'I'm sorry, I didn't mean it like that.'

'It's all right. I know what you meant.' She smiled reassuringly. 'I'm sure to the Coroner it *is* pretty straightforward. Please, do have some more to eat. Louise makes the cake and the scones herself.'

I took a slice of fruitcake. It was rich and dark, thick with fruit, and even at a distance I could smell the aroma of brandy.

Mrs Sutton got up suddenly and went to the window. She stared out at the overcast sky and seeping drizzle. Her face and blonde hair caught the light.

She said: 'I hope you don't mind my asking you out here.'

'Not at all.'

'You probably think it a little strange.'

I waited.

'You seemed sympathetic when you were here on Tuesday. I don't know much about these things, but you're a reporter. I thought perhaps you would.'

'Know what?'

'In a case like this, Richard's crash I mean, what would the verdict usually be?'

'The Coroner's verdict? Accidental death, in most cases.'

I wondered why she was asking me and not the Coroner's Officer.

She came back to the settee and sat down again.

'It gave me a shock this morning to find out he was drunk. A terrible shock. Richard was teetotal. I never saw him touch alcohol the whole time we were married.' She watched for my reaction.

'Never?' I said.

'He was very disciplined about things like that.'

'Through religious conviction?'

She shook her head. 'He lost his faith long ago. He wasn't always an abstainer. He rebelled against his Quaker up-bringing in his twenties. I think he did a few foolish things under the influence of drink—haven't we all?

'He never talked about it much, but he had a girlfriend at that time who got drunk at a party and fell off a third-floor balcony. She was killed. It wasn't Richard's fault, but he felt partly responsible for it. He gave up alcohol after that and he stuck to his vow until the night he died.'

'Why are you telling me this?'

'Would it make any difference to the inquest verdict? The fact that he was teetotal.'

'Does the Coroner know?'

'No. I don't know whether to mention it. I spoke to Nigel this morning, Nigel Sinclair. He was Richard's financial director. He said I should let sleeping dogs lie. What do you think?'

I rounded up the last crumbs of fruitcake on my plate and popped them into my mouth. Whatever Mrs Sutton wanted of me I was pretty sure it wasn't advice about inquests.

'I think I'd tell him,' I said. 'Let him decide whether it's relevant. Tell Bob Davis first, he's an understanding man.'

'Would it influence the verdict?'

That was a more interesting question. And one I felt she must already have considered herself. She was too intelligent not to have.

'I've been to a lot of inquests,' I said. 'Quite a few of them road traffic accidents where drink was involved. The verdict was nearly always accidental death.'

'Nearly always?'

There was no way to be gentle about it. 'In the others it was suicide.'

She nodded very slowly. 'And telling the Coroner Richard was teetotal would open up the possibility of a suicide verdict?'

'The possibility is there already. It happens. People get drunk and crash their cars deliberately. The Coroner will

already have considered that, so will the police. The fact
that your husband didn't drink is just another factor to take
into account.'

'An important one?'

'I'd let the Coroner be the judge of that.' I leant towards
her and touched her hand reassuringly. 'Mrs Sutton, I can
understand your concern. It's traumatic for relatives to consider the possibility that someone they loved may have
taken their own life. The Coroner knows that too. He
doesn't reach a verdict without thorough consideration of
the evidence. There's no reason to believe your husband
killed himself, is there?'

'He got drunk.'

'There are a thousand reasons why people get drunk.
And very rarely do they do it with the intention of commit-
ting suicide.'

'It was way out of character.'

'Do you have any other reason to suspect the crash might
have been deliberate?'

She shook her head.

'Was he depressed?'

'No.'

'Was he under pressure of any kind?'

'No more than usual. As you can imagine, he was always
under pressure of some sort. What businessman isn't? But
he'd been handling that kind of stress for years.'

'Did anything happen that day that might explain why
he had a few drinks in the evening?'

'I asked Nigel that after the inquest. He said there was
nothing out of the ordinary about Monday. Nothing happened at the office. No catastrophes or rows. Richard was
a very calm man. He didn't let things upset him and that's
how he worked. If problems arose, he dealt with them. He
didn't let them get on top of him.'

'You know there was a fire at his office on Monday night?'

'Yes. The police came here yesterday. A detective-
sergeant from Sheffield.'

'Short, fat, moustache?'

'Do you know him? Strange, he said his name was.'

'We've met.'

'He asked me a lot of questions. He was, well, rather abrupt.'

'That sounds like Strange.'

'He implied that Richard might have started the fire.'

'Did he now?' I thought about my conversation with Strange in the Two Chuffs a few hours earlier. He hadn't seemed too keen on that particular theory then. Devious sod.

'Why would your husband do that?' I asked.

'He wouldn't. I told the Sergeant it was preposterous.'

'Did you speak to your husband on Monday? Did he give you any inkling that something might be wrong?'

'No. We had breakfast together that morning. He seemed in good spirits. He drove to the office as usual, then—' she swallowed and screwed up her eyes as if they hurt—'I never saw him again.

'You know, I could cope. I could . . .' The words weren't coming out.

She let out a tiny sob and started to cry. Not a gentle release of tears but something much more intense.

I tried to look away but my eyes kept coming back to her face all crumpled up with grief. It was impossible not to be moved by her suffering. She was only a foot or two away from me. I did the only thing I could. I reached across and took her into my arms.

She came willingly, seeking the comfort of human contact. She was frailer than she looked. Her body pressed against mine. I smelt shampoo in her hair and perfume on her skin.

She tried to speak but I cut her off. 'Later. Just let it out now.' She lay against my chest, shaking, and I held her until the sobs began to subside.

In time she pulled away. She picked her handbag up from beside the settee and fumbled in it for a handkerchief.

'I'm sorry. I didn't mean . . .'

'It's all right.'

'I've embarrassed you now.'

'You haven't.'

'Thank you for . . . you know. I've ruined your shirt.

I smiled. 'It'll dry. Are you all right?'

She nodded and blew her nose. Even with tears on her face she looked beautiful. But the sadness went deep in her. She must have truly loved her husband. I wondered if he had appreciated it.

'I'm so sorry,' she apologized again. 'I hate doing things like that.'

'Please, Mrs Sutton, you don't have to say anything.'

She smiled. 'You're very understanding.' She dabbed at her face. 'My make-up's ruined.'

She took a mirror out of her handbag and looked at herself in it. She wiped away the tears and smudges of mascara with that total lack of self-consciousness women exhibit when tending to their looks. My presence didn't trouble her in the least; she seemed only worried about her appearance.

She touched up her eyes and cheeks. 'Forgive me,' she said.

'Don't apologize.'

'It's just that Richard and I were very close. We hadn't been married all that long, three years, nearly four. I'm coming to terms with the fact that he's dead, but what I cannot bear to think is that he died with some terrible burden on his mind.

'I can't think of any other reason why he would get drunk like that. It would hurt me deeply if there was something he hadn't told me about, he always used to confide in me absolutely.'

She looked me straight in the face. 'You're a journalist You know people round here. You pick things up from all over the place, I'm sure.'

'What are you trying to say?'

'The police aren't being very communicative. They seem to suspect Richard of something. If you hear anything, anything that might touch on Richard or his business, would you let me know? I've had too many shocks over the last few days. I don't want anything to come out without at least some kind of warning. Can you understand that?'

'Perfectly. If I hear anything, I'll be in touch.'

'Thank you. Would you like some more tea?'

I shook my head. 'I have to be going.'

She gave me her hand again. It was much less formal this time. The direct look and gentle pressure of her fingers left me in no doubt that we were no longer mere strangers.

On the drive back into Sheffield I wondered about her. I was puzzled. She had asked me a number of questions but at no time, I felt, had she explained the real reason why she'd asked me to the house. Yet somewhere in our incoherent conversation there must have been a subtle motive.

Sensible, intelligent people do not confide in journalists. If they want to talk, they turn to friends, relatives, the local vicar, the Samaritans. You'd have to be crazy to confide in a reporter, especially one you hardly knew. Yet that's what she'd done. It was almost as if she were inviting me to poke my nose further into her husband's affairs. If that was the reason, I could have saved her the effort. I'd already decided to do just that.

The second post had brought me yet more unwanted mail. A wad of promotional junk from the *Reader's Digest*, a package from a mail-order house telling me I could win a car if I ordered their catalogue, and a letter from my bank manager asking me to come in to discuss my 'unauthorized overdraft'.

I filed them all in the wastepaper bin and went into the kitchen to look for something to eat. I already knew I wouldn't find anything but went through the motions of checking the cupboards and fridge just in case I'd overlooked a stale biscuit or shrivelled lettuce leaf. There was nothing.

I sighed and sat down for a moment to prepare my body for the forthcoming ordeal. I'd put it off for days but now

I had no choice. I was going to have to go shopping.

Tesco's was bedlam. I'd hit the early evening rush hour and every aisle was a jam of frantic consumers: mothers with kids in tow, men in suits buying a pint of milk and a loaf of bread on the way home from work, smart women in high heels with baskets full of cottage cheese and low-fat yoghurt.

I raced around filling my trolley with tins of beans and cream crackers and ready-prepared meals, anything that took less than ten minutes to cook, and broke my own personal best by forty-three seconds.

Then I waited in the check-out line for half an hour behind five women who appeared to be feeding families of fifty. By the time I reached the front, my frozen TV dinners had almost thawed out and I was looking for someone to murder. If men had to do most of the shopping in this world, supermarket check-outs would be like Beirut on a bad day.

I had pre-packed stick-in-the-oven-and-frazzle lasagne and apple-flavoured cardboard pie for dinner, then drove to Debbie Nolan's house.

As I turned off Attercliffe Road towards the canal, I saw blue flashing lights ahead of me. Two police cars and a police van were parked by the bridge, half on the pavement, half on the road. I couldn't see over the parapet but the surrounding buildings were illuminated in a bright light which could only have come from the canal towpath.

Some faint premonition touched me and I shivered involuntarily. I didn't know what it was. I drove across the bridge and parked, then walked back.

An old man with a dog on a leash was leaning over the parapet. I stopped by him and looked down. The section of canal below us was lit up by floodlights. The water which in daylight was a cloudy yellow, was an impenetrable strip of charcoal black. In the middle of it, two dark heads bobbed up and down, occasionally disappearing altogether beneath the inky surface. When one of the heads turned, I saw the mask and aqualung mouthpiece on the front. Police divers.

At the side, on the cordoned-off towpath, other police officers were waiting. Not talking or doing anything, just waiting. The light bathed them in an unnatural whiteness, but beyond, the darkness folded round obliterating all detail. There was no sound except the hum of the generator for the lights and the splash of the divers searching the water.

'What happened?' I said to the old man.

'Body in t'water.'

'You see it?'

'Naow, they took it away afore I got 'ere. But one of t'coppers told me.'

'He say who it was?'

The old man shook his head and wiped his nose with the back of a gnarled hand. 'Just some girl. He didn't know 'owt else.'

An icy chill suddenly constricted my breathing and I felt slightly sick. I leaned my weight on the parapet and closed my eyes until the spasm passed. There was no evidence, but I knew that the girl in the canal had been Debbie Nolan.

CHAPTER 7

There was a stench in the air, a pungent, sour odour which pricked the inside of the nostrils. It was the sharp industrial smell of coke and sulphur and soot which you can still find in parts of the city on damp winter nights and which, thirty years ago, gave rise to the jokes about Sheffield people waking up to the sound of birds coughing.

I left the car and walked the last hundred yards to Debbie Nolan's house. The terraces followed the bend in the road and the end house curved right round the corner, a common feature in the area as many of the houses were built by

brickies who were used to constructing cylindrical cemen-
tation furnaces for the steel industry. The lights were on
inside Debbie's house. I rang the bell.

The door was opened by a uniformed police constable,
confirming my guess about the body in the canal. Why else
should he be there?

'I'm expected,' I said, taking a step inside.

The copper blocked my path. 'Sorry, sir, you can't come
in.'

I could hear the murmur of voices from the back of the
house.

'What's going on?'

'Who are you?'

'It was Debbie, wasn't it? The body.'

The copper hesitated but didn't move aside.

'Could I have your name, sir?'

A voice from down the passage said: 'Don't bother, I
already know it.'

Chris Strange was standing in the shadows at the far end.

'Hello, Chris. Got a minute?'

'Push off, McLean. I've nothing to say.'

'What happened down at the canal?'

Strange gestured curtly at the constable. 'Williams,
escort Mr McLean out into the street. And don't let him
back in.'

I edged away from the constable's outstretched arm.

'Now wait a minute. Since when was this your house?'

'Throw him out, Williams.'

'What about a statement first?'

'You'll get a statement from the press office in the morning. You're getting nothing now.'

'What about the other people in the house?' Debbie had
told me she shared.

'What other people?' Strange said.

'Don't tell me those voices I heard just now were only
you talking to yourself. They might want me to stay.'

Strange took a deep breath. 'No one in their right mind

would ever want you to stay anywhere, McLean. Now do you leave, or do we boot you out?'

'It's all right, he can stay.'

It was a girl's voice. She'd come out of the room behind Strange and was standing half hidden behind his not inconsiderable bulk. I recognized her as the girl who'd been at Richard Sutton's inquest with Debbie.

Strange glowered and turned his head to look at her.

'You know he's a reporter?'

'I don't mind.'

'Look, Miss Hughes, we wouldn't advise you to talk to the press at the moment. We're conducting an investigation.'

'All the same, Sergeant, he can stay.'

Her manner was firm. I had to admire her guts. Strange could be intimidating when he chose to be.

Before she was persuaded to change her mind I said: 'I'll wait in the front room until you've finished.'

It was cold and unwelcoming. The main light was harsh and there were no table lamps to soften its glare. The furniture was old and soiled, the carpet worn away in patches and in one corner the wallpaper was peeling away. It smelt of damp; a typical run-down rented house. I huddled in an armchair and shivered.

It was ten, perhaps fifteen minutes later that the door opened. Strange came in alone. He put his notebook away in his pocket and eased himself into the tatty chair opposite me. His moustache shone as if it had been slicked down with Brylcreem. He looked at me.

'You know, a bloke could get to hate you without too much difficulty, McLean.'

'Some people find it easier than others.'

'That girl's in a state of shock. You going to ask her questions?'

'You did.'

'That's different. This is a police matter.'

'You heard her. She said I could stay.'

'How did you get here?'

'My car's up the road.'

'That's not what I meant. None of this has been released so how come you show up?'

'I was just passing.'

'Oh yeah, pure coincidence?' He screwed up his nose and shook his head. 'You show up a lot of places you're not wanted. It has to be someone on the force. And when I find out who, I'll have his balls.'

'Too late, they're already in my pocket.'

I had no intention of telling him I'd been invited there. Let him think I had a mole at police headquarters.

'So what happened?' I said. 'At the canal?'

'Why the hell should I give you any help?'

'It'll save my having to ask the girl out there too many painful questions.'

Strange sneered. 'Jesus, you're a bullshitter.'

'An old bloke on the bridge said you'd pulled out the body of a girl.'

'He should have minded his own bloody business. I suppose he told you she lived here, too.'

I didn't deny it. 'An accident?'

'Everything's open.'

'Suicide?'

'I said everything's open.'

'Murder included?'

'Don't shoot from the hip, McLean. I'm not making any speculations.'

'But there are suspicious circumstances.'

'Says who?'

I shrugged. 'People don't fall in canals accidentally.'

'She could have been walking along the towpath, tripped and banged her head on the edge. Fallen in and drowned.'

'Did she have a head injury?'

'We don't know until the pathologist's done the PM.'

'Ah. Didn't you look to see?'

'The body had gone by the time I got here.'

'What are the divers looking for?'

'Anything that might be relevant. We haven't found her handbag yet.'

'What makes you think she had one?'

'Women tend to.'

'Got a name?' I had to ask the obvious questions, even ones I knew the answers to.

Strange thought it over. 'Wait until morning,' he said eventually.

'Age?'

'Same answer.'

'OK.' I could see he wasn't going to tell me any more.

'One last thing,' Strange said. 'Her friend out there, Sonia Hughes, is very upset. Leave her alone, will you, for once in your life.'

'She doesn't have to talk to me.'

'You're a callous little shit, aren't you?'

'Someone has to do the dirty jobs.'

Strange pulled himself up out of the chair.

'You're like a vulture, scavenging for titbits. Feeding off other people's misfortunes.' He buttoned up his trenchcoat. 'I see a lot of things in this business that turn my stomach, but it's people like you who really make me sick.'

He went out of the room. The venom lingered behind in the musty atmosphere. He was right on all counts. I was a vulture. I did feed off the misfortunes of others. Sometimes it made me sick too.

I talked to Sonia Hughes in the large kitchen at the back of the house. It was clearly the communal living-room. Chairs were gathered around the gas fire and there was a portable television on the table. The shelves above the worktops were lined with jars full of pasta, rice, sultanas, different kinds of beans and pulses. It was warm and smelt of garlic and spices.

Sonia was in her mid-twenties, like Debbie, but there all resemblance ended. Debbie had looked like a conventional secretary; smart, well-groomed and particular about her appearance. Sonia had black hair cut in the shape of a crash helmet, a deathly white skin and lots of black eye make-up and lipstick. It was fashionable but made her look like the Bride of Dracula.

Her clothes too were all black; a baggy man's pullover and skin-tight leggings which emphasized the thinness of her legs. She seemed in need of a square meal.

'Do you feel up to talking?' I asked.

'I want to. That's why I said you could stay. The Sergeant didn't like it.'

'He wouldn't. Did he tell you what happened?'

Sonia nodded. Her face was pallid but it was hard to tell whether it was due to shock or the pancake make-up.

'How did they know it was Debbie?'

'One of the neighbours saw her . . . floating there. She recognized her.'

'Where had Debbie been?'

'Been?'

'To be out there.'

'She was coming home from work.'

'Along the towpath?'

'I don't think so. Not in the dark. She usually caught the bus from town and walked the last bit up the road.'

I looked at her gently. 'Are you all right? Did the police put you through it?'

'It was such a shock. It hasn't sunk in yet.'

'Do you want a drink?'

'I wouldn't mind some tea.'

I put the kettle on to make a pot of that great English palliative. Sonia sat listlessly at the table. She seemed utterly drained of energy.

I tried to keep the conversation matter-of-fact.

'Were there just two of you here?'

'Three. Janet, she's the third, is out at the moment.'

'What do you do? For a living I mean.'

'I work at the Crucible.'

'What, an actress?'

'No, backstage. Design, set painting.'

'Enjoy it?'

'Yes.'

'How long've you been there?'

'Couple of years, since I left college.'

Then she blurted out suddenly: 'Please, what's going on? Tell me!'

I sat down again next to her and pressed one of her hands on the table.

'Easy now. Don't get excited.'

But it was not excitement I saw in her eyes, it was fear.

'Debbie's dead!' Her voice rose unsteadily. 'She's dead.'

'Sonia, please.'

'You must tell me. Somebody killed her.'

'You don't know that, Sonia.'

'What else was it?'

'It could have been an accident.' I didn't believe it, but I had to calm her down. It didn't work.

'Accident? How can it have been? She was walking home from the bus stop. She couldn't have fallen in the canal.'

'What if she was on the towpath?'

'Why would she be there? It only leads to the Canal Basin one way and Tinsley the other. She had no reason to be on the towpath.'

'Was it a short cut from anywhere?'

'No. And even if it was, Debbie wouldn't have used it. Have you seen it? There's no lighting, just those creepy buildings and all that murky water. No woman would go there in the dark, it's terrifying.'

I went back to the kettle and filled the teapot with boiling water.

'Where are the mugs?'

'What?'

'Mugs.'

'Oh, in the cupboard, that one.'

I brought the teapot and mugs to the table.

'You take milk?'

'It's in the fridge.'

'Sugar?'

She shook her head. I poured the tea.

'And before you ask me,' Sonia said abruptly, 'she didn't kill herself either. The police asked me all that. She had no grounds to.'

'You sure?'

'She was perfectly balanced. And she wasn't the type. She would never take that way out.'

'She must have had a traumatic few days. She was pretty upset about Richard Sutton.'

Sonia let out a violent exclamation. 'You don't kill yourself because your boss crashes his car.'

'What if he was more than a boss?'

She looked at me and shook her head. 'No way. She worked for him, that was all.'

'Did she talk about him much?'

'Of course. Everybody talks about the people they work with. She admired him, but she wasn't in love with him, if that's what you're getting at. By all accounts he was totally devoted to his wife. He didn't sound the type to play around.'

Sonia took a quick gulp of tea, the mug held in the palms of both hands.

'The only way she'd have ended up in that canal is if someone put her there.'

The knuckles of her hands were white. She was taut as a violin string, but controlling the tension. If she'd been going to snap, she'd have done it already.

She turned to me. 'Why did Debbie ask you to come here tonight?'

'How do you know she did?'

'Please, don't mess me around. I was there when she wrote you the note. Why else would I let you stay here? What's happening?'

'I was hoping you might tell me that.'

Her eyes probed my face, suspicious that I was holding back on her.

'I don't know.'

'Did she not say anything to you?' I asked.

'No.'

'Nothing at all?'

'Well . . .' She changed tack quickly, the fear resurfacing. 'She was killed, wasn't she? Why would anyone do that?'

I ignored the outburst. 'At the inquest this morning, did she say anything about me?'

'Only that you were a reporter she'd spoken to.'

'Did she say why she left me the note?'

Sonia hesitated. 'Not specifically.'

'But you have an idea?'

'It was something to do with work. Oh, it was all so vague. I didn't really understand it. I don't think Debbie did either, that was the problem. She was funny all week.'

'In what way?'

'Jumpy, nervous, that wasn't like her.' Sonia leaned towards me earnestly. 'She was frightened, I think.'

'Of what?'

'I don't know.'

'A particular person? Something in general?'

'I think it was just a feeling she had.'

'You say she might have wanted to talk to me about something at work. What makes you think that?'

'Because it was work that seemed to be worrying her. She said you'd asked her about the fire.'

'It was arson. Did Debbie know who started it?'

'If she did, she didn't say. In a way I don't think she did know. But it was all connected; the fire, her boss's death, work. She seemed to link them all together.'

'But without saying why?'

'I'm not sure she really knew. I'm sorry, this all sounds pathetically vague. I did ask her what was bothering her. I asked her again this morning but she wouldn't give a proper answer. She just said, "Oh, maybe I'm imagining it all," and dismissed it. You know, the way people do when they think they're being silly.'

'When did you first sense she was frightened?'

Sonia thought for a while. 'The beginning of the week, I suppose. Monday, maybe Tuesday.'

'Did anything happen which might have caused it? 'Phone calls, threatening letters?'

'Not that I know of.'

'Did she mention any incident at the office?'

'Well, the fire, obviously. And her boss's crash. She talked a lot about those. To be honest, I didn't listen much. We lived together but we weren't all that close.'

'You went to the inquest with her.'

'It's my day off. She was upset by the thought of it all so I offered to go with her.'

'Did she talk about anything else that happened this week, anything unusual?'

Sonia tapped a fingernail on the table, her forehead creased in thought.

'Well, she came home very upset one day. Something about her boss throwing a fit. Apparently he was almost never angry.'

'Her boss? That must have been Monday. He died later that evening. Did she say what he was angry about?'

'I don't think she knew. The anger wasn't directed at her. It just upset her. That's all I can remember.'

'Did you tell the police she'd been acting strangely?'

Sonia nodded. 'Just what I've told you. I'm not sure they believed me. It sounds like the ramblings of an emotional woman.'

She took another gulp of tea and swallowed hard. 'It scares me like hell. Debbie walking home in the dark, someone attacking her or dragging her down on to the towpath, then . . .' She shivered and wrapped her arms around her body.

I said gently: 'Don't get carried away with your imagination, Sonia. You've absolutely nothing to fear.'

'But for Christ's sake, she was murdered, wasn't she?'

'Let's wait for the police verdict on that.'

'I know she was. The other possibilities are too unlikely.'

'Leave it to the police.'

'Who could have done it?' She stared dully at her empty mug. 'Do you think it was just a random killing, some lunatic on the loose and Debbie was in the wrong place at the wrong time? Or did it have something to do with whatever it was she was going to tell you this evening?'

'I don't know, Sonia.'

But I did. There were just too many coincidences. A man getting killed, his offices catching fire, his secretary ending up dead in the canal. They had to be connected and the one common link was Richard Sutton.

I drove slowly back to my flat. The shock of Debbie's death had not yet worn off and I drove in a semi-trance, thinking about the evening's events.

There was not much doubt in my mind that Debbie had been murdered. Sonia Hughes was right: the alternatives were too unlikely. But I had no idea why she had been killed, or by whom.

I tried to piece together all the facts. Richard Sutton had crashed his car on Monday night while under the influence of alcohol. The sudden death of his secretary only a few days later made me wonder a bit about that crash. Yet there were no suspicious circumstances. I'd been to the inquest. The police had made no mention of foul play and the pathologist who did the autopsy had found nothing to suggest it. So it was either a straight accident, or possibly suicide.

What *was* suspicious, however, was the fact that Sutton, an abstainer, had got drunk in the first place. Why had he? And if indeed it was suicide, why had he done it? I had no answers.

Then the fire. It had been reported shortly after nine o'clock. By then it had been visible from outside the building but had not spread to engulf the whole office block. I'd seen the damage for myself. A few rooms had been gutted but not much else. Given the speed with which flames spread, that seemed to imply the fire hadn't been burning all that long. So it was probably started some time between eight and nine o'clock. Where did that get me? Not very far at all.

And who did it? The police seemed to think Sutton himself was a likely candidate, but I couldn't see what evidence there was to incriminate him other than the fact he was the head of the company. The police, of course, knew more than I did, but I doubted they had conclusive proof of anything. For the moment it was probably an open question. No one knew for certain who had started the fire. Or why.

Now back to Debbie Nolan's murder, and the same two key questions: who? and why? The who was impossible to answer. The why was not much easier, but I could make a few educated guesses. Assuming she hadn't been killed by a maniac or a mugger after her handbag, it was not stretching the bounds of credibility to link her death with the fire at the RPS offices, or Richard Sutton's crash, or both.

Had Debbie known why Richard Sutton got drunk? Had she known who started the fire and why? Or had she known something else, something I hadn't thought of, which meant she had to be killed?

And why now? Sonia Hughes said Debbie had been on edge since Monday, so presumably, whatever it was she knew had been on her mind since then.

That lent itself to two possibilities. Or only two I could think of at the moment. One, the killer had only just discovered Debbie knew something dangerous and so took immediate action to silence her; or, two, the killer had been aware all along that she knew but wasn't worried by it until she started talking to someone who might have made more of it than she could. Someone like me, a nosey bastard who'd already been asking questions. If that was the case, I was partly responsible for her death.

But no one knew Debbie had wanted to talk to me. No one except Sonia Hughes and the receptionist at the Medico-Legal Centre that is, and they seemed highly unlikely suspects. No one else had seen the note she left me after the inquest. At least no one I was aware of.

In short, I could make guesses and postulate speculative theories, but I knew nothing for certain about any of it.

I pulled up outside my flat behind the remains of an
Escort XR3i someone had been unwise enough to leave
there a few days earlier. It had lasted only a couple of hours
before someone had jacked it up on bricks and nicked the
tyres. It was still there, gradually diminishing in size as
various parts were cannibalized. The wing mirrors and
number plates had gone, as had the radio cassette player
inside. In a few weeks' time it would just be a small heap
of nuts and bolts nestling in the gutter. Neighbourhood of
character, mine.

As I opened the door of my flat, there was a soft scuffling
sound inside. I flicked on the light and caught a glimpse of
a wiry brown tail disappearing under the skirting board.
One of my sitting tenants: an extended family of mice.

When I first discovered them, I told the landlord but all
he said was, 'Think yourself lucky it's not rats,' and did
nothing. So I put down traps myself and knocked a few of
them off. But it made me feel like a murderer so I stopped.
We now have a tacit agreement, the mice and I. When I'm
in residence they keep out of the way; when I'm out they
have the run of the place.

I made a pot of tea and a cheese sandwich and slumped
down in front of the television. There was a new sitcom
on BBC1 starring a nondescript, middle-aged actor whose
name I could never remember but who seemed to appear
in every sitcom on television. I munched my sandwich and
prepared to have my brain anæsthetized by the exhumed
jokes.

The nondescript, middle-aged actor was playing a
widowed father with two rebellious but infinitely lovable
teenage children who bore as much relation to real teenage
children as Thomas the Tank Engine does to British Rail.

In this first episode, the teenage daughter had brought
home her new boyfriend, a long-haired, bearded 'hippy' she
must have found in a museum, probably the same one in
which the writers found the plot.

Naturally, the father finds the boyfriend highly unsuit-
able and the ensuing conflict between him, the daughter,

the boyfriend, the vicar (yes, there was a vicar) and the right-wing retired colonel next door leads to what the *Radio Times* called 'hilarious consequences'.

However, just as the 'hilarious consequences' were about to begin there was a knock at my door. I don't get many visitors. Usually it's one of the neighbours telling me they've had a break-in and asking if I've seen anything suspicious. Like a bunch of kids legging it down the road with the TV and video.

The knock came again. Reluctantly I left the nondescript, middle-aged actor and his lovable kids and opened the door.

The two men pushed me back and came in slowly; they were too big to move very fast. Besides, they didn't seem to be in a hurry. I looked up at them. They were like sofa beds in suits.

'No Jehovah's Witnesses,' I said.

The first one hit me in the face with a fist the size of a baseball glove and I went over backwards. Clearly they weren't Jehovah's Witnesses. A Jehovah's Witness would have hit me with a copy of the *Watchtower*. I stayed where I was, feeling my cheek numb with pain. At least on the floor I couldn't fall any further.

'Jesus, what a shitty dump,' one of them said.

'Like the rest of this shitty town,' the other replied.

They both had strong London accents. I hate cockneys who come up here and badmouth my home. I'm allowed to do it because I'm a native, but it gets up my nose when other people do it.

They were taking books out of shelves now and ripping them in two before hurling them around the room. They stacked my records on the floor and jumped on them, then snapped the legs off my desk and smashed my typewriter. One of them went into the kitchen and I heard crockery and glass shattering. I struggled into an armchair. Two of my front teeth were loose.

'My cleaning lady's not going to be very pleased,' I said, looking at the mess.

One of the Sofa Beds picked up a chair and smashed in the front of the television set. The right-wing retired colonel who lived next door to the nondescript, middle-aged actor disappeared in an explosion of white light.

'It wasn't that bad,' I said lamely.

The Sofa Bed came over and tore the phone book slowly in half—across the front, not down the spine—a few inches from my face. A show-off.

'Do you juggle as well?' I asked.

He hit me in the stomach then and I felt as if my guts had been crushed in a mangle. I whooped for breath and he hit me twice in the face. Not hard, I'd have passed out if he'd used his full strength, but enough to hurt. They obviously wanted me conscious. I watched them demolish my flat and wondered why.

Eventually they got tired of the carnage and sat down on the settee. They watched me recover in a half-interested way. One of them scraped dirt from under his fingernails.

When I could summon enough air to speak, I said: 'You guys collecting the poll-tax?'

'A smart-arse, eh? Yer fink we're just fucking around?'

'Don't worry, lads, it's all you're capable of.'

It was the wrong thing to say. One of them took a pair of electrical pliers out of his pocket and attached them to the end of my nose. He twisted them. A searing pain shot up my forehead and down my neck. Hot blood trickled from my nostrils and over my lips. I wished I'd kept my mouth shut.

'Watch yer lip, sonny boy,' he said, leaning close so I could smell the stale booze on his breath. 'We dahn't like cocky bastards.'

He pulled the pliers off roughly and sat down again. I took out my handkerchief and held it under my nose, it was too painful to actually touch. The blood was pouring out now, my shirt smeared scarlet.

'Now button yer mouf and listen,' he continued.

I saw them through a red haze of pain. They had ugly faces that were somehow hard and pudgy at the same time, like two overgrown pug dogs. Small, glinting eyes, hair cropped short around cauliflower ears, too much muscle in their necks. They had fancy suits and diamond tiepins but the trappings didn't conceal what lay beneath: pure, un-adulterated thug.

'There's somefink else we dahn't like,' he said. 'Reporters with big noses.'

'It's not my fault, it's hereditary,' I said. 'My father was an anteater.'

The second Sofa Bed hit me across the mouth. 'Shut it. Just fink about yer nose next time yer feel like sticking it into somefink what dahn't concern you. It hurts now, but that's nuffink to what you'll get if yer dahn't back off.'

I sniffed back the blood, hoping it would clot. 'You mind telling me what you're talking about?'

'We 'aven't come for a conversation.'

'What am I supposed to keep my nose out of?'

'Fings what's none of yer business.'

'Who sent you?'

'You're sticking yer nose in again. We dahn't like that.'

He leaned across with the pair of pliers again. I could have kicked him in the groin and got a bit of pleasure, but it would only have lasted a few seconds. After that they would have really done me over and I don't like hospital food.

He stuck the pliers on my nose again. 'You're putting blood all over my nice pliers. That's naughty.'

He tugged at my bruised flesh. I bit back a yell and grasped the pliers, trying to release myself. But the pain only increased.

'OK, OK. Jesus, let me go.' My nose was on fire, tears of agony in my eyes.

'Just remember,' he said, jerking the pliers off. 'Next time it won't be yer nose. It'll be your dick.'

They stood up and walked casually out of the flat. They even closed the door after them.

I struggled out of the armchair and crawled across the

debris to the front window. I pulled myself up on the sill and peered out. Blood dripped on to the paintwork.

The two men came out of the house and got into a black BMW parked on the opposite side of the road. I blinked hard, trying to focus my eyes on the number plate. The letters were blurred, hidden in shadows. It was only when the car pulled out into the full light of the streetlamps that I saw it. H370 EGB.

I dragged myself to my feet and staggered into the bath-room where I was sick. With pain, and with fear, and with anger. All the time I was retching I was repeating the registration number of their car to myself.

CHAPTER 8

'My God, Michael, what's happened to you?'

Maria came round from behind her desk as soon as I walked into her office. It was almost worth the pain in my nose to see the concern on her face.

She pulled out a chair. 'Sit down. You look awful.'

'It's just a bad cold,' I said manfully, wincing slightly to let her know I was really in agony. I can milk sympathy with the best of them when I want to.

She bent down by the chair and examined my face, touching my cheeks with cool fingers. It was the first time she'd ever touched me.

'Have you been to the hospital?'

'Last night. It's just bruised, nothing broken.'

'Are you sure? It's terribly swollen.'

'It looks worse than it is.'

'Is there anything I can do? We've got a first aid kit.'

I thought about asking her to rub in some soothing oint-ment, but my nose was so sensitive the pleasure of her touch would be more than outweighed by the pain it would cause.

'It just needs time,' I said.

She touched my face again, shaking her head, her eyes

worried. I wanted to take her hand but she straightened up suddenly and went back behind her desk.

'How did it happen?'

'I walked into a door.'

Maria smoothed her cream skirt over the backs of her thighs in one of those automatic gestures women do unconsciously but men find slightly erotic. She sat down.

'I'm not stupid, Michael.'

I picked up the plastic carrier bag I'd brought with me.

'I thought I'd drop in my accounts for you.' I put the bag on the desk.

'Don't change the subject. Have you been in a fight?'

'I told you.'

'Don't bullshit me. You don't get an injury like that from walking into a door.'

'I'm a fast walker.'

'Who did it?'

'It's nothing.'

'Michael, don't shut me out. I'm worried.'

She was genuine all right. It gave me a warm glow inside.

'You don't always have to make a joke of things,' she said.

'I know.' Maybe that was my problem. Maybe that was what had ended my marriage: too much joking, not enough talking. Women don't like that.

'A couple of blokes came to see me,' I said.

'They beat you up?'

I told her what had happened. Her eyes opened wide in horror.

'A pair of *pliers*?'

'Snub-nosed. With wire strippers on them.'

'Jesus! But why?'

'I don't know.'

'You mean these two brutes just roughed you up and left without saying a word?'

'They told me to keep my nose out of other people's business.'

'Have you been poking it in?'

I started to grin but stopped. It hurt my nose too much. 'I do it all the time, it's my job. But what they didn't say was *whose* business.'

'You should go to the police.'

'It wouldn't get me very far.'

'Men like that are dangerous.'

'They struck me as pretty thick.'

'That makes them even more dangerous.' She leaned over the desk. 'Don't get out of your depth, Michael, please. If they can do that kind of thing to you, they can do worse.'

'That's what *they* said.'

'Are you going to take any notice?'

I didn't say anything.

'You're going to carry on with whatever it is, aren't you? Out of pride and stubbornness.'

She got up and went to the coffee machine on the side table. She filled two china cups and brought them over. I took one of them.

Maria said: 'You going to tell me?'

I looked at her, trying to read her eyes. There was sadness there, behind the smoke.

'You got time?'

'You know I have.'

I stirred my coffee. 'I think it has something to do with Richard Sutton. The fire I told you about at Sutton's office. The police have confirmed it was arson.'

'Why would anyone want to do that?'

'I don't know. Nothing of any significance seems to have been destroyed.'

'Maybe it was just vandalism. Hooligans doing it for kicks.'

'I can't see it. A derelict building or a bus shelter perhaps, but not an office block.'

'What about an employee? Or an ex-employee? Someone with a grudge against the company. Doing it purely out of malice.'

'The fire started on the fourth floor. If I were someone who had it in for RPS Trading, I'd start the fire in the simplest location I could find, probably the ground floor, and get the hell out.'

'Where's all this leading?'

'Probably down a big dead end, but I'm sure there's something there.'

'Why?'

I lifted a finger to the red and purple pulp in the middle of my face. 'My nose tells me.'

Maria leaned back in her chair, swinging her reading glasses by one of the arms. Light glinted on her mother-of-pearl earrings.

'You move in financial circles,' I said. 'You heard anything about RPS Trading? Debts, cash flow problems?'

'No.'

'Nothing that would make Sutton take his own life?'

Maria stared at me. 'You think he committed *suicide?*'

'He got drunk, abandoning the principles of a lifetime. That sounds pretty deliberate to me.'

'And then he crashed his car deliberately? Isn't that a bit fanciful?'

'Dutch courage. Life became unbearable so he ended it.'

'Why?'

'I don't know. But something major must have happened. What if his company was bust?'

'Bust? Come on, Michael, we're talking about one of the most successful companies in the north of England.'

'All bubbles have to burst. He was pretty overstretched, wasn't he?'

'How do you know?'

'Well, most industries are suffering from high interest rates, debts and falling sales in this economic climate. And on top of that he was shelling out fifty million on a huge recycling plant in the Don Valley.'

'And the fire?'

'Maybe Sutton did it.'

'You have evidence for any of this?'

'No.'

'Just trying not to let the facts spoil a good story, eh?'

'It's what I do best.'

'You want some more coffee?'

I shook my head. 'I haven't finished this one yet.'

She went to the coffee machine. I studied the lines of her figure as she bent over the table. She turned round suddenly and caught me at it. I didn't avert my eyes. She gave me a long look, not at all embarrassed, more amused. Her poise was intensely annoying.

'I think you're looking for motives, for crimes, for something sensational where nothing exists,' she said, walking back to her desk and sitting down. 'Sutton was killed in a simple road accident and it has no connection with the fire in his office. You're imagining the whole thing.'

I pointed at my nose again. 'Am I imagining this?'

That stopped her. 'Are you sure it's connected to this?'

'The only other thing I've done this week is a couple of features on loft insulation and waste disposal. You think maybe the loft insulation people sent a couple of heavies round because I recommended the wrong kind of fibreglass roof foam?'

Maria laughed softly. 'OK. So why did they do it?'

'I wondered about that.'

'It's pretty stupid to warn off a journalist.'

'I told you, they *were* stupid.'

'It would only encourage you.'

'Maybe they thought I was a cheap local hack who frightened easily.'

'It's easy to get that impression.'

'That's not funny. Besides, there's another thing which tells me something peculiar is going on.' Maria squinted at me questioningly. 'Sutton's secretary was murdered last night.'

Maria sat back heavily, one hand going involuntarily to her mouth.

'She was found floating in the canal.'

'Oh God. But why?'

'I don't know. But she left a note for me after Sutton's

inquest yesterday. She asked me to go round and see her in the evening. She was dead before I got there.'

'And you think . . .'

'There has to be a link. She had something, I don't know what, information, a hunch, a suspicion, something she wanted to tell me.'

'Why you, not the police?'

'I don't know that either.'

The implications of it came home to Maria. 'Michael, if that's true, then—'

I interrupted her. 'I'm not in any danger. They only beat me up. It was a warning. They could have gone further.'

Maria's telephone rang. She waited, unsure whether to answer, then picked it up quickly.

'What is it, Muriel?' She listened for a second. 'All right, put him through.'

She held a hand over the mouthpiece. 'Sorry, this won't take long.'

I strolled over to the window while she talked to a client. The rain was falling in a depressing drizzle. Grey sky, grey streets, grey people. My bruised ribs hurt each time I moved and my whole head ached from the damage to my nose. Each breath I took stung the inside of my sinuses like acid. I wondered where the two men with the pliers were. Pliers with my blood on them.

Maria said: 'Sorry about that. I had to take it.'

I turned to see her replacing the receiver. I said: 'Let's forget about the possibility of suicide. Assume Sutton's crash was an accident. If you lived in Hathersage, which way would you go home?'

She blinked. 'What?'

'Which way would you go home?'

'What's this . . . ?'

'From the city centre.'

Her brow furrowed. 'Well, up Ecclesall Road, I suppose.'

'Then?'

'Straight out on the A625. Past the Fox House Inn. The main road. Why?'

'That's not the way Richard Sutton went the night he was killed. He went round the back over the moors.'

'Is that so odd?'

I shrugged. 'It's a much longer route, a poor road and not very pleasant at night, particularly in November.'

'Maybe he liked the solitude up there, the lack of traffic.'

I sat back down and took a sip of my coffee. It had gone cold.

'Or maybe he wasn't coming from the city centre,' I said.

Maria narrowed her eyes. 'What are you talking about now?'

'According to Sutton's secretary, he left the office with her about six o'clock on Monday evening. He died around ten, ten-thirty.'

'How do you know?'

'The police found him at ten forty-five. They tried to revive him. They'd only do that if he was still warm, if there was some chance of bringing him back. And I saw his body. It was limp; rigor mortis hadn't set in.'

'I'm still not with you.'

'What if something happened in those four hours? Something which made Sutton get drunk. Maybe he went somewhere, met someone, who knows? Where might a businessman go between finishing work and going home?'

'I know where my husband used to go.'

She smiled sardonically. There was a very deep hurt somewhere there. A hurt that made her wary.

'But Sutton wasn't like that,' I said.

'What's this got to do with the murder of his secretary?'

'I'm not sure.'

'You're not sure about much, are you? I think you should go to the police.'

'And tell them what? This is just speculation. In any case, if there's a story, I'm not giving it to the flatties.'

Her eyes seemed to cloud. 'Pig-headed sod, aren't you?'

I took it as a compliment. 'I try.'

'And if those men come back and hurt you again? Maybe put you in hospital?'

'I hope you'll bring flowers.'

She half opened her mouth to say something but shook her head instead. A touch angrily.

Then she noticed the carrier bag I'd put on her desk. She pulled it towards her and glanced inside.

'What's all this?'

'My invoices and receipts. You wanted to see them.'

She gritted her teeth and seemed to count to ten.

'I told you not to do this to me, Michael.'

'Do what?'

'Bring me shoe boxes full of paper that I have to sort out.'

'They're not in a shoe box.'

She narrowed her eyes at me. 'I'm starting to see why people beat you up.'

'I'm not very good with financial things,' I said. 'You have to make allowances.'

'Oh, I will. But I promise you one thing, Michael. When that nose of yours is better . . .'

'Yes?'

'I'm going to punch you on it.'

I'd been going to ask her out again, but I think I just blew it.

CHAPTER 9

I spent the afternoon in a laundrette off Pitsmoor Road, watching my clothes spin round in a washing-machine and thinking. Laundrettes are the most boring places on earth but they make you sit down and do nothing for a time. In the past I would have stuck my clothes in and gone away to do some work. But then someone stole my washing in my absence, all my shirts and underwear and socks. Even now, two years later, I still keep my eyes open in the vicinity, hoping to spot someone in my dark blue Fred Perry or luminous green socks with the hole near the big toe. But I don't leave my washing unattended.

I thought about Richard Sutton, the very much admired, very respectable and very dead millionaire businessman. The ache in my injured nose helped concentrate my thoughts. It made me angry, determined. I wanted to know why the two heavies had done me over. And I wanted to know where Sutton had gone the night he died. I was certain it was important. To a restaurant? A pub? To see friends? He could have gone anywhere.

Yet for some reason two things Maria had said kept coming back to me. One was in her office that morning. '*I know where my husband used to go.*' That's what she'd said when I asked what businessmen did after work. It was a clear reference to her husband's womanizing.

The other was something she'd said when we had dinner at The Frog. What was it? Again about her husband. '*He didn't look like a womanizer. Most people thought he was a straight, earnest sort of man.*' Something like that.

It started me thinking about Sutton, another straight, earnest man with an apparently unimpeachable reputation. I wondered about that. Was he really as strait-laced as he appeared? Indeed, was it humanly possible for anyone to be as virtuous as that? Just because he didn't drink and managed his business affairs with probity, did that mean he had no vices whatsoever?

I took my plastic bag of clean washing back to my flat and tipped the contents out on to the armchair in the sitting-room. The tumble driers at the laundrette never seemed to dry anything completely no matter how many 20p pieces I put in. Most of my clothes were still damp. I draped them around the room to air, adding to the mess left by my visitors the previous night.

The flat looked like a scene from the aftermath of an earthquake, if an earthquake could just hit the inside of a building and leave the walls and roof intact. Furniture was smashed, bookshelves had toppled, mounds of paperbacks and broken records lay everywhere like rubble.

I sifted through it, trying to salvage something from the debris. Only one LP was untouched, Murray Perahia playing Mozart. I would have put it on but the stereo was a heap of crushed plastic and metal. Those boys had certainly known what they were doing when it came to demolition.

I pushed the wreckage to the sides to clear a passage through the room. The kitchen and bedroom were equally bad but I couldn't face clearing it all up at the moment. I simply needed a bit more space to breathe.

As I kicked the ripped books and splintered shelves out of the way, a piece of brightly-coloured plastic caught my eye. I picked it up. It was vivid green, about the size of a credit card but thicker and more rigid. It had £10 on the front in raised white letters. I turned it over. Stamped on the back in barely legible black ink was the word Casanova's.

Interesting. Casanova's was a casino in the centre of town. The piece of plastic was a gambling chip of some sort. I knew it wasn't mine, I'd never been to Casanova's in my life. It must have fallen out of the pocket of one of my cockney chums.

I put it in my jacket. So they'd gone gambling and forgotten to cash in the chip. I didn't give it any more thought. First things first. Right now I was still on Richard Sutton.

I wanted to know where he might have gone on Monday evening and that meant talking to someone who knew him rather better than I did. He must have had many friends but there was only one I knew would talk to me for certain: Stuart Sutherland.

Stuart and his wife Alison, my ex, lived on a tree-lined avenue on the south-western fringes of the city where professional footballers and company chairmen rubbed garden fences with minor showbusiness celebrities. Well, one or two at least; showbusiness celebrities, even minor ones, are not exactly thick on the ground in Sheffield.

The houses out there are all different, yet they're all the same. The architecture varies but they all have two-car garages and burglar alarms at the front, patios and pergolas at the rear and screwed-up people inside.

Alison was no exception.

When she answered the door, I knew immediately she'd been drinking. Not enough to make her drunk, but plenty all the same. A couple of gin and tonics in the afternoon, a glass or three of wine while cooking dinner. She handled it well but her eyes were glassy and slightly vacant.

'Michael!' She seemed pleased to see me but I knew she'd have been pleased to see anyone: milkman, meter-reader, door-to-door brush salesman. Anyone to alleviate the boredom and loneliness.

'You got a minute?' I asked.

'For you, darling, any time.'

She threw open the door and waved her arms to usher me in. She was a shade unsteady on her feet. I hoped she wasn't going to embarrass me.

'Come into the lounge.'

We went into a large room running all the way from front to back with french windows at the garden end. It was big enough to house three settees, several armchairs, tables, bookcases and an enormous bar in one corner. I wouldn't have minded a bar as big as Stuart Sutherland's bar. I wouldn't have minded a flat as big as Stuart Sutherland's bar.

Alison said: 'Drink?'

'No, thanks.'

'Sure?'

'I'm driving.'

'You don't mind if I do.'

It wasn't a question, she was already pouring herself a gin. She was past the stage of concealing it.

'So how are you, Michael, my dear ex?' she said, in the faintly mocking tone she used with me now. As if being married to me had been some mildly amusing aberration she could no longer fathom.

'Fine.'

'Still slogging away at the births, deaths and marriages?'

I smiled thinly. 'Same as usual.'

'How boring.' She squeezed her eyes into slits and

examined me. 'Your hair needs cutting. And you're still wearing that abominable windcheater. Has no woman taken
you under her wing yet and made you tidy yourself up?'

The assumption that only a woman could change me, or
that I'd let her, irritated me.

'What happened to your nose?'

'I fell over.'

'You been to a doctor?'

'It's not serious.'

She nodded automatically. She wasn't really interested.
No cool fingers touching my cheeks, no concern in her face.
I was glad. I no longer wanted her solicitude.

Alison sipped her drink and tried to look coy.

'Have you come round to relive the good old days, then?
Shall we go upstairs?'

She'd drunk more than I thought. She giggled. Jesus.
What was she, thirty-eight years old, and she still tried to
flirt like a schoolgirl.

'Stuart home yet?' I said.

She pouted, annoyed. She didn't like the way I got on
with her new husband. She had some primitive idea that
we should be at each other's throats, fighting over her. I
was sure she liked to think I was still in love with her. For
a while after our divorce I had been, but that had long
faded. I felt nothing now, neither love nor hatred, just indif-
ference. It was a sad reflection on the transience of human
feeling.

Alison stood up and adjusted her dress, bringing my
attention back to her.

'What do you think?'

'About what?'

'The dress, of course. I got it this morning.'

She turned so I could admire the side view. I played
along out of old habit. I'd spent years pretending to like
her dresses.

'It's very nice.'

'You're not looking.'

I ran my eyes over her. The dress was dark maroon with

a wide collar and lapels, and a waistline nearer the hips than the waist which gave it a Twenties look. It was too young for her, but then no woman ever feels she's as old as her passport says.

'Well?'

Alison was watching me, chin tilted, lips forming a tiny 'O', back arched to show off her breasts. What she really wanted me to admire, of course, was her figure. I had to admit she was still in good shape. She went to an expensive gym in town and worked at it to give herself something to do. Lifting weights and pounding the treadmill to keep time at bay.

'It looks good.'

'I'm still a twelve, you know.'

'Twelve stone's not bad for someone your age.'

She gave a sour smile. 'How much do you think it cost?'

'You mean how much is it worth? Or how much you paid for it?'

'You don't change much.'

'Nor do you.'

She sat down again. 'Four hundred pounds.'

'Are we talking about your weight again?'

Alison ignored me. 'Pure wool isn't cheap. You have to spend to get quality.'

'And you always did enjoy spending, didn't you? Preferably someone else's money,' I added drily.

'Fortunately Stuart's got plenty. He likes me to look good.'

She was taking another dig at me. Not very subtle, but Alison had never been subtle. Money had always been a problem in our marriage. Mostly because I didn't have any. She was acquisitive, she liked to spend. In the early days she'd accepted our relative poverty, but as the years passed she'd found it hard to reconcile my income with her ambitions. She'd realized I would never be rich and traded me in for a more affluent model.

'Where is Stuart?' I asked.

'Is that why you've come?'

'Still at the office?'

'He's always at the bloody office.'

I felt sorry for her. The money hadn't bought her companionship.

'What do you want to see him about?'

'Business.'

She raised her eyebrows wearily. 'Not more business. Yours or his?'

'Mine. When do you expect him home?'

She threw up her arms in an exaggerated shrug. 'Whenever he can drag himself away from that fascinating factory.'

'Business booming?'

'No. Orders are falling and he's being undercut by the bloody Koreans and Japanese. Stuart's quite worried, actually, although he's not admitting it.'

'I'm sure he'll sort it out.'

'I hope so. He merged with some engineering company last year. It's not working out the way he expected.'

'He rationing your dresses?'

'Things aren't that bad yet. But I'm stocking up just in case.'

We were silent for a time. It's strange, I thought, I was married to this woman for three years and we have nothing to say to each other. I remembered the early days, the incessant chatter, the constant new discoveries that sparked off conversation, the delights, the pleasures of living together. It was a long time ago.

She was still an attractive woman, but all desire had evaporated. If you lust you do not need to love. But if you have loved and it has died, the lust dies with it. We were strangers now. More than strangers, for we didn't have the stranger's curiosity to learn more. We already knew too much.

She stood up and poured herself another gin.

'You sure you won't have one?' she asked.

'OK,' I said, to alleviate her guilt at drinking alone.

'What?'

'Same as you.'

She poured the gin and added tonic to fill the glass. She splashed some in her own drink and topped it up with more gin, not caring if I noticed. She handed me my glass.

'Are you all right, Alison?'

'What do you mean?'

'Well . . .' I tried to put it tactfully. 'You don't think you're drinking a little bit too much?'

Her eyes flashed. 'Mind your own damn business.' She took a swig of her gin defiantly.

I cursed myself. I wanted to help if I could but it had sounded like a recrimination. I hadn't intended it that way.

'It wasn't meant as a criticism,' I said.

'You're not my keeper any more. It's none of your business what I do.'

This wasn't going to lead anywhere. I changed the subject.

'Did you know Richard Sutton?'

Alison looked at me suspiciously, as if trying to see if this was a devious way of returning to her drink problem.

'Why?'

'I just wondered. I'm doing a piece on him.'

'Yes, I knew him. I knew his wife, Jackie, better.'

'She's not from round here, is she? Where did they meet?'

'At a dinner in London, I think. Some charity event. Jackie used to be a model.'

I nodded. I could have guessed that.

'Were they married long?'

'Three, four years.'

'About as long as us.' I smiled to show it wasn't another reproach. She smiled back. We'd had some good times together.

'But you didn't go to the inquest.'

'Jackie asked me not to. She said she didn't want it to be a spectacle with an audience. Stuart went, though.'

'I know. I saw him there.'

'She was terribly upset about it all. She was devoted to her husband. His death was bad enough but then all that stuff in the papers—Tycoon was drunk—all that. She was distraught. I suppose you wrote some of it if you were at the inquest.'

'Not in the *News*.'

'It was in the nationals too.'

'Yes, I wrote some of that.' I didn't make any excuses. I'd done that too often in our marriage. 'Do you see Mrs Sutton often?'

'We go to shows together.'

'The theatre, you mean?'

'Fashion shows.'

'In Sheffield?'

'Good God no! How many fashion shows do you get in Sheffield? In London of course.'

It seemed a long way to go shopping, but what do I know?

'Tough life.'

'It's an exhausting business filling all this leisure time.' It was a joke, but only just.

'Did they have a good marriage?'

Alison eyed me archly. 'What kind of article are you writing?'

'Just background,' I said.

'If you mean, what was their sex life like, I haven't a clue. And if I had I would hardly tell you, would I?'

I grinned. It still hurt my nose. 'You always used to tell me about your friends' sex lives. I seem to remember it was one of your favourite topics.'

'I was younger then. It's not so interesting now.'

'I thought it got more interesting with age.'

'That depends how lucky you are.'

'What about him, Richard Sutton?'

'An extremely boring man. Always working. Stuart saw him fairly often. They were on some tedious Chamber of Commerce committees together.'

'Did they socialize with each other?'

She guffawed. 'Socialize? My dear, have you any concept

of what these businessmen are like? Their idea of socializing is reading Board minutes aloud in bed.'

'Would you say they knew each other well?'

Outside on the drive, car wheels crunched on gravel.

'Ask him yourself. That sounds like Stuart now.'

She made no move to get up and go to the door. They were beyond the stage of welcoming each other home. Maybe they'd never done it. We waited for Stuart to come in.

'Michael,' he said when he saw me slouched in the armchair. 'How nice to see you.'

He shook hands and smiled warmly, the patrician manner of the successful businessman manifesting itself again. He must have pressed a lot of flesh in the course of his career and was very good at putting people at their ease. Yet I always felt there was something insincere in his greetings. He was wearing a dark grey overcoat with a black collar. Add a fur hat and he could have passed as a fairly junior member of the Soviet Politburo.

'What happened to your nose?' he asked.

I wished people would stop asking about my nose. 'You should see the other guy,' I said.

'Staying long?'

'I wanted a word.'

'Of course. If I can be of any service. I'll just remove my coat.'

He went back into the hall.

Alison said: 'You can stay for dinner, you know.'

'No, thanks. I won't keep Stuart long.'

'There's plenty. It's cauliflower cheese. One of your favourites.'

'I have to get off.'

I hate cauliflower cheese but I didn't say so. Early in our marriage Alison had made it one night and, anxious not to upset her, I had forced it down and pretended to enjoy it. Then, when she made it again, I could hardly admit I'd lied the first time—she had little enough confidence in her cooking as it was—so I'd continued the pretence. The

longer I kept it up, the harder it became to confess I loathed cauliflower cheese. So for three years I'd stoically eaten the stuff, with the not surprising result that Alison was convinced I liked it. Such are the frailties and misunderstandings of marriage.

Stuart came back in, still carrying his leather attaché case.

'You'll stay for dinner, I hope.'

'I can't.'

'That's a shame. What are we having, by the way?'

'Cauliflower cheese,' Alison said.

'Splendid. Come into the study, Michael. I've got a few things to do.'

Alison looked irritated. Perhaps because she was being excluded from our talk, perhaps because it delayed their meal.

'How long are you going to be?' she asked sharply.

'Not long,' Stuart said.

'Ten minutes,' I added. 'No more.'

'Pour yourself a drink, dear,' Stuart said. 'We'll be out in a minute.'

He hasn't noticed she's drinking too much already, I thought. Strange how a man so perceptive in business can be so unobservant at home.

I picked up my gin and tonic and followed Stuart to his study. It looked out over the garden, all neat flowerbeds and a lawn unscuffed by children. They employed a gardener, of course. And a cleaner and a handyman. That's why Alison had nothing to do except drink. She could have hired someone to do that for her as well, but some things you just have to do yourself.

The study walls were lined with unread books and a few cheap prints: Stuart was too busy to bother much with literature or art. It was really an extension of his office rather than a study. The same sort of desk and swivel chair, the VDU, even a fax machine. These days executives don't just take their work home, they take their surroundings.

I sat down in a high-backed leather armchair and

watched Stuart unpack his briefcase. He was taking out wads of documents and dumping them on the desk.

Suddenly I sat bolt upright. The briefcase. Jesus, could that be it? I remembered the list of the contents of Richard Sutton's Rolls-Royce I'd copied after the inquest. I'd sensed that something was missing from it. Was it a briefcase? Sutton had been a successful businessman going home after work, and if there is one item a businessman almost always carries it's a briefcase. Yet there had been no briefcase in his car.

'Are you all right, Michael?'

'What?'

'You look startled.'

'Yes, I'm fine.'

'Excuse me while I do this. I didn't have time at the office.'

'You busy?'

'Very. Can't keep up with the orders.'

That wasn't what Alison had said, but I didn't expect Stuart to tell me the truth. Businessmen are rarely honest about their companies, and never to journalists.

'I thought the cutlery industry was suffering.'

'It is. But if the market's poor, you work doubly hard to make sure you increase your share of it or you expand overseas. Only way to maintain profits.'

'You export much?'

'More and more. It's a bloody nightmare dealing with all the paperwork but it's worth the effort. Just made a big sale in the US.'

'Don't they make enough of their own?'

'Cutlery? Of course. But not the way we do it here. Quality is quality. And at our end of the market they'll pay for it. You want cheap rubbish you go to Korea. You want silver plate or craftsmanship that'll last generations you still come to Sheffield.'

I toyed with my glass, waiting to get his full attention. He was sorting though the documents, putting them in different piles.

'Stuart, how well did you know Richard Sutton?'

Stuart glanced up sharply. 'Is that why you're here?'

'I'm just curious. I thought you might have been close to him.'

'I don't think anyone was particularly close to him. Except his wife.'

'Really?'

'He wasn't that kind of man. He worked too hard to have much time for friends and he was slightly intimidating.'

Stuart intimidated. I found that hard to believe.

'In what way?'

'Well, he was a formidable man. Awesome intellect, not always an easy companion. All that Quaker upbringing.'

'He didn't practise though, did he?'

'No. I don't think he ever believed. But the work ethic rubbed off on him. I'll miss him. So will this city. He's done a hell of a lot for it.'

'Was his company in trouble?'

Stuart stopped what he was doing and looked up at me very slowly. He sat down in his high-backed chair and took off his spectacles. He began to polish them with a handkerchief. A stalling tactic. I wasn't convinced he actually needed spectacles. He seemed to see all right without them, but they gave him the correct sober Chairman of the Board image. They also gave him time to think. I suspected the frames contained clear glass, not lenses. It was the sort of thing Stuart would do.

'Trouble?' he said cautiously.

'Financial trouble.'

Stuart laughed. 'I wish my business was as sound as his.' His tone was full of contempt for such a notion.

'What about his project in the East End, the recycling plant? Isn't that costing fifty million?'

'Yes, it's a large investment but it's well covered. RPS isn't highly geared. It can easily cope with a debt like that.'

'The cash is coming from the European Community, isn't it?'

Stuart pursed his lips cautiously. 'Some of it, I believe.'

He put his spectacles back on and blinked at me like some benign professor. Only I knew him too well to be deceived. His mind had caught up with me and by now was probably running way ahead.

'Suppose you tell me what you really want to know.'

'Sutton got drunk on Monday night. A strange thing for him to do, as you know. Any idea where he might have gone to do it? Or why?'

Stuart took a long time answering. 'I haven't a clue, I'm sorry.'

'Was he a member of a club of some sort? Did he eat regularly at a particular restaurant.'

'Not a club. He wasn't a clubby person. As to restaurants, I don't know. He probably ate out all over the place.'

'What if he ate in?'

'Pardon?'

'Dinner at someone's house.'

'What are you fishing for, Michael?'

I got to the point. 'Did he have a mistress?'

Stuart said: 'Ah.' Then said nothing.

I waited.

Finally he said: 'That is a very indiscreet question.'

'But I'm not an indiscreet person, you know that. Did he? Or any regular lady friends?'

'No. If you knew his wife, you wouldn't have to ask a question like that. They were a very happy couple. And Richard was not a womanizer. The idea's ridiculous.' His voice hardened. 'I hope you're not trying to dig up dirt on him.'

'You know I'm not that kind of journalist.'

'Then why?'

'Wouldn't you like to know why he got drunk?'

'Let it be, Michael. He's dead. There was enough bad publicity after the inquest. I don't want any part of creating any more.'

He stood up. 'Alison will be getting impatient.' He

opened the study door and walked me down the hall to the front of the house.

'Thanks for your help, Stuart. There *is* one last thing, though.'

He opened the front door pointedly. 'You like to wring people dry, don't you?'

'Will you answer me something truthfully?'

'What is it?'

'Do you like cauliflower cheese?'

He started, taken aback, then glanced around furtively to check that no one could hear.

'No,' he said. 'I hate it. But I daren't tell Alison.'

I went away feeling rather reassured. He was a wealthy man, distinguished captain of industry, God knows what. Yet when it came to cauliflower cheese he was as gutless as I was.

CHAPTER 10

The two bouncers were arm wrestling with each other across the front counter when I arrived at Casanova's casino. I watched them grunt and grimace, eyeball to eyeball, biceps straining at the seams of their dinner jackets, then cleared my throat to let them know I was there. One of them glanced round and while he was distracted his mate jammed his arm down hard on to the counter top. He grinned triumphantly.

'Two one to me.'

'Bollocks. That dun't count, I weren't looking.'

'Tough shit. One up to me.'

'I'd turned round, 'adn't I?'

'Fair and square it were.'

'Fuck off . . . Good evening, sir,' he said to me.

You have to wonder about bouncers. Where do they get them? Nobody can be that thick naturally; they have to be taught. Is there a training school somewhere, perhaps, where they show them how to grow a moustache, give them a clip-on black tie and remove their brains?

'Good evening,' I said.

'You want to play?'

He meant the tables. I refrained from giving a smart reply. Bouncers don't like jokers. They tend to butt them in the face first and laugh later.

'Yes.'

'You a member?'

'No.'

'You want to join? It waint cost you nowt.'

'Do I have to be a member to go in?'

'Aye.'

I joined. At Casanova's they have an exclusive clientele but anyone can become part of it. It's that kind of place.

I went downstairs into the gaming room. Behind me, the bouncers started their argument again.

The casino was done out like an eighteenth-century bordello, or rather what a deranged interior designer thought an eighteenth-century bordello looked like. Red carpets and drapes, rococo ceiling, fake gilt ornaments, glass chandeliers and, round the walls, framed erotic prints, cracked and yellowing like true antiques but manufactured, I guessed, about 1975 when the casino opened. The waitresses and female croupiers were dressed like courtesans, long dresses, hair up, breasts out. The bar-tender wore a periwig and stockings and looked a right prat. It was the tackiest place I'd ever seen.

I wandered over to one of the roulette tables and watched a few spins of the wheel. The minimum bet was 25p. We weren't talking Las Vegas here. The croupier, a petite blonde with powdered breasts doing their best to fall out of her dress, called out the numbers in French. Her accent was one part Paris, nine parts Rotherham.

'Does monsieur wish to bet?' she said to me.

'Not at the moment.'

I looked at the chips on the table. They were different sizes and colours but none matched the rectangular piece of plastic I'd found in my flat. I crossed to the blackjack tables and casually examined the chips in front of the dealer. Again, none matched the chip I had in my pocket.

Puzzled, I went to the bar and sat down on one of the eighteenth-century bar stools.

I ordered a beer from the period barman. His costume was pretty good. The wig looked genuine, the embroidered coat and wool breeches like originals. The pock marks on his face were authentic too. He was even bigger than the bouncers, but then, in an outfit like that he probably had to be.

'Have one yourself,' I said.

'Thank you, sir. I'll have a half later.'

The drinks came to £3.20. They certainly weren't charging eighteenth-century prices. The barman started washing some glasses at the sink under the counter. I took the plastic chip out of my pocket and showed it to him.

'This come from here?'

The barman glanced at it. 'Yes, sir.'

'I don't see any others like it on the tables.'

'It's one of the high-stake chips. From the back room.' He indicated a pair of gilt double doors set in the end wall.

'There are more tables through there?'

'Yes, sir.'

'Can I just walk in?'

The barman shook his head. 'You'd have to ask Mr Moranis. Invited guests only in the back room.'

'Mr Moranis?'

'He owns the casino.'

'Where do I find him?'

The barman reached under the bar and pressed something. There was a delay, then a mirror on the end wall clicked open and a short, swarthy man came out of an office. He crossed the room towards us. He waddled rather than walked, taking short steps and swinging his stubby arms. His jet black hair was carefully parted and blow-dried in a bouffant wave. Diamonds glinted on his fingers and he wore a frilly cream shirt under his midnight blue dinner jacket. He looked like a lizard on his way to the opera.

His perfume reached us a couple of minutes before he did.

'What is it, Jack?' he said to the barman.

'This gentleman was asking about the back room, Mr Moranis.'

Moranis turned his dark eyes on me. They were so deep-set they were barely visible in the cavities behind the heavy lids and fleshy cheeks.

'I'm sorry, sir. The back room is for invited guests only. The general membership is not admitted.' His voice was low and rasping, with a lacing of a foreign accent.

'How do I become an invited guest?'

Moranis studied me carefully. 'That depends. You wish to play for the higher stakes?'

I could see this would end up an expensive night if I didn't watch out.

'Actually, I don't want to play at all.'

'Then . . .' He frowned and made a gesture of impatience with his hands.

'It's for a magazine article,' I said. 'Would you be prepared to give me an interview?'

His face relaxed a fraction. 'An interview?'

'For a colour piece on your casino. I'd like to arrange for a photographer to come one evening, if that's convenient for you.'

'For which magazine?'

'The *Tatler*,' I said without hesitation, choosing a magazine I knew he'd have heard of but probably never read. Not that anyone actually reads the *Tatler*, they just stick it on coffee tables.

'The *Tatler*, eh?' He ran the words around his palate and seemed to like the taste. 'What kind of interview?'

'Well, our readership likes a glimpse of the high life,' I said, making it up as I went along. 'We usually concentrate on the London social scene but we're starting a series of articles on provincial trendsetters. We thought you would make an ideal subject.'

'But why did you not 'phone me first?'

'I wanted to take a look around beforehand, to get a feel of the place. That's why I wanted to see the back room.'

Moranis beamed. I'd found his weakspot. Vanity.

'Come into the office. We do the interview first, then I show you the other tables.'

I congratulated myself on my cunning but then began to regret it as Moranis, once ensconced in the leather chair behind his reproduction Regency desk in his reproduction Regency office, launched forth on his life story. He was a voluble interviewee who could talk at length about all manner of subjects, all of them himself.

Fortunately, I'd brought a notebook with me in which I doodled assiduously, pretending it was shorthand. Periodically I nodded and asked a question, not so much to encourage him as to let him know I was still there. Most of the questions he asked himself, and then answered himself. 'You want to know how I made my first fortune? I tell you how I made my first fortune . . .'

The one thing that made the ordeal bearable was the presence in the room of a slender young woman on a lyre-end sofa next to Moranis's desk. She lounged back in the red velvet cushions throughout the interview, one hand resting on the end of the sofa, the other holding a fluted glass of champagne from which she occasionally sipped. Her legs were crossed but her red sheath gown, slit up the side, had fallen away to reveal a sliver of tanned thigh.

Whenever Moranis's self-centred bragging became to insufferable, I turned to the woman for a brief respite. Her serene expression never changed and her mind seemed elsewhere. That was probably the only way to deal with Moranis: not listen to a word he said. She'd been introduced to me as his secretary and personal assistant. I wasn't sure about the secretarial bit, but she looked as if she'd be pretty good at personal assistance.

After an hour or so of terminal boredom I closed my notebook and stood up.

'Don't you want the rest?' Moranis said, the disappointment apparent in his face.

'Thank you, but I've enough to be going on with.'

'OK, so what about the photographer? When he going to come?'

'I'll have to check availability. I'll 'phone you to fix it up.'

'Make it a Saturday night. That's when the high rollers are in. You get lots of good pictures then.'

Moranis came out from behind his desk. 'I show you the back room now. You get a much higher class of pun . . .' He'd been about to say punter but stopped himself. '. . . customer in there.'

'Would you mind if I looked around on my own?'

He took a pace back. 'Sure. If that's what you want.'

'I'll just have a drink and soak up the atmosphere.'

'Whatever you like. You want some chips on the house? Play the tables a bit.'

'No, thanks.'

'OK. Which month you say the article going in?'

'Not for a while, I'm afraid. We have a long lead time.'

'But you let me know?'

'Of course.'

'Good.'

I shook his hand. It was soft and squelchy like a dead toad. I went out of a second door on the other side of the office and into the back room of the casino. I took a deep breath to clear my lungs of Moranis's aftershave and headed for the bar. The things I did to get a story.

I ordered a beer from the girl behind the bar and twisted round on my stool to survey the room. The bordello theme had been continued and I couldn't see much difference between this and the front room. There were perhaps more mirrors, a few more velvet curtains, but it was essentially the same. Only the clientele differed. They were smarter dressed in here. Some of the men were in dinner jackets, some of the women in long evening dresses. And there was more money. Most of it going straight down the drain.

'Your beer, sir.'

I turned. 'Will I get change from a fiver?'

'It's on the house. All the drinks in here are.'

'I should have had champagne.'

The girl smiled. 'It's not too late to change your mind.'

I shook my head. 'The bubbles would only get up my nose.'

She could only have been about nineteen. She was wearing the same tarty outfit as the female croupiers, showing a lot of cleavage but not much taste.

'You like getting dressed up like that?' I said.

'It's part of the theme, sir. Everyone dresses like this. Mr Moranis likes us to fit in.'

'I can imagine. Do you work here every night?'

'Five nights a week.'

'Tell me, do you remember a couple of guys? Big, ugly, short-cropped hair, maybe wearing black suits, looked like extras from a Hammer horror film. Came in here fairly recently.'

She thought for only a moment. 'Yes, sir.'

'You do? Can you remember which night?'

'Last Monday, I think. Yes, I'm pretty sure it was Monday.'

'You've a good memory.'

'They were new, that's why I remember. Most of the people in here are regulars. I'd never seen them before.'

'How did they get in? I thought this room was for invited guests only.'

'Mr Moranis makes exceptions for people who, well . . . like to spend a lot.'

'You mean like to lose a lot.'

She grinned. 'That's what most of them do.'

'Including those two?'

'I think so. They were hard at it for a couple of hours. A big group of them. The two men, and some of the regulars, Mr Coulton, Mr Sutton, Miss Myers.'

The room seemed to go suddenly quiet. I was acutely aware of my own heartbeat and nothing else.

'What did you say?'

'They were hard at it for . . .'

'After that. Did you say Sutton?'

'Yes, he's one . . . well, he *was* one . . .'

'Richard Sutton?'

'That's right.'

The surrounding world came back. I heard voices again, laughter, the click of roulette chips.

'Richard Sutton came here?'

'Yes, frequently.'

'Richard Sutton, the businessman who was killed last week?'

'Is that so odd?'

So he did have some vices. Suddenly he was becoming a much more interesting character.

'And he was with the two men I described?'

She screwed up her brow, trying to remember. 'Well, I'm not sure about that. They were playing roulette at the same table but I don't know if they came in together.'

'Are you sure it was Monday night?'

'Yes. It was my first night back after my weekend off. I only get one off in four, it must have been Monday. Why?'

'Do you remember what time Mr Sutton left?'

'I didn't notice. Early I should think. He never stayed much after nine or ten.'

No, of course not. He had a wife to get back to.

'You could ask Miss Myers if you really want to know. I think he used to give her a lift home quite often.'

'Miss Myers?'

'She's over there. Stephanie Myers. She plays a lot here.' She nodded towards one of the tables. 'In the green dress.'

I looked across at Stephanie Myers. It was no hardship. She was tall with long auburn hair and a striking figure. Not thin, not even slim, but verging on the voluptuous. Very unfashionable by modern standards but it looked all right to me. The green silk dress was expensive without being showy and she was wearing very little make-up. Not a woman to overdo her appearance. Her features were no more than attractive but even at a distance she seemed to exude a distinct sensuality. The one word that came to mind when you looked at her was not beauty. It was sex.

She was playing roulette with the intense concentration of an habitual gambler, the emotions showing clearly in her face. When she won, her eyes shone with unashamed greed; when she lost, she was like a disappointed little girl. She seemed to conceal nothing and that openness was deceptively alluring.

Once, she lifted her eyes from the table and saw me staring at her. She gave me an equally frank appraisal in return, not remotely angry or embarrassed. She was probably used to men staring at her.

Then she returned her attention to the green baize and the relentless spin of the roulette wheel. The casino was not crowded. It was still early. Maybe the majority of the gamblers came in later. Apart from Stephanie there were only four others at her table: a blowsy woman in a halter-neck dress and three men in dinner jackets, all different in appearance but all alike in manner—brash, loud, flashy. The kind of men who would wear gold medallions in their pubic hair. Stephanie appeared to be on her own.

I tried to imagine Richard Sutton in this glossy, skin-deep environment. The apparently staid, respectable business-man throwing £50 chips across the table, exchanging small talk with men who permed their hair, peering down the dresses of teenage croupiers. I couldn't see it.

If you have a fixed image of someone in a particular surrounding, it is difficult to transpose it to an altogether different place. Yet that doesn't mean they couldn't fit in there, and it doesn't mean your original perception of them was wrong. There are always some aspects of a person that remain forever hidden, either because they choose to hide them or because our own prejudices prevent us seeing them. I'd met enough to realize it was foolish to make any assumptions whatsoever. Unlikely people are always found in unlikely places.

After some time, Stephanie Myers collected up her chips

and came to the bar. She sat down on the stool next but one to mine and ordered a dry white wine.

I watched her discreetly as she opened her handbag. She took out a small glass bottle with a red and gold cap and sprayed scent on to one of her wrists. Then she rubbed her wrists together, transferring the perfume. I glanced casually at the bottle and started violently. I looked again. On the front of the bottle, in gold letters, it said Yves Saint Laurent, Opium. It was the same perfume that had been in Richard Sutton's car the night he died. I straightened up and paid attention.

Stephanie had taken a cigarette out of a pack and was lighting it with a slim gold lighter. She put the cigarette packet, the lighter and perfume spray back into her handbag.

'Winning?' I said.

She turned slowly and ran cool eyes over me. 'About even. You're not playing?'

She seemed willing to talk. There was none of the hostility or plain boredom I've seen in women habitually chatted up by men.

'Not for the moment.'

'Just enjoying the view, eh?'

'Pardon?'

'The view.' She lifted her finely-plucked eyebrows at the girl behind the bar. 'And the others. That's why a lot of men come here.'

'I'm not sure . . .'

'Don't tell me you haven't noticed the costumes. Or the pictures.'

She pointed at one of the erotic prints on the back wall of the bar. It depicted a semi-naked man and woman engaged in a bizarre coupling in an eighteenth-century boudoir. I tilted my head to try to work out what they were doing.

'It doesn't look anatomically possible,' I said.

'You've led a sheltered life. Moranis thinks they're

tasteful. You've met him, I take it. I saw you coming out
of his office.'

'Yes, I've had that pleasure.'

'So have I.' She said it archly, as if there were a double
meaning there. 'You a friend of his?'

'First time I've been here. I gather you come quite often.'

'I like to gamble.'

'That must be expensive.'

She smiled patronizingly. 'Don't worry, I can afford it.'

There was something about her manner I didn't like. A
harshness, a coldness, some internal hardness that belied
the obvious softness of her body.

'You were here last Monday,' I said. 'Do you remember
a couple of big blokes, played roulette at your table, London
accents, looked as if someone had hit them in the face with
a shovel and forgotten to remove the shovel?'

'Yes, I remember them. Why?'

'Know who they were? I'm trying to find them.'

'I'd never seen them before.'

'So they weren't friends of Richard Sutton's?'

She let smoke trickle out of the corner of her mouth. 'He
had more taste than that.'

'Were you close to Sutton?'

She laughed suddenly. It wasn't a warm laugh either; it
was more cruel.

'You could say that.'

She gave me a coy, amused look. There was no mistaking
the expression. I was sure then she had been his mistress.
The facts were all there. They'd gambled together regularly, he'd given her lifts home and she'd left a perfume
bottle in his car. She had an expensive lifestyle, Sutton had
been wealthy. I couldn't see them being just good friends.
Stephanie was not a woman you wanted to simply look at
or engage in the noble arts of conversation.

'Were you with him all last Monday evening?'

'What's it to you?' Some thought came to her and her
mouth curled into a sneer. 'You plainclothes?'

'Do I look like a cop?'

She examined me. 'No, cops dress better than you.'

That hurt. I was wearing a tie, wasn't I?

'Then who are you? Why're you so interested?'

I shrugged. 'He was killed that night. You must have talked to him at the roulette table. Was he depressed, worried about anything?'

'Why should he have been?'

'He was drinking heavily, wasn't he?'

'He had Perrier all evening, he always did.'

I took a sip of my beer and gazed at the erotic print on the wall. It still didn't look anatomically possible.

'You know he was drunk when he crashed?' I said.

Stephanie hesitated. She looked down at the bar. Her hair shielded her face.

'I read it in the paper.'

'You told the police he only drank Perrier the whole time he was with you?'

'It's nothing to do with me, none of it.'

I could see that. The other woman. I could see why she might not want to step forward.

'Didn't it strike you as odd?'

'Look, who the hell are you?'

I told her. 'You didn't care very much about him, did you?'

Stephanie finished her wine in a gulp and picked up her handbag and stack of plastic chips.

'Did he have a briefcase with him?' I asked.

I knew from the stiffening of her posture and the widening of the eyes that I'd hit home.

'I don't know what you're talking about,' she said.

She was lying. I couldn't fathom why. But I knew instinctively the briefcase was relevant. Her devious reply was enough to tell me that.

'It could be important,' I said. 'Do you know where it is.'

Her voice became a harsh whisper. 'Mind your own fucking business.'

She climbed down off the stool and went back to the roulette table.

'Nice talking to you, too,' I murmured softly to myself.

I was getting used to being told to keep my nose out of other people's business. She hadn't been particularly pleasant about it, but at least she hadn't reinforced her displeasure with a pair of snub-nosed pliers.

I wondered what Sutton had seen in her. He had an intelligent, beautiful wife, apparently perfect in almost every way yet he still went elsewhere for his pleasure. Maybe that was it: Jacqueline was too perfect. Maybe he wanted someone who would be more fun, who would take her dress off without putting it on a hanger. Who could tell why he did it? Maybe he no longer desired Jacqueline, maybe she no longer desired him. Sex is rarely very simple.

I watched Stephanie throw a few chips carelessly on to the roulette board. The wheel spun. The ball rattled around the numbers and stopped. Stephanie lost. The croupier gathered in the chips. Stephanie didn't move a muscle. She didn't seem to mind.

She came out of the casino at 2.0 a.m. She'd been in there a long time. I'd half dozed off in the car but roused myself when she appeared in the doorway in a knee-length grey fur coat. Probably real fur too; I couldn't see her worrying much about dumb animals. She got into the waiting taxi and I pulled out after them.

We headed out of town up West Street and Glossop Road. The nightclubs were emptying and practically the only traffic on the road were the convoys of cabs taking drunken revellers home. We turned up Manchester Road, past the Hallam Towers Hotel, and climbed the hill to Crosspool. I could see Stephanie slumped sideways on the back seat in the beam of my headlights.

At Crosspool we turned west along Sandygate Road and after about a mile and a half took a road to the left. This was Lodge Moor, the high land between the rivers Porter and Rivelin. Freezing cold in winter but the people here can afford the heating bills.

Stephanie's house was set back from the road behind a low beech hedge. I drove straight past as she was getting out of the taxi and parked a distance away. I gave her time to get inside, then went back and had a look. Not a bad little place. Four or five bedrooms, a conservatory at one side, garage at the other, maybe an acre of garden. She had expensive tastes. I wondered how she was going to satisfy them now her sugar daddy was gone.

I didn't drive home straight away. I took a map out of the glove compartment and found the most direct route from Stephanie Myers's house to Hathersage. Then I followed it. Down the hill, skirting the sides of the valley, across the River Porter very close to its source and along Fulwood Lane to Ringinglow Road. A right turn and then the long, lonely stretch across Burbage Moor, a vast plateau of heather and peat bog and the occasional sheep.

Beyond Burbage Brook the road curved around the north side of Higger Tor before falling away steeply to the point where Richard Sutton had crashed. I parked on the narrow verge and climbed out.

I knew now why Sutton had been out here the night he died. He'd been at the casino with Stephanie Myers. The two thugs who'd beaten me up had been there also. That wasn't a coincidence.

Later, Sutton had driven Stephanie home. Maybe he'd gone into her house, maybe they'd made love, maybe he'd left his briefcase there, I could only guess. But when he left her house he came this way, the simplest route home to Hathersage.

More importantly, when he left, he'd been sober. Yet when he reached this point on the road, perhaps ten minutes later, he'd been drunk enough to crash his car. Or had he?

I examined the road with a torch. There were black skid-marks on the tarmac, but they stopped sixty or seventy yards before the point at which Sutton's car had careered off down the hill.

I walked to the exact spot where he'd left the road. The fence on the verge had not yet been replaced but the Rolls-Royce had long since been towed away. I could see the dark furrows in the grass where a tractor had dragged it back up the slope. The wind gusted in my face and I cupped my hands over it to protect my aching nose. It was a lonely spot, sinister in the dark, but the fresh air cleared my head.

I still didn't know what had happened that night. Every new bit of knowledge I acquired seemed only to confuse me further. I'd considered Sutton's death from the perspective of accident or suicide. Yet now I was almost certain it had been neither.

CHAPTER 11

If you want to get an idea of what death really means, go and visit a pathology lab. Take a look at the long, shallow, trough-like tables they use for cutting up bodies, the hoses for washing away the blood, the array of saws and knives to slice through lifeless flesh. The glass jars full of diseased organs, the filing cabinet drawers for the cadavers, the excrement, the bits of putrid corpses. The men and women in white coats and rubber gloves dissecting the remains of someone's loved one, chopping them into bits to be peered at through a microscope and then dumped in a plastic bag. It gives you a good idea of what it's like, the straight honest facts of physical extinction with nothing hidden for the squeamish. It's almost enough to make you turn religious.

Carl Byeswater was sitting at a bench reading the newspaper and eating his lunch. He was a big, jolly man with a ginger beard, a hill walker as full of life as his lab was of death. He grinned and waved me over.

'Coffee?' he boomed.

'Sure.'

He stood up and went to the sink, spooned instant coffee into mugs and filled them with hot water. The milk he got from a refrigerator under the bench. It was on a shelf in between jars of unidentified tissue. I said I'd take mine black.

Carl sat down and pushed over a stool for me with his feet. He took a bite from a thick wedge of granary bread and chewed.

'What's in the sandwiches?' I asked.

'Egg mayonnaise.'

My stomach turned over. 'You always eat in here?'

'Easier than going to the canteen. Provided you don't pick something up off the bench and eat it by mistake.' He gave a low chuckle. 'You're looking under the weather, Michael. Had a bad cold?'

My nose again. It was becoming a severe embarrassment. 'I'm fine.'

'You should come on another walk with us. Do you good.'

'You think I'm a masochist?' A couple of years back I'd gone on a day's hike in the Peaks with Carl, his wife and their little daughter, Annie, who was only seven but could walk the legs off a slob like me. Edale skyline, Kinder Scout, fifteen miles of agony in Britain's longest rainstorm. Annie thought it was fun. For me, never again.

'We're going to Ullswater in December. Cottage underneath Helvellyn. Plenty of room if you want to come. We thought we'd do Striding Edge now Annie's a bit older.'

'Well, you can do it without me,' I said. 'I'm not being humiliated by that daughter of yours again.'

'No stamina, you journalists. You can tell that from your colleagues we get in here.'

'What?'

'Well, bits of them anyway.' He nodded at some glass containers on a shelf. Dark brown objects floated inside them. 'Cirrhosis of the liver. We use them for teaching. Journalists are the best examples. Saves labour too as they're already well preserved in alcohol when we get them.'

I said it was old.

Then I asked him, as we were on the subject, what he could tell me about the absorption of alcohol.

It's best to do it with a rump steak and chips and a salad on the side,' he said.

'You finished?' I said.

I took out my photocopy of the post-mortem examination on Richard Sutton. I'd cut the top off it to conceal the source and Sutton's personal details.

'You got time to read this?'

'No problem. I'm just waiting for the forensic entomologist to arrive. He's giving a lecture to the students.'

'The what?'

'Forensic entomologist. Insect expert.'

'I know what an entomologist is. What's the forensic bit?'

'You really want to know?'

'I like to broaden my education.'

'He looks at the insects that colonize a body, maggots, weevils, termites, that sort of thing. Different insects take over at different points in the decomposition so he can work out how long the person's been dead.'

'I bet he gets a lot of job satisfaction from that.'

'Very specialized field. He's coming from London. Glad you asked?'

I gave him the photocopy. He scanned it superficially.

'I think you've been a naughty boy, Michael. This is an autopsy report.'

'Yes.'

'You're not supposed to have these.'

'I can't imagine how I got it.'

'You think I haven't done enough PMs for the Coroner to know where this came from?'

'But you won't tell, will you? That's why I came to you. You'd never shop a man who'd struggled up Grind's Brook in the pouring rain with you.'

'I seem to remember we pulled you up.'

'Yeah, well, I didn't want to show you up too much on our first hike.'

Carl read the post-mortem report. 'It's not one of mine. Is it from here?'

'The Hallamshire.'

'Looks like a drunk driving to me. RTA.'

I nodded. 'That's why I asked about absorption of alcohol. Does it look normal for a traffic accident?'

'What do you mean, normal?'

'The injuries, the alcohol, are they consistent with an accident?'

'The pathologist who did the autopsy thought so.'

'What do you think?'

'What is this, Michael?'

'The injuries, are they what you'd expect in a man who'd crashed his car on a hillside?'

Carl tugged at the ends of his beard and studied the sheet some more.

'Yes,' he said finally.

'Sure?'

'It has all the classic signs.'

'What are they?'

'Well, a ruptured spleen for a start. That's almost inevitable in a car crash. The body jolts forward and the steering-wheel crushes the spleen. Same with the fractures of the hip sockets.'

'How does that happen?'

Carl stretched his legs out. 'That's how your legs are immediately before the crash. Feet on, or near, the pedals. Bang! On impact your legs get rammed back hard. The thigh bones are pushed straight out the back of the sockets, fracturing them in the process.'

'What about the other injuries?'

'Multiple leg breaks. Only to be expected if the front of the car crumples.'

'And the head injuries? What's this here? Contrecoup.' I pointed at a paragraph.

'It's French.'

'And in English?'

'It's a type of bruising on the brain.'

'Suspicious?'

Carl gave me a wry look. 'Sorry to disappoint you, Mike. No, extremely common in accidents.'

'What kind of bruising to the brain?'

'Well, think of the brain as a ball floating in a pool of fluid inside the skull. If there's a blow to the front of the head, the brain bounces back and hits the opposite side, causing a bruise there as well as at the front. That's contrecoup.'

'In this case, what would be the blow to the front of the head?'

'Impact with the windscreen. That's clear. His body is hurled forward. The seat-belt restrains him to some extent but the front part of the cranium—' he touched his hairline above the forehead—'hits the windscreen and you get a contusion, contrecoup, on the rear of the brain, here, as well.'

'Could it have been caused by a different sort of blow?'

'Like what?'

'Like someone hitting him with something.'

Carl picked up a Kit-Kat from the bench and unwrapped it. He broke off one of the wafers.

'Want a bit?'

I shook my head.

'This for a story?' he asked, licking the chocolate from the wispy hair around his lips.

'Yes.'

'Spill it?'

'Is that possible? That he was hit with something else. An instrument of some sort.'

'It would have to have been very blunt.'

'Why?'

'Because of the type of fracture. You hit someone on the forehead with a hammer or something sharp, it leaves a hole in the skull. Any half awake pathologist would notice that.'

'And think it odd?'

'In a car crash, of course. But he didn't have that kind of fracture.'

'If he'd been hit and then pushed down the hill in his car, could you tell the difference between the initial blow and the subsequent injury from impact with the windscreen?'

'No. Certainly not from this.' He nodded at the photocopy. 'I didn't examine the body.'

'What about the alcohol in his bloodstream?'

'High. He was way over the limit. Two hundred milligrams per hundred millilitres of blood. The legal limit's eighty.'

'Could he drive in that condition?'

'Yes. Not safely, of course—presumably that's why he crashed—but he wasn't so drunk he would have been incapable of driving.'

'How much is two hundred milligrams?'

Carl shrugged. 'Half a bottle of spirits, something like that.'

'So nothing strikes you as odd about this case?'

'No. I've seen dozens of others just like it. All RTAs. And the police didn't see anything odd either.'

'How can you tell?'

'The autopsy was done by a local pathologist. Hallamshire, you said.'

'So?'

'If there'd been any suspicious circumstances, they'd have called in a Home Office pathologist, a forensic pathologist. That's the procedure.'

He screwed up the Kit-Kat wrapper and tossed it towards a plastic dustbin under the bench. It missed.

'Why do you think something's wrong with it?'

'The guy was teetotal.'

'You're adding two and two and making five, Michael. All this about him being hit on the head. You trying to make it a murder? The Coroner sees a case like this he thinks of two verdicts: either accidental death or suicide. There's nothing to indicate foul play.'

'What about this for a scenario?' I said.

I outlined it for him and he listened, his expression sceptical.

When I'd finished, he sighed. 'That's pure speculation.'

'But possible? It could have happened like that?'

'I suppose so.'

'Nothing in the medical evidence would contradict it?'

'No. It would fit the facts all right. What's going on?'

'I'm trying to find out.'

'There's more, isn't there? Things you haven't told me.'

'You've been a great help, Carl.'

I got up off the stool.

'Hey, you change your mind about Ullswater, let me know.'

'I don't think I will.'

'One Sunday, then. We could do Kinder again. Annie still talks about you, you know.'

'Really? She's a nice kid.'

'She calls you "that man who goes up mountains on his knees".'

'Funny how quickly you can go off someone.'

'You want to know *what*?' Harry Raymond said.

'How to burgle a house.'

'Jesus Christ, you serious?'

I nodded. 'I need a few tips.'

'Tips? You need your 'ead examining.'

He opened the safe in the corner of his back room and took out some cans of Stone's bitter. That's all the safe contained. He tossed one to me.

'I just want you to tell me something about locks and alarms,' I said.

'I'll tell you summat about alarms. They make a loud noise and can get you five in Armley.'

I smiled. 'For a first offence?'

'You planning to make an 'abit of it?'

Harry pulled the ring cap off his can and flopped down into a shabby armchair, pushing a cardboard box out of the way to make room for his feet. The back room of his locksmith's shop was crammed with safes, tools, different types of alarms and piles of stocks.

'Is there a simple way of opening a locked door?' I said.

'For you, yes. Use a key.'

'Come on, Harry. I want to know. Can you use a credit card?'

'You been watching too many films. I can't even get money out of a cashpoint with *my* credit card.'

'So what do I use?'

'What kind of lock?'

'I don't know.'

'Jesus.' Harry raised his eyes until they almost disappeared under his eyebrows. 'I don't believe I'm 'earing this.'

'I'm not kidding, Harry. I need some help.'

'Aye, from a psychiatrist. What d'you want to burgle an 'ouse for?'

'Business.'

'You're a journalist, for Christ's sake. You don't know the first thing about 'ousebreaking.'

'That's why I've come to you.'

He shook his head. 'Look, stick to what you do best, Michael. I don't think I could learn to be a journalist in 'alf an hour. For one thing I'm barely literate when it comes to writing.'

'You could get a job at the *News*.'

'So don't you think you can learn about burglary in 'alf an hour.'

'It's only a simple job, Harry.'

'Simple jobs are the ones you get caught on.'

'What's the best way to disable an alarm?'

'You're determined to do this, aren't you?'

'Do I cut the wires or something?'

He sighed. 'What kind of an alarm?'

'I don't know.'

'Bloody 'ell! You don't know much about this, do you? Where's the 'ouse?'

'Lodge Moor.'

'You really are crazy. You taken a close look at them places up there? Every kind of trip device, dead lock, guard dog you've ever seen.'

'There isn't a dog.'

'You sure?'

'Well . . .'

'Never touch an 'ouse wi' a dog.'

'Couldn't you drug it?'

'Drug it? What d'you think you do? Give the Doberman two sleeping tablets and a glass of water?'

'I'm almost certain there isn't a dog.'

'You cased it?'

'Not exactly.'

'Then you might as well ring Snig Hill now and make an appointment for the plods to meet you there.'

'It can't be that hard, Harry.'

'You knocking my old profession?'

'What about all the kids who do it? They don't know much.'

'That's why they get caught. You ever been down the Magistrates' Court of a Monday morning?'

'OK,' I said. 'Forget it.'

I started to get up. The bell on the front door tinkled and Harry climbed out of his armchair.

'You stay here,' he said and went through into the shop. I admired the damp patches on his walls and wondered how I was going to break into Stephanie Myers's house.

Harry was back in a few minutes. 'A couple of Yales needing cutting,' he explained as he picked up his can of beer.

'Thanks anyway, Harry,' I said. 'I'll find a way myself.'

''Ang on a sec. What's in this 'ouse?'

'A briefcase, I think.'

'Important to you?'

I nodded.

'You going to do something stupid?'

'Maybe.'

'Meaning yes.' He gave it some thought. 'I'll come wi' you.'

'No, Harry. I wanted advice only. I'm not getting you involved.'

'You think I'm going to let you do it on your own when you don't know the first thing about it? When you doing it?'

'It's not your affair, Harry. I'll take a chance myself.'

'When?'

'It's not fair on you.'

'*When?*'

'Tonight.'

'I owe you one.'

'I'm not asking, Harry.'

'It'll be like the old days. I must be round the bend but I'm fed up being a shopkeeper.'

'I can't let you. It's too much of a risk.'

'That's what I miss.'

'If we're caught, you'll be sent down again.'

Harry grinned. 'What the 'ell. I could do wi' a break from the wife.'

We sat in my car watching Stephanie Myers's house. It was ten o'clock at night. A light was on upstairs.

'How d'you know she's going out?' Harry asked.

'She will, don't worry. She's not the type to stay in and crochet table mats.'

'Big 'ouse. You been inside?'

'No.'

'A lot of antiques up here. I did an 'ouse once somewhere round 'ere. Near the golf course, I think. Beautiful rosewood furniture. Fetched a tidy price.'

'You stole the *furniture?*'

'We don't go around with swag bags, you know. We brought a van.'

'And no one noticed? In the middle of the night?'

'It weren't night. The owners were out at work. We came

in a removal van and cleared the 'ouse. Me and a couple of mates.'

'What about the neighbours?'

'One of them came out while we was doing it. Shit, we thought. We've 'ad it now. But all she said were, "I think it's very rude of the Taylors not to let us know they were moving."'

Harry chuckled. 'That were twenty year ago, of course. You couldn't do it now. People are more suspicious. Neighbourhood Watch schemes, all that kind of crap.'

'How did you get in when you used to do it?'

'All sorts. Pick the locks if they were easy enough, jemmy the door, break a window. I never liked the smash and grab stuff much, not very skilful. Estate agents, that was the one I liked.'

'Estate agents?'

'Aye. When an empty 'ouse was up for sale, I'd go along to the estate agents and ask to look round it, like a prospective buyer. Most of the time they'd be too busy to come wi' me so they'd give me the keys instead. I'd make copies, then wait until the 'ouse was sold. Wait a few months after that and then just use the keys to get in. It took a lot of patience but it were dead easy.

'Bit of advice. If you buy an 'ouse what's been empty for a while, always change the locks.'

A taxi had pulled up outside the house. Stephanie had obviously been waiting, for she came out at once and got in. She was wearing another fur coat. Not the grey one but a dark colour which glistened when it caught the light. She probably had a wardrobe full of them.

We waited for the taxi to go, then Harry said: 'I'll just check it out.'

'I'll come with you.'

'Uh-uh. On my own.'

He slipped out of the car and crossed the road. I saw him disappear into the drive of the house.

I waited.

It was twenty minutes before he returned, strolling casually down the street like a man out walking the dog.

'No problem,' he said.

'Is there an alarm?' I asked.

'Not any more. And no dog either. I opened the back door for us.'

'How?'

He gave an exaggerated wink. 'Trade secrets. Now this briefcase we're looking for. What's it look like?'

'I don't know.'

'You're not making this any easier.'

'Probably some sort of executive attaché case.'

'This woman, is she trying to hide it?'

'Maybe. It won't be lying around but she won't have a safe or anything to put it in.'

'Aye, she doesn't seem very security conscious.'

'How do you know?'

'Flimsy locks, cheap, out-of-date alarm system. These rich people. Fill their 'ouses with pickings and then skimp on the security. It should be a crime.'

We went round the back of Stephanie's house, skirting the glass conservatory and an ornamental pool. The back door Harry had opened led into a sort of laundry-cum-storage room containing a washing-machine and tumble drier, a deep freezer, central heating boiler and several cup-boards.

'How long we got?' Harry asked.

'Hours. She'll have gone to the casino for the night. Won't be back until two at the earliest.'

Harry gave me a pair of thin gloves.

'Are these necessary?' I asked.

'I've got a record, remember. You brought a torch?'

'Yes.'

'Try not to use it too much.'

'How am I supposed to see?'

'Turn on the lights. The curtains are all closed. Lights in an occupied 'ouse aren't suspicious, torches are.'

'How we going to do it?'

'I'll take the downstairs, there are more 'iding places. You check the upstairs.'

'Harry,' I said. 'It's not the briefcase I'm interested in so much as the contents. They might have been taken out of it.'

'What are they?'

'I don't know.'

'Then 'ow are we supposed to find them?'

'I'll know them when I see them. Sorry to be so vague.'

Harry sighed heavily. 'I think I'm going to regret this.'

I went through the kitchen into the hall, then up to the first floor. I tried the smallest room first, the toilet. Not many hiding places there. The cistern was too small for a briefcase but it was just possible Stephanie might have removed the contents, sealed them in a plastic bag and weighted them down inside. I couldn't really see her going to the trouble, but I wanted to be thorough. I lifted off the lid of the cistern. Nothing but a ballcock and a dark blue block of disinfectant. The bathroom drew a similar blank.

I went into the master bedroom. An archway led through into an opulent en suite bathroom. The carpet was thick enough to polish your shoes as you walked and the purple sunken bath could have accommodated half a football team. On the shelves were all the usual appurtenances of female hygiene: perfumes, bath foams, scented soaps, talcum powder.

I opened the mirror-fronted cabinet on the wall. There were various medicines and pills inside, two contraceptive caps in green plastic containers, several tubes of spermicidal cream and—I counted them—ten packets of twelve Durex Nu-form Extra Safe condoms, 'spermicidally lubricated with Nonoxynol-9 for added protection'. Definitely a woman who took no chances.

The bedroom was decorated in shades of pink and white, very frilly and feminine. I looked in the bedside cupboard and pulled out two books, Stephanie Myers's nighttime reading.

One was a soft porn blockbuster about a heroine who

managed to build a global business empire, raise five children, sleep with a different man every chapter and still find time to make her own gazpacho. The other was a paperback entitled, *How to Manage Your Investments*. The two books somehow summed up the two faces of modern woman; the romantic and the practical. Of the two, the Investment book was the more thumbed. That seemed in keeping with my perception of Stephanie. Also in the bedside cupboard were another five packets of condoms. What did she do, buy them wholesale?

I opened one of the fitted wardrobes. It was overflowing with clothes, untidily arranged. I flicked through the dresses, then rummaged in the stacks of shoes in the bottom. Sheffield's answer to Imelda Marcos. It reminded me of being married to Alison. She had racks of clothes which spread like parasites, gradually encroaching on empty spaces until the whole house threatened to be swamped by them. Yet she never had anything to wear.

The chest of drawers was filled with underwear. I felt like a pervert raking through the layers of knickers and bras. One drawer contained nothing but black lingerie: suspender belts, teddies, basques, all the wrappings and trimmings that bind a woman into a man's view of her sexuality.

But no briefcase, and nothing that looked as if it might have been deliberately hidden.

I opened the other wardrobe and recoiled in shock. I'd been expecting more clothes but the inside was lined with racks and hooks bearing a variety of sado-masochistic instruments. Ropes, bracelets, whips, canes, a whole panoply of pain. I began to see a different side to Stephanie Myers, and perhaps another reason why she might not have wanted to get too involved with the police inquiries into Sutton's crash. I began to see also why Sutton might have visited her.

I closed the door quickly, feeling faintly sick. I searched the rest of the room but found nothing. Nor did the other bedrooms yield anything of interest. I went downstairs to find Harry poking around the sitting-room.

'Nothing upstairs,' I said. 'Not that I can find, anyway.'

'No luck 'ere either. There's some nice stuff, though. Look at the silver in that cabinet.'

'Tempted?'

Harry grinned. 'I've gone straight.' He picked up an antique jade ornament from the table and put it in his pocket. 'But not that straight.'

'You should have brought the van,' I said.

'You going to give me an 'and?'

'What's left?'

'Just this room. I've done t'others.'

I checked all the furniture, removing the cushions from the armchairs and settees and unzipping their covers. I felt down the backs, I tipped them over and examined them underneath. Then I took books off shelves and looked behind them. Plenty of dust, but nothing else.

'You sure this briefcase is in 'ere?' Harry said.

I began to wonder. Maybe it had never been there, or maybe Stephanie had moved it elsewhere after I'd asked her about it at Casanova's.

'Where else is there?' I said. 'What about under the floorboards?'

Harry shook his head. 'Fitted carpets. No one puts things under floorboards these days. There's the garden.'

'Buried, you mean? No, she'd never dirty her hands digging the hole and, judging by the look of it, she's got a gardener. She'd never risk him digging it up by accident.'

'What's so special about this case?'

'I don't know until I look in it. You checked every room?' Harry nodded. 'Conservatory?'

'Yep.'

'Cellar?'

'There isn't one.'

'Garage?'

'Ah.'

'You haven't done the garage? Let's take a look.'

We switched off all the lights and went through to the back of the house. There was an inside door to the garage from the laundry room. Harry shone his torch on it. It was locked.

'Can you pick it?' I asked.

'There's an easier way.' He lifted a key off a hook near to the door and inserted it. The lock opened smoothly.

'Glad I came wi' you?'

The garage was full of clutter, a lawnmower, garden tools, tins of paint, a stepladder, but in the middle was a red Mercedes 280SL. Harry looked at it.

'I think I'd like to meet this woman,' he said.

'She doesn't mix with people like us, Harry.'

'I bet she'd quite like a bit of rough trade. Women do.'

'Yes,' I said. 'But not as rough as us.'

Harry peered inside the Mercedes. 'Can't see anything there.'

'Try the boot.'

We went round to the rear of the car. As we reached it a light flashed over us suddenly through the glass panels in the garage door. I pulled Harry down, my heart pumping rapidly. A car had pulled into Stephanie's drive.

'Jesus, she's back,' Harry whispered. 'You said we had 'ours.'

'Her car's here,' I said.

'So? Someone's given her a lift. Let's get out of 'ere.'

He started to crawl round the side of the car. I pulled him back.

'The boot, Harry.'

'You out of your mind? She'll be in the 'ouse any second.'

Car doors slammed outside. We crouched in the darkness and listened to footsteps approaching the house.

'She's brought friends 'ome, that's all we need,' Harry said.

'The boot, we have to open the boot,' I said, trying hard to control my nerves.

'The 'ell we have. We've got to get out of 'ere. Me first.'

'Give me your tools, then.'

'What?'

'Your tools for the lock. I'll meet you back at the car.'

'Don't be stupid, Michael . . .' He stopped. The front
door of the house slammed. We both looked towards the
rear of the garage. A light came on somewhere in the house
and a faint glimmer penetrated through to us.

'If we don't go now we'll be trapped.'

'Your tools, Harry. I'm not going until I've looked in the
boot.'

'You stubborn bastard.'

He pulled a leather pouch out of his jacket pocket and
unrolled it. He selected a thin metal implement from the
row of tools and started to work on the boot lock.

'You remember to switch all the lights off upstairs?'

'Yes,' I said.

'Everything the way it were?'

'She won't know we were there.'

'What if she comes in 'ere?'

'Why should she come into the garage? It's midnight.'

The lock made a sharp click and the boot popped open
on its spring. I knelt up and shone my torch inside. There,
in the middle of the boot, was a black attaché case. I
reached in and pulled it out.

'Is that it?' Harry said.

I examined it. By the two combination locks were the
gold initials RPS. Richard Percival Sutton.

'This is it.'

'I should have thought of a car boot earlier. It's the kind
of place people use when they want to 'ide something but
can't be bothered to think of anywhere really clever. Now
let's get the 'ell out.'

I pushed the boot shut and followed Harry to the rear
door. He was peering through the glass panel. It was
opaque so he couldn't see much.

'Kitchen light's on,' he whispered. 'But I don't think
anyone's in there.'

'We going to chance it?'

'Unless you want to spend the night in here.'

He turned the handle and gently opened the door. When
a crack appeared he stuck his eye to it and looked through.

Then he pulled the door wide enough for us to slip into the laundry room. The kitchen door to our right was ajar. I stepped over and peeked through. I could hear voices faintly. A woman's, then a man's.

'You staying to introduce yourself?' Harry asked, his voice more unsteady than usual. He had the back door already open.

I went out with him on to the terrace. The lights were on behind the curtains in the sitting-room.

'Over the fence,' said Harry.

We went down the garden, away from the house, and I gave Harry a leg up.

'I'm getting too old for this,' he gasped, struggling to drag himself over the top.

He pushed an overhanging branch out of the way and dropped over the other side into the next garden. There was a sudden splash and a muffled tirade of obscenities. I balanced the attaché case on top of a fence post and scrambled over after him. It was pitch dark under the trees and I couldn't see him.

'Harry? You there?'

A gurgle came from somewhere near my feet. 'Harry?'

I felt around. The ground seemed to end just in front of me. I reached further and something grabbed my hand. Something wet and slimy. My heart dropped to somewhere near my knees.

''Elp me out, for Christ's sake,' Harry spluttered.

'Don't do that, Harry. What's happened?'

'I've fallen in a bleeding swimming pool, that's what's 'appened.'

I helped him out and we went back to the car. Harry sat in the passenger seat and dripped water on to the floor.

'Remind me never to go 'ousebreaking wi' you again,' he said.

CHAPTER 12

I was making a late lunch when there was a knock at the door. After my last visitors I was wary about opening it. The flat still bore the marks of their short stay: piles of ripped books, smashed crockery, a broken desk. I hadn't got round to tidying it up yet.

'Who is it?' I called.

'Open up, McLean.'

I recognized the voice. I opened the door. Chris Strange's beer gut came into the room, followed by Chris Strange himself. His mouth was set tight.

'You're pretty cautious about opening your door, aren't you?'

'It's a rough neighbourhood. You never know what wide boys are going to come calling.'

'Well, it's only me.'

'See what I mean.'

'Don't piss me about, McLean. I'm not in the mood.'

I closed the door behind him. 'I take it this is an official visit.'

'Too bloody right it is.'

He was angry, but holding it in. I hadn't seen Chris Strange angry very often.

'You want to do it here?' he said. 'Or do we go down Snig Hill and put it all on the record?'

'Let's stay here,' I said. 'The coffee's better.'

I filled one of my few remaining cups and gave it to him. I sat down opposite with my own.

'You know a woman called Stephanie Myers?' Strange asked.

I took my time. 'Stephanie Myers?'

'I'll make it easy for you, McLean. I'd hate your memory to fail at a time like this. Night before last she was at Casanova's—goes there quite a lot by reports. Fellow comes in asking questions. Scruffy bloke, looks as if he's slept in his clothes. Talks to her at the bar, has a drink with her.

'We check the bouncers, couple of heavies, thick as pig-shit but they remember him all right. Joined that night. We check the membership list for a name.'

'Yes,' I said. 'I think I might have met her. But since when has my social life been police business?'

'You don't socialize at a place like Casanova's, McLean. For one thing you don't have the money. You were there, you were working.'

'That's pretty smart detective work. Why you so inter-ested in Stephanie Myers?'

'She was murdered last night.'

I knew he was watching for my reaction, but I didn't have to fake it. It stunned me cold. Strange waited for me to say something.

'How?' I said.

'Beaten to death.'

'Jesus!'

'In her home. You know where she lives?'

'No,' I said, my brain running back over the previous night's activities. Had I accidentally left something behind which might incriminate me? I couldn't think of anything. Thank God for Harry, the professional. If he hadn't made me wear gloves, my fingerprints would have been all over Stephanie Myers's house.

'Were you one of her clients?'

'Clients?'

'I'll go along with you playing dumb only so far, McLean. You knew she was a prostitute.'

I'd already guessed that from the wardrobe in her bedroom.

'I didn't know that,' I said.

'The hell you didn't. Good-looking woman, wears expen-sive clothes, jewellery, drives a Mercedes, big house in Lodge Moor, gambles every night with different men. You thought maybe she took in laundry?'

'Two nights ago was the first time I'd met her.'

Strange watched me narrowly.

'You said it yourself, Chris, I don't have the money to mix with a woman like her. Call girls are a bit beyond my pocket, never mind my inclination.'

'So what were you doing there?'

'More coffee?'

'Answer the question.'

'For a story I'm working on.'

'Ah yes. We talked to the owner too. Slimy little creep called Moranis. Since when did you work for the *Tatler*?'

'I work for all sorts of people.'

'Sure. You're just perfect for all that Home Counties deb and piss-up scene. I can see you now, nobbing it with all those upper-class dickheads.'

'A bloke has to earn a living.'

'You don't work for the *Tatler* any more than I do.'

'You haven't been moonlighting, have you?'

'I'd stake my pension that if I rang them now, they'd say they'd never heard of you.'

'You've rung them already, haven't you?'

'Yes.'

'And what did they say?'

'They'd never heard of you.'

'Why would anyone kill Stephanie?' I said.

'Girls in her line of work meet a lot of weirdos.'

'You think a client killed her?'

'What's the story you're really working on?'

'She was only incidental to it.'

'You hold out on me and I'll stitch you up.'

'You think I'd withhold evidence?'

Strange leaned forwards holding his coffee cup in two hands between his knees. 'That's exactly what I think.'

'Am I going to be charged with something? Or am I helping with inquiries?'

'Look, McLean, I haven't come here to go round in circles with you. You cooperate or I'll take you in.'

'On what charge?'

'I'll think of something.' He gave a sour smile. 'I always do.'

In a curious way I respected Strange. He was uncouth and arrogant but he did his job well. He caught criminals. No fancy trimmings, no degrees in sociology or law like the modern graduate intake who got the promotion but not the results. He knew what a villain looked like; he'd grown up in the same streets as them.

'You remember Richard Sutton, the businessman killed in a car crash? He was one of Stephanie's clients.'

Strange opened his eyes a little wider. 'Was he now?'

'Does that surprise you?'

'Not much. She probably laid every businessman in the city. They're the only ones who could afford her prices.'

'Expensive?'

'We checked her bank account. She paid in one, two thousand a week.'

'You have had a busy morning. What time was the body found?'

'Half-eight. When the cleaning lady came in.' He glanced around the room. 'You could do with a cleaning lady here.'

He picked one of my ripped books up off the floor.

'I'm sorting through a few things,' I said.

Strange nodded. He knew when a room had been done over but he let it pass. He'd come back to it later; that's how coppers work.

'So why were you talking to her in Casanova's?'

'For a piece I'm doing on Richard Sutton.'

'Piece?'

'A sort of long appreciation for a finance magazine. Tragic death of tycoon, that kind of thing.'

'Really? And you think readers of this magazine want to know about his taste for bondage, do you?'

'I don't know what you mean.'

'Stephanie Myers didn't deal in just straight sex. Not with the gear we found in her house.'

'I was talking to her as a friend of Sutton's. Background, that's all.'

'You think I'm going to believe that?' He turned his head and pulled back one of his ears to show me. 'See any water there?'

He changed tack. 'Where were you last night?'

'You telling me I'm a suspect?'

'We went round the neighbours first thing. See if they heard anything last night. They keep themselves to themselves up there but one of them said she saw two men walking down the street about midnight. She was coming home from a bridge party.'

'Wild lives they lead at Lodge Moor.'

'Noticed them because one of them was dripping wet.'

'Where's this leading?'

'They got into a parked car. Clapped-out old banger. Cortina, the lady thought. You've got a Cortina.'

'You don't seriously think I killed her, do you?'

'You know something, McLean? You're a very irritating person. You always answer a question with a question.'

'Do I?' I said.

'What happened to your nose?'

'Cut myself shaving.'

He waited, watching me benignly. He was too shrewd to get tough with me; he saved that for the punks they pulled in on a Saturday night. He'd try something more subtle.

'I've done you favours, McLean. I'm calling in a few now.' Playing on my gratitude.

He was right. He'd helped me in the past, often with a degree of self-interest, but help nevertheless. There was a certain obligation there which I couldn't ignore.

'You got anywhere with the death of Debbie Nolan?' I asked.

'Don't you know?'

I looked at him blankly.

'I assumed you went to the press conference this morning. The inspector was appealing for witnesses.'

'I had a lie-in.'

'Did you? Up late, were you?'

'Witnesses to what?'

'She was hit on the head and thrown in the canal. It's a murder inquiry now.'

I nodded. Steam from my coffee cup drifted up into my eyes. As I'd assumed from the beginning it was murder, I wasn't surprised. I'd forgotten the police had to wait for a post-mortem report before reaching the same conclusion.

'Any leads?'

'What's this got to do with Stephanie Myers?' Strange said.

'You must see the connection.'

'Sure I do. Sutton. Nolan was his secretary. Myers, I find out from you, was his piece on the side. You certain about that?'

'She was his mistress.'

'But not exclusive. There were other men.'

'She was that type.'

'Why were you at Casanova's talking to her?'

I went to my jacket and pulled out my wallet. I opened it and took out a piece of paper on which I'd written the registration number of the black BMW belonging to the two heavies who'd beaten me up.

I handed the paper to Strange. 'It's a car number. Will you let me know who owns it?'

'What?' Strange shook his head, close to losing his temper. 'You've some bloody nerve, McLean. I ask for some cooperation and the first thing you do is look for another favour from me. And one that's against regulations.'

'It could be important. I was warned off the other night by a couple of blokes. They were driving that car.'

'Warned off?'

'That's where I got my Technicolor nose. They beat me up.'

'Well, good for them. I know a few people who would have given them a hand.'

'I thought you wanted some help from me.'

'I'm still waiting.'

I went back to my chair. The broken springs twanged as I sat down.

'They told me to keep my nose out of other people's business.'

'I've been telling you that for years but it hasn't got me very far. What business?'

'They didn't say. But I think it was the fire at Sutton's office. I was asking questions. You know who started it yet?'

'Not for certain.'

'Tell me something, Chris. If somebody broke into the RPS Trading offices, why didn't the alarms go off?'

'They did.'

'And no one came to see why?'

'A night watchman from down the road. That's when he saw the fire and rang us.'

'So the fire had already started when the alarms went off? I don't get it.'

Strange said nothing. He stroked his moustache with his thumbnail, mulling something over.

'This is all off the record,' he said after a while.

'Sure.'

'The alarms didn't go off when someone entered the building. They went off when they left.'

I squinted at him. 'What?'

'The night watchman went to investigate a couple of minutes after the alarm bells started to ring. When he got there the fourth floor was already well ablaze.'

'There was no time for someone to have broken in, set the fire and got out before the watchman arrived?'

'No. Which leaves two possibilities. Either whoever started it was already in the building. They set fire to the storeroom and smashed the front door to get out, setting off the burglar alarms.'

'Or?'

'Whoever did it had keys to the building, and the alarms. They used the keys to get in, switched off the alarms and started the fire. Then they reset the alarms on their way out and deliberately smashed the lock on the front door to set them off.'

'Why would they do that?'

'To make it look like a break-in, an outside job.'

'I seem to remember suggesting that possibility to you in the Two Chuffs,' I said.

'Did you?' Strange said, trying a look of virgin innocence which didn't come off.

'Who has the keys to the building?' I asked.

'Sutton had. And Nigel Sinclair, the Finance Director.'

'No one else?'

'Only the security men at Sutton's factory in the East End. They checked the holding company's offices at intervals during the night.'

'And the fire started when they weren't around?' Strange nodded. 'Convenient. Is this why you think Sutton started the fire?'

'He's a leading contender.'

'What about Sinclair?'

'He has an alibi. He was at a dinner all evening.'

'Watertight?'

'He was sitting next to the Assistant Chief Constable.'

'Ah. Sutton has an alibi too.'

Strange looked up sharply. 'How do you know?'

'He was gambling at Casanova's all evening with Stephanie Myers.'

'You sure?'

'She confirmed it when I spoke to her two nights ago. Check with the staff there. Rules out your primary suspect a bit, doesn't it?'

Strange scowled at me. 'Any better suggestions?'

'No.' I'd thought about the two thugs with the battered faces but they'd also been at Casanova's when the fire started. It hadn't been them.

'What got destroyed in the fire?' I asked.

'I've told you that already.'

'Office furniture and carpets, you said. What else?'

'That was about it.'

'What else?'

Strange looked away, trying to seem casual. 'A few files, bits of paper, nothing much.'

'What sort of files?'

'I don't know.'

Like hell he didn't. I tried a different line.

'Where did it start?'

'Fourth floor, you knew that too.'

'I meant which office.'

'Something clerical, I think.'

'Which department?'

He put his little finger in his right ear and twisted it around, scouring for wax. I waited for him.

'Which department, Chris?'

'Accounts.'

Ah. I didn't say anything. I didn't need to. Strange pulled his finger out and wiped it on his trouser leg.

He said: 'You think the fire and Debbie Nolan's death are connected?'

'I don't believe in coincidences.'

'And Myers? Where does she fit in? Why were you talking to her?'

'I was asking her about Sutton's crash. You know the facts?'

'Yes.'

'You look into it? Since Debbie Nolan was murdered.'

'We didn't know she was murdered until yesterday afternoon when we got the lab report. Why should we look into it?'

He was playing me along on the end of a line, acting dumb to see what I said. Strange was pretty good at acting dumb. Sometimes he didn't even seem to be acting, but I knew him too well to be fooled. The stupid coppers are the ones who act smart.

'Didn't you know he was teetotal?' I said.

'Who?' Strange replied, overdoing it a little. He knew all right.

'Sutton.'

'So?'

'Stephanie Myers said he didn't drink anything but mineral water all the time he was with her. Yet he was drunk when he crashed.'

Strange peered across the room as if he were staring into a hot sun. The skin wrinkled beside his eyes and across his forehead.

'If I remember correctly, wasn't there a bottle of whisky in his car? Maybe he got drunk after he left the casino.'

'Oh yes,' I said slowly. 'I'd forgotten about the bottle. That explains it.'

Strange had turned his gaze to me and was studying me suspiciously. He very rarely believed anything I said without independent corroboration, but then as I almost never told him the truth it was probably the best course to take.

'So you don't know anything about why Myers was killed?' he said.

'Sorry.'

He got up out of the chair and pushed some of the debris on the floor out of the way with the toe of his shoe.

'Messy, aren't you?'

'Sending a few things to a jumble sale.'

'They won't want ripped books or smashed records. Or a broken desk.'

I waited.

'Looks like Stephanie Myers's place. Funny coincidence that, isn't it? Someone went through it with a sledge-hammer. Someone looking for something.'

'Did they find it?'

'If it was there, I think so. She'd have told them all right . . . after what they did to her.'

I went suddenly cold. I didn't want to hear the next bit but I knew he was going to tell me.

'That's why I want this one badly. She was tortured before she was killed. If you're holding out on me, McLean, just think about that.'

He went to the door and opened it. 'Someone played around with her before they killed her. There were marks all over her. Some kind of tool. The police doctor said it looked like a pair of pliers.'

Harry Raymond was not a happy man. He was blowing his nose and drinking Lemsip when I walked into his shop.

'I've probably got pneumonia,' he said, looking for sympathy.

I obliged. 'Take a few days off, Harry. You've earned it.'

'I would,' he said morosely, 'only the wife won't 'ave me in the 'ouse. She said it were me own fault for going swimmin' on a November night.'

I felt guilty. 'Did she know where you were?'

'Naow. But she knew I were up to no good. I suppose you've come for the case. It's in the back.'

We went through. I'd left the briefcase with him so he could work on the combination locks.

'Did you have any trouble?' I asked.

'Naow.'

'Easy combinations?'

He put the briefcase on a table. The lid was hanging off at an angle.

'I used a jemmy,' he said.

'The silky skills of the professional,' I said.

I pulled back the lid and took out a thin wad of papers, maybe ten sheets in all. From the print I could tell they were photocopies. They were covered in figures.

'You had a look at these,' I asked Harry.

'Aye. Couldn't make 'ead nor tail of them.'

I flicked through them. They looked like RPS Trading accounts. Or rather copies of accounts. It didn't take much brainpower to figure out that the originals had almost certainly been destroyed in the fire.

'I really appreciate what you did last night, Harry,' I said. 'You took a big risk.'

'It were fun,' he said. 'Apart from the last bit. Stupid bastards. Who 'as water in a swimming pool in November?'

'I'll buy you a few pints.'

'I'm not well enough at the moment to drink beer.' He

blew his nose again to emphasize the seriousness of his condition.

'Lock up the shop,' I said. 'I'll buy you a hot toddy and a bottle of aspirin instead.'

I couldn't make head nor tail of the figures either. After I'd dropped Harry back at the shop I sat in the car for a while and studied the photocopies. They looked like ledgers, records of moneys paid and received by RPS Trading. But I could see nothing of any significance in the columns; they were simply meaningless numbers to me.

Yet I knew there was something in them, something I could not immediately identify. Sutton must have had a reason for copying them, a reason for leaving them at Stephanie Myers's, and Stephanie must have had a reason for hiding them. Whatever it was eluded me.

I started the engine and drove away from the city centre. The buildings, the undergrowth of concrete and tarmac oppressed me. I wanted to feel the air of the countryside, air untainted by the pervasive smell of car exhaust and hamburgers. And I wanted to see Jacqueline Sutton. I drove into the Peak District.

There was a canopy of black cloud over the Hope Valley and the hills were soggy from a recent downpour. The sun was just starting to break through, piercing the disintegrating clouds with rays of white light. A rainbow arched across the valley sides, disappearing into the rooftops of Hathersage. The pot of gold would have been somewhere about Andy's Nosh-Up, a cafeteria beloved of climbers and ramblers. Whoever it was decided the location of the pot of gold had obviously never eaten there.

The Suttons' maid let me in and took me to a room at the side of the house which overlooked a well-tended kitchen garden. It was smaller, warmer in every sense than the formal drawing-room I'd been in before. A gas fire, with concealed jets and imitation logs, was burning in the hearth. The maid said she'd let Mrs Sutton know I was there.

I sat down by the fire and stretched my legs. The alcoves on either side of the chimney breast contained shelves bearing an assortment of paperback books, mostly popular fiction. Below that were a hi-fi system and several rows of LPs and compact discs. I flicked through them. The range was pretty catholic: a lot of classical, Mozart, Chopin, Brahms, and quite a bit of lighter stuff, Kate Bush, Paul Simon, Aretha Franklin, Demis Roussos. Jesus, Demis Roussos? I couldn't imagine Jacqueline Sutton listening to Demis Roussos. I couldn't imagine anyone listening to Demis Roussos.

It was ten minutes before Jacqueline came in. She was wearing a peach-coloured towelling bathrobe and slippers. Her legs were bare. Strands of wet hair clung to her neck and forehead. Her cheeks were slightly flushed. She smelt of bath lotion.

'I'm sorry, I wasn't expecting you,' she said. She shook hands. Her skin was warm and damp.

'I should have rung. Am I disturbing you?'

'No. I was in the bath. I've been out riding,' she added.

She sat down opposite me and crossed her legs. Her robe fell away and I caught a brief glimpse of thigh. She didn't appear to be wearing anything underneath the robe. I wasn't about to complain.

'Can I offer you anything?' she said.

'No, thanks, I won't keep you long.'

'You have something to tell me?'

She flicked her hair away from her face and rested one hand on her cheek, her elbow propped on the arm of the chair. Her eyes were pale, very still. The aura of grief around her had dimmed since our last encounter.

'Did your husband have many enemies?' I asked.

She barely moved. 'Enemies?'

'People who didn't like him.'

'I expect so. People as successful as Richard was always have enemies. No doubt a lot of people didn't like him.'

'Enough to kill him?'

Jacqueline sat up very straight. There was a mark on her

cheek where her hand had been resting. Her eyes opened
wide, then narrowed into a puzzled frown.

'What are you talking about?'

'Had threats been made against him?'

'Threats?'

'Did he ever say anything, anything to indicate he
thought his life might be in danger? Particularly in the few
days leading up to his death.'

She leaned forward urgently. The front of her robe gaped
wide. It took some doing but I kept my eyes on her face.

'What are you saying? That someone killed Richard?'

'It's possible.'

'You mean murdered him?'

I nodded.

'Why haven't the police let me know?'

'It's my theory, not theirs. It's not official.'

'And do you know something they don't?'

'It's only a possibility, Mrs Sutton. Would anyone have
wanted your husband out of the way?'

'I don't understand this. Why do you think he might
have been murdered?'

'You think it unlikely?'

'Well . . .' She held out her hands in a gesture of helpless-
ness. 'I don't know what to think. No one, to my knowledge,
had made threats. Richard never said anything. Who would
want to do that?'

'That's why I asked if he had any particular enemies.'

'But for God's sake, everyone has enemies. That's no
reason to suppose those enemies are going to murder you.'
She sat back and stared at me. The flush of the hot bath
had left her skin. She was pale now.

'Do you have proof?' she said.

'No. I'm just exploring all the possibilities. Did he ever
say anything to you about his accounts?'

'Accounts?'

'The company accounts.'

'What are you talking about now?'

'He didn't say anything recently? About RPS Trading,

the accounts, the business. Anything odd or unusual.'

'Why should he? He discussed his accounts with his accountants, not me. I don't understand financial matters. Please, what is going on?'

'He photocopied some accounts before he died. I don't suppose you know why? Or could guess why?'

Jacqueline shook her head blankly. 'You could ask Nigel. He was in charge of the financial side of the business. I'm sure he'd be glad to help. But what's all this got to do with Richard's death?'

'That,' I said after a pause, 'is what I'm trying to find out.'

I stood up and looked down at her. She pulled her robe closed, tightening the cord around her waist. It was still a nice view.

'One other thing,' I said. 'Have you ever seen a couple of men, ugly, cropped hair, built like brick outhouses, London accents.'

'Seen them where?'

'Anywhere. Recognize the descriptions? Did you ever see them with your husband? Did he ever mention anyone like that?'

'I don't think so. Who are they?'

'That's another thing I'm trying to find out.' I went to the door. 'Thank you. I'll let myself out.'

I left her there by the fire before she could ask me any more questions. Questions I couldn't answer. Not yet, at any rate.

I drove out of the gates and back through the village. At the junction with the main road I slowed to give way and a black saloon car cut across the corner in front of me. I gave it a fleeting look and jammed on my brakes suddenly. It was a BMW. The driver was the blond man with the hook nose I'd seen at Richard Sutton's inquest. I spun round in my seat and read the car's number plate before it disappeared. H370 EGB, the same car Pinky and Perky had driven when they came to beat me up.

I rammed the gears into first and swung out into the

main road, doing a U-turn to go back the way I'd come. I put my foot down through the village but there was no sign of the BMW. I drove on for a couple of miles without spotting it. It had either outstripped me—perfectly possible given the knackered state of my car—or . . . it had stopped somewhere in the village.

I turned round in a farm gateway and went back into Hathersage. There was only one place I could think it had gone. I parked on the verge just beyond the entrance to the Suttons' house and walked up the driveway, keeping near the rhododendron bushes at the side. On the gravel fore-court, next to the portico outside the front door, was the BMW.

I looked at it for a moment, then crept away back down the drive. I took my time returning to the city, I had a lot on my mind.

Maria was busy with a client when I reached her office so I sat and annoyed Muriel until she was free. I'd brought the photocopies in with me and a large bunch of flowers I'd acquired hurriedly from a shop near the Town Hall. I gave her the flowers first. She looked at me suspiciously.

'What are these for?'

'You like flowers, don't you?'

'That depends on who gives me them. And why.'

Such mistrustful people, women. 'It's a peace offering,' I said. 'To make up for last time. You know, my receipts and invoices.'

'If you're trying to get round me, Michael, it'll take more than flowers.'

'Did I mention how beautiful you're looking today?'

'Or sham flattery.'

'I meant it,' I said. I did too, although I knew she didn't believe me. I've never yet met a woman who genuinely thought she was beautiful. She was wearing a light grey skirt and a cream silk blouse, open at the neck. It suited her perfectly, but then I guessed most things did. I considered trying to kiss her but knew I wouldn't get within two yards of her.

'How about dinner, then?'

'Well, that's more tangible than words, but I've had one of your dinner invitations before and it worked out very expensive.'

'It's on me this time.'

'Really? You booked a table at McDonald's, did you?'

'No more *haute cuisine*,' I said. 'Let's go Chinese this time.'

She half smiled at me, playing with a silver fountain pen on her desk. 'And?'

I looked at her blankly. 'And?'

'What else?'

'How do you mean?'

'You haven't just come here to give me flowers and invite me to dinner.'

Was I that obvious? And I thought I had my deviousness well covered.

'I've been doing your accounts for seven or eight years, Michael. You learn a lot about someone in that time.'

'Honest,' I said. 'I just wanted to say sorry for landing you with all those bits of paper. I know how busy you are.'

'And?'

Damn the woman. How did she know? She was looking at me with an air of smug superiority. It would have been annoying if it hadn't been so bloody sexy.

'Well,' I said. 'There is one thing.'

'Now we're getting there.'

'If you've got a moment this afternoon, you couldn't have a glance at these, could you?' I put the photocopies on her desk.

'What are they?'

'Accounts. From RPS Trading.'

'Where did you get those?'

'Contacts,' I said vaguely. I didn't dare tell her the real way I'd got them. She's under the impression I have principles and it doesn't do to disillusion your accountant.

'Why do you want me to look at them?'

'You understand that kind of thing. The figures are meaningless to me.'

'RPS Trading accounts?' I nodded. 'What am I looking for?'

'I don't know. Anything that looks unusual.'

Maria sighed gently. 'If I have time.'

'Thanks. Eight o'clock OK for tonight?'

'All right.'

'I really will make it up to you. No expense spared.'

'I'll bring my credit cards. Just in case.'

It was dark by the time I got home. There was no parking space outside the flat so I drove round the corner and left the car there. Walking back, I called in at the newsagents and bought a loaf of bread and a bottle of milk before going into the house.

I pressed the light switch by the front door. Nothing happened. The communal lights on the stairs and landings were always going but the landlord was too mean to replace the bulbs. I felt my way along the hall and up the stairs to the first floor. I put my groceries down on the floor while I fumbled in my pocket for the key to my flat. There were no windows on the landing and I could see nothing in the pitch darkness. I turned the key and pushed the door open, then crouched down to pick up the milk and bread.

They were waiting inside. I caught a tiny movement, a silhouette against the window, then they came for me. The thugs with the pliers. They were big but they were slow. And I had the advantage of the darkness. They couldn't see me and they certainly didn't expect me to be squatting when the door opened.

I straightened up quickly, catching the first thug under the jaw with the top of my head. It hurt like hell but he came out of it worse than I did. The second attacked from the side, grasping me around the waist in an attempt to bowl me over. I lashed out with the milk bottle and heard the clunk of glass on bone. He yelled and fell over, pulling me with him. I kicked out and my foot sank into something soft.

The first thug got a grip on my arm and half pulled it out of the socket. I gasped and spun round on the floor towards him. He was taken by surprise. They weren't going to find me such an easy victim this time. I brought my elbow up sharply and jabbed him in the face. He grunted and let go of my arm. I rolled over and snaked out of the door on to the landing.

I tumbled down the stairs but the thugs weren't delayed for long. They came after me. At the bottom I turned towards the back of the house and went down another flight of stairs into the basement. Feet thumped heavily behind me. The house was built on a slope, lower at the back than the front. I kicked open the fire exit and ran out into the rear yard, panting more with fear than exertion.

At the far side was a brick wall. I sprinted for it, jumped on to a dustbin and vaulted over, rolling to break my fall. I was in the timber yard that extended practically the full length of the next street. I ran across it into one of the covered stacks of seasoning wood. I ducked down behind some lengths of pine and poked an eye over the top.

They were still behind me, but the wall had slowed them down. I watched them climb awkwardly over it, too big and ungainly to manage it easily. They drew breath and had a discussion, looking round the yard. They hadn't seen where I went and there were about two acres of timber sheds to search. In the dark and without torches.

I hoped they might give up the chase but they were more determined than that. They split up and started to search the stacks of wood. I edged further back into the shed, keeping low and trying to deaden the sound of my feet.

The two heavies had started at opposite ends of the shed, working inwards. If I stayed where I was they would eventually trap me between them. Yet whichever way I moved would take me nearer one of them.

I risked a peek out, contemplating running back to my flat. But there were thirty yards of open ground to cross first and then an eight-foot wall to surmount. There had been dustbins on the other side to help me over. On this side there was nothing. They would almost certainly catch me before I could get over the wall.

My heart was thumping like a kettle drum and somewhere in the pit of my stomach was a lead ball. They were getting desperately close. I was completely hemmed in; by them, by the walls of the shed, the towering shelves of timber. I looked up into the gloom. Planks of wood were stacked on metal brackets reaching almost to the roof. They were my only hope. I began to climb.

The rough wood grazed my hands, spiking my skin with tiny splinters. I tried to climb slowly, but the planks were loose and rocked together under my weight. My right foot slipped suddenly and two planks banged together noisily. I knew the sound must have been audible throughout the shed. There were footsteps below and, glancing down, I saw Pinky and Perky run up and stop beneath me.

I scrambled higher, pulling my legs out of reach of their straining arms. But I had nowhere to go. They started to climb up after me. I was trapped on the top shelf.

I squirmed to the back of the shelf and squeezed my fingers under one of the planks. If I could run no further at least I could stand and fight. The plank was two inches thick and some twelve feet long. It was unwieldy but not too heavy to lift. I gripped it in the middle and pulled it up, clutching it to my body. Then I leaned over the edge and hurled it down at the two men. One end caught the nearer of them on the head. It stunned him but he held on to the stack.

The second man was higher, just a few feet below the top. I could see the fierce expression of determination on his face. He got one hand over the edge. I stamped on it hard and he yelled. I lashed out with my foot but he dodged to the side and grabbed my shoe, pulling me down hard on to the planks. The shelf shuddered under the impact and before I could move I felt the brackets give way and the whole top shelf collapse.

The thugs cried out as the mound of timber toppled down on to them. I rolled backwards into the wall as the support gave way and fell with a jarring thud on to the shelf below, clutching for something to stop myself tumbling even further. My hands found the bracket of the adjoining shelf and I clung on, my legs dangling half in space. Wood dust choked my lungs and a for a few seconds all I could hear was the sound of planks hitting the concrete floor.

I pulled my legs up and swung my body on to the next section of shelving which was still standing. Below me the two thugs were disentangling themselves from the planks piled on top of them. I scrambled down quickly before they recovered and stumbled out of the shed, my legs shaking.

Climbing over the main gates of the timber yard, I glanced back and saw the thugs stagger out, obviously bruised and in pain, but not seriously injured. I felt a small pang of regret.

I dropped to the street and ran round the corner to my car. I could barely insert the ignition keys, my hands were trembling so much. I pulled off and drove flat out for five minutes, not caring where I went.

CHAPTER 13

Maria picked up a slice of crispy Szechuan duck with her chopsticks and popped it delicately into her mouth.

'How do you do that?' I asked.

'Practice.'

I tried to do the same. The duck slithered out of my chopsticks and landed on the tablecloth, splashing my shirt with sauce.

'Shall I ask the waiter for a bib?' she said.

'No,' I said. 'A knife and fork.'

'Coward.'

'I'll starve if I have to use these things all night.'

'Hold them lower down. Use your forefinger to move the top stick. Keep the bottom one rigid.'

I retrieved the slice of duck from the tablecloth with my fingers and slipped it quickly into my mouth before any of the other diners noticed.

'Cheat,' Maria said.

'Listen, you're half way through the meal and I've yet to get a decent mouthful.'

'Hold your bowl nearer your mouth and shovel it in. That's how the Chinese do it.'

I tried it without much success. 'I've had a great idea for a diet book,' I said, salvaging another piece of duck from the tablecloth. 'You tell people to eat whatever they fancy, chips, cream cakes, stodge, anything they like only they have to eat it with chopsticks.'

'Sounds like a bestseller,' Maria said. 'But not in China.'

She picked up a porcelain spoon and leant towards me. Between us, resting on heated metal trays in the centre of the table, were dishes of chicken Cantonese-style, fried beef with green pepper and black bean sauce, prawns in spring onion and ginger sauce and crispy Szechuan duck. She helped herself to some of the chicken, spooning the small pieces of meat and the accompanying orange, slightly sweet sauce into the porcelain bowl in front of her.

'You want some?' she asked.

'I'm still trying to dispose of this duck.'

'You're way behind, Michael. I can't eat all of this myself.'

'You seem to be making a pretty good effort,' I said sourly.

Maria smiled and expertly picked up a morsel of chicken with her chopsticks. She slipped it between her lips without losing a drop of sauce on the way, then followed it with a ball of fried rice, just to rub it in.

'I hate you,' I said.

We were in an alcove at the side of the restaurant, partially screened from our neighbours by a bamboo trellis and a small jungle of plastic plants. On the wall above our table was a watercolour of a Chinese fisherman in straw hat and half-mast trousers, sitting in a sampan with a couple of cormorants. Behind the boat the river was a ripple of glistening silver, tinted orange at the edges by the setting sun. The fisherman had an ageless face and his expression was calm and serene, the smug look of a man who could more than hold his own with a pair of chopsticks. I hated him too.

'I looked at those accounts for you,' Maria said.

I turned to her. She was sipping jasmine tea from a tiny, handle-less cup, holding the cup between thumb and forefinger. Her turquoise teardrop earrings swayed gently as if caught in a breeze. Below that her blouse was turquoise and aquamarine, blended in subtle waves of colour. It reminded me of a tropical lagoon in the white midday heat.

'Find anything?'

'Nothing out of the ordinary. What's so special about them?'

'Sutton copied them before he died. I'd like to know why. You got them with you?'

She nodded. 'In my bag. I'll show you after the meal.'

'The rate I'm going that could be the day after tomorrow.'

'They don't look like general accounts to me.'

'How d'you mean?'

'They're too narrow. There aren't enough entries for general business accounts. It looks as if they come from an isolated, more specific account, maybe one set up for a particular purpose.'

'Any indication what?'

'A lot of the entries are regular payments to one other account.'

'A person?'

'A company.' A thought came to her. 'Hey, you don't think someone was extorting money from Sutton?'

'Well, he had one or two pastimes which might have made him vulnerable to blackmail.'

'Pastimes?'

'Of a sexual nature.'

Maria's mouth dropped slightly. 'Really?' Her interest was aroused now. Amazing what sex can do. 'Tell me more.'

'It's not important.'

'Come on, you can't leave it there. What pastimes?'

'You don't want to know.'

'Try me.'

'You'd be shocked.'

'Michael.' She looked at me sideways, daring me to stall her further.'

'OK, he had a mistress.' I told her about Stephanie Myers and the contents of her bedroom wardrobe. Maria's mouth dropped further.

'How can you know that?'

'The police told me,' I said, obscuring the truth very slightly.

'And he might have been blackmailed because of that?'

'Possibly. But blackmail doesn't explain why he was murdered.'

A king prawn fell from Maria's chopsticks, narrowly missing her jasmine tea. She really was stunned.

'Hold your bowl nearer your mouth,' I said. 'That's how the Chinese do it.'

'Murdered? Where do you get that from?'

'Just another of my theories.'

I spooned egg fried rice and fried beef into my bowl, taking my time. The slices of green pepper with the beef were large and unevenly cut. Even I could pick them up with chopsticks. I put a couple in my mouth and crunched them noisily.

'I'm getting better at this,' I said with just a hint of triumph.

Maria watched me, an expression of weary tolerance creeping over her face.

'I know you're dying to tell me, Michael, so why don't you just get on with it?'

I grinned, blatantly transparent to the last. 'OK. What

do you think to this?' I paused. 'You want some fried beef first?' Maria closed her eyes and sighed heavily. 'All right, get this, Sutton was with Stephanie Myers on the evening he died. They played roulette together at Casanova's for a couple of hours, then went back to her house in Lodge Moor. He didn't drink anything all evening. Yet when he crashed on his way back to Hathersage from her house, there was alcohol in his bloodstream.'

'Maybe he stopped at a pub.'

'There aren't any pubs on Burbage Moor. There was a broken bottle of whisky in his car when he was found, but I don't think Sutton put it there.'

'Then who did?'

'The person, or persons who killed him.'

'Wait a minute, you're losing me here. Start at the beginning.'

I put down my chopsticks. 'This is what I think happened. Sutton was crossing the moors on his way home when he was stopped by someone. I don't know how, maybe they forced him, maybe they said they'd broken down, run out of petrol, something like that. However they did it, Sutton had to brake hard to stop. That's why there were skidmarks on the road, but *not* where he careered off. They were sixty or seventy yards further back up the road.

'I think there was more than one person. It would need at least two to do it. They opened Sutton's car door, held him down in his seat, rammed a whisky bottle into his mouth and poured it down.'

'That's just speculation, Michael.'

I shook my head. 'I've a pathologist friend. He looked at the post-mortem on Sutton. He drank a half bottle of spirits just before he died. Can you see a total abstainer doing that?'

'But that didn't kill him.'

'No. He was killed by the multiple injuries sustained in his crash. The killers knocked him out with something blunt —a blow to the forehead—after they'd filled him with whisky, maybe before, it doesn't make any difference. Then they turned on the ignition and pushed his car down the hill. It's very steep there. It would have gathered enough pace to smash through the fence and down the slope. But before they pushed him they left the whisky bottle in the car to make it look as if he'd been boozing. They wanted it to look like an accident.'

'Why?'

'They didn't want a murder inquiry. The first thing the police would do would be to poke around in Sutton's business and private life. Looking for a motive. I don't think they wanted anyone looking too closely at Sutton's business affairs.'

'Why not?'

'I hoped you might be able to help me there. From those photocopies.'

'I told you, there didn't seem to be anything suspicious about them.'

'Were they audited accounts?'

'No, they're too recent.'

'So there might be discrepancies that no one has noticed?'

Maria shook her head. 'Not in a company like RPS. There might have been no external audit yet, but there'd have been internal safeguards in the accounts department.'

She spooned the last of the beef with green pepper and black bean sauce into her bowl and took a mouthful. She licked her lips.

'This is all pretty far-fetched. Surely the police would know if he'd been murdered.'

'Not on the basis of his injuries alone. He really did die in a car crash, you see. Only he was unconscious when it happened.'

'Couldn't they tell that?'

'Not according to my friend. The circumstances of the crash, the injuries, were all consistent with an accident. But if he was deliberately filled up with whisky first, knocked out and pushed over the edge, that would make it murder.'

Maria pursed her lips doubtfully. 'If you're right, why

fill him up with whisky? They could just have pushed him down the hill.'

'There had to be a reason for the crash. There was no fog or ice that night, there was nothing wrong with the car. Something had to cause it.'

'All right, but if they wanted him dead, why choose a car crash in the first place?'

'You think about it. It had to look like an accident. What kinds of accident are there? Accidents which are common enough to be accepted at face value.

'Most accidents happen in the home, or on the road. It's not easy to stage an accident in the home. What do you do? Try and electrocute him with a faulty toaster? Drop a radio in the water when he's taking a bath? No, the road is much easier, and much more plausible. They could have pushed him in front of a bus, but I think whoever did it is far too cautious for that. Anything in a city is likely to be witnessed by other people. So they chose a car crash on a deserted country road at night. No witnesses, no questions. And they made him drunk because alcohol is the commonest cause of road accidents. It had to look like all the others.

'Their only mistake was picking the one man in a thousand who was a genuine abstainer. That's an easy mistake to make. Everyone assumes you drink. How many teetotallers do you know? It's a rarity. It probably never crossed the killers' minds that Sutton might be teetotal.'

I poured jasmine tea into our cups. Black leaves floated around in it like fragments of charcoal.

Maria sipped hers, deep in thought. 'This is all guesswork, isn't it?' she said.

'Not all.'

'You're making the facts fit your theory. That's the wrong way round.'

'Am I?'

'Sutton might have stopped on the moors, drunk the whisky himself and then accidentally crashed.'

'That's hardly credible. Why would he have done that?'

'Why not what you thought the other night? Dutch courage to commit suicide. It's just as likely as your murder theory.'

'In isolation, yes. But there are other facts to consider. Debbie Nolan's death for one. Now that definitely was murder. That has to raise a few suspicions about Sutton's death.'

A Chinese waiter crossed to our table and began to clear away the empty dishes. He asked if we wanted to see the menu again. I shook my head. Or coffee? Maria declined. I asked him to fill the teapot with hot water.

When he had gone, Maria said: 'Who would want to murder Richard Sutton?'

'I think the people who actually did the deed were the two heavies who beat me up. But they were just the hired help. I don't know who paid them.'

'Someone who benefited from his death? His wife? She presumably inherits his money.'

'I might go for that if it weren't for one thing. She knew he was teetotal. She wouldn't have chosen that way to bump him off. Whoever did it didn't know him very well. That would seem to rule out most of his friends and work associates.'

Maria gazed at me sceptically.

'It fits all the facts,' I said. 'I know it's right.'

'There's a major flaw,' she said. 'The whole thing depends on the murderers just happening to be on Burbage Moor at the time Richard Sutton was crossing it. That's an unbelievable coincidence.'

'They didn't just happen to be there. They followed him. Sutton went to Casanova's with Stephanie Myers. The two thugs followed him there. That's why I think they did it. They even had the nerve to go in and play roulette at the same table as him. Then they followed him to Stephanie's house and when he left there, they followed him across the moors, overtook him somewhere near Higger Tor and forced him to stop.'

'Why would anyone want Sutton dead?'

'The answer's in those photocopies. Photocopies of

accounts which were destroyed in the fire at Sutton's offices. Those are the only record of whatever it is Sutton knew that meant he had to die.'

Maria shivered. 'Where did you get them, Michael?'

'Sutton left them with Stephanie, for safekeeping, I'd guess.'

'And she gave them to you?'

'She's dead.'

'What?'

'She was murdered last night.'

'Now hang on, slow down here.' Maria leaned across the table. 'Someone else was murdered too?'

I nodded. 'Not an accident this time. She was beaten to death.'

'Oh my God!' She put a hand to her mouth.

'Which makes Sutton's death even more suspicious, wouldn't you say?'

'But why? Because she knew who killed Sutton?'

'Maybe. Or because she knew about those photocopies.'

'So how did you get them?'

'I paused as the waiter brought our fresh pot of jasmine tea. I filled both our cups and half drained mine.

'Michael.' Maria's voice was urgent. 'You're saying she might have been murdered because of those papers? Papers which *I'm* carrying around in my handbag.'

'Yes.'

'God almighty, you might have told me.'

'You're quite safe.'

'Do the police know?'

'Not exactly.'

'How stupid can you be, Michael? If they'll kill Stephanie whatever-she's-called for them, they'll kill you. Or me.'

'They don't know I've got them.'

I didn't want to alarm her. Someone knew I had them all right. That's why the two heavies had been waiting inside my flat. And only Jacqueline Sutton could have told them.

Maria was fumbling in her handbag. She pulled out the photocopies and threw them across the table.

'Take them. I want no part of this.'

'Don't get upset, Maria. You're not in danger.'

'And what about you? Why won't you go to the police?'

'It's *my* story.'

'Story?'

'It could be a big one.'

'Jesus! You stubborn bastard. What use is a posthumous scoop?'

'You want to go through the accounts now?'

'Yes. No. What am I saying? I'm out of this.' She caught a waiter's eye and asked for the bill.

We said nothing until it arrived. I paid and we went out to my car. She was very quiet on the journey home.

'I need your help, Maria,' I said when we reached her house.

'Go to the police, Michael.'

'I haven't got the whole picture yet. When I've pieced it together, I'll go. Will you run through those accounts with me?'

'No.'

'Please.'

She turned to look at me.

'The answer is somewhere in those figures,' I said. 'I need you, Maria.'

She opened the car door. 'I must be mad. Come inside.'

I sat next to Maria at the kitchen table and looked through the columns of figures.

'They're ordinary ledgers,' she said. 'The kind of day-to-day payments and receipts any large company would have.'

'You sure there's nothing peculiar about them?'

'Like what?'

'I don't know, you're the accountant. Is it possible to spot discrepancies, missing money, something like that?'

'Not from these sheets alone. They're just a record. There's nothing to cross-check them against.'

'Sutton must have had a reason for copying them.' I

scanned the pages and pointed a finger. 'Is this the company you mentioned?'

'Yes. Fieldsend Consultants plc. A lot of the payments are to them, most in fact.'

'Ever heard of them?'

'No.'

'Me neither. Doesn't get us much further. They've had a lot of money over the past few months.' There were several dozen debits for amounts varying from £25,000 to £250,000.

'I totalled it up on the last page,' Maria said. She checked a pencil scribble at the bottom of the final sheet. 'Nearly eight million pounds since April.'

'Quite a lot.'

Then I noticed something. 'Just a minute. Look at this. Some of those debits are to a different company, not Fieldsend Consultants plc but Fieldsend Construction plc.'

Maria leaned over. 'You think that's significant? It's probably a subsidiary or a different part of the same company.'

'Who's had the most?' I did a few sums in the margin. 'Fieldsend Consultants has taken the bulk, six million plus. The rest has gone to Fieldsend Construction.'

'For doing what?'

Each line gave the date of the transaction, the name of the payee, the nature of the payment and the amount. Beside both Fieldsend Consultants and Fieldsend Construction the nature of the payment was always described as 'IRP construction'.

'What does that mean?' I said. 'IRP construction.'

'No idea.'

'Some kind of accounting jargon?'

'Not that I've ever seen. Of course there may have been internal codes unique to RPS Trading, to identify particular items. You'd have to ask someone in the company.'

I flicked through the sheets and found one which looked different from the others.

'What's this?'

'They're credits. All the other sheets are debits.'

There were only a few entries on this particular sheet, but for large sums of money. One payment for two million pounds in April and two more for three million pounds each in July and September. Each payment was labelled 'ECSC advance'.

'That's eight million too,' I said. 'The same amount coming in as going out. Is that odd?'

'Not at all. Books tend to balance themselves over a period.'

'ECSC. What could that stand for?'

'Could it be a customer? Sutton must have had some pretty big orders. He exported all over the world, Europe, the US.'

'Hmn.' I studied the print-outs. Two sets of initials we didn't understand, IRP and ECSC. The first set meant nothing to me but the second, ECSC, was familiar.

I stood up and went to the sink by the window.

'Mind if I make some coffee?'

'I'll do it.' She seemed to have forgiven me after her little outburst in the restaurant.

'No, you stay there. You got any instant?'

'Cupboard next to you.'

I took a jar of Nescafé and filled the kettle. While I waited for it to boil I ran the initials over in my head. Maria said something I only half caught.

'Sorry, what was that?'

'ECSC,' she said. 'Is that European something or other? That's what "E" usually stands for.'

I stopped, spoon of coffee poised in mid-air over the mugs.

'Jesus, you're right. ECSC. European Coal and Steel Community.'

'That doesn't mean anything to me.'

'It's some Brussels outfit. They lend money for projects in areas depressed because of the decline in the coal and steel industries. For the creation of new jobs, that kind of thing.'

'They lent money to Richard Sutton?'

'You bet your life they did. For his East End project. That's what IRP is, Integrated Recycling Plant. He's building one in the Don Valley.'

'So the credits are payments to Sutton's company from the ECSC,' Maria said. 'And the debits are payments to a firm involved in building this recycling plant. That sounds pretty legitimate.'

'It does, doesn't it,' I said. 'But worth checking out. You sure there's nothing in any of the other entries?'

'Not that I could see.'

I gathered the sheets in and put them in a pile. 'Thanks, Maria, that's been a big help.'

'Michael, I'm worried. It's dangerous having those papers.'

'I told you, you're quite safe.'

'I'm worried for *you*. Someone is prepared to kill for those accounts.'

There was genuine concern in her voice. I took her hand. She didn't try to pull it away.

'I know what I'm doing,' I lied. 'But look, if it'll make you feel better, why don't I sleep here on the couch tonight? Then you'll know where I am. And you'll feel safer too.'

She went over it silently, her woman's mind working out all the angles, all the possible motives. I came out clean. I could tell by her expression.

'That's sweet of you. I'll get you a couple of blankets,' she said.

When she came back downstairs into the sitting-room, she said: 'Will you be all right here? You could use the spare room, but the bed's not made up.'

'I'll be fine.' I took the blankets. 'Good night.'

I kissed her gently on the cheek. She looked at me, just a little uncertain. She didn't seem to mind. Maybe I was getting somewhere after all.

'Good night,' she said softly and went out.

I arranged the blankets on the couch and crawled under them, using a couple of cushions as a pillow. I felt bad about deceiving her, but I cope well with guilt. The real reason I wanted to stay, of course, was that I was terrified of going home in case the two heavies were waiting there to kill me. If Maria ever found out, she'd murder me herself.

CHAPTER 14

I awoke to the smell of toast and fresh coffee. Maria came in from the kitchen and smiled at me.

'Breakfast?'

She was already dressed, make-up on, hair brushed. I knew she'd be the early morning energetic type. It made me feel exhausted just looking at her.

'I'll be right through,' I said.

I crawled out from the blankets, bleary-eyed, crumpled, unshaven. I glanced in the mirror over the mantelpiece. I looked like the leading candidate for the Dosser of the Year Award.

I splashed water on my face in the downstairs toilet. It was spotlessly clean and smelt of sandalwood soap. I thought to myself: There's no way you're going to get very far with a woman like this, McLean. It did nothing for my spirits.

Maria had mugs and plates laid out on the kitchen table. She was nibbling toast and stirring her coffee, very composed and efficient. I wondered what she'd have done if I'd gone sleepwalking in the night.

'Toast's under the grill,' she said. 'You want some cereal?'

I shook my head and sat down opposite her. She poured me some coffee. She didn't try to make conversation. I liked that. We sat there together, comfortable, munching toast, listening to the hum of the refrigerator.

Then Maria went upstairs and I heard a toilet flush. She had her coat and bag in her arms when she came back in.

'I want you to go to the police today, Michael.'

I said nothing.

'Will you?'

'Yes,' I said.

'Promise?'

'I'll ring them at nine,' I said. 'Thanks for breakfast.'

She hesitated, unsure of something. 'Will you let me know what they say?'

'Yes.'

'Well . . .'

We were both awkward now. I didn't know what to say either.

'I'll have to go,' she said. She smiled uncertainly. I smiled back. She went out and the front door clicked shut. I wished I'd said something but I didn't know if it was the right moment. I never know.

At nine I rang the police headquarters and got Chris Strange.

'I tried you last night,' he said.

'I was out. Any luck with that registration number?'

'I want you to come in.'

'About the number.'

'This morning, McLean. I don't want to have to come out and get you.'

'OK,' I said, having no intention of going anywhere near police headquarters. 'Who owns the car?' There was a silence. 'I'll come down, Chris, and tell you anything you want. Who owns the car?'

'A Charles Whitfield, address in London. Know him?'

'What address?'

'I'll tell you when you come in.'

I knew he'd play coy.

'Who is he?' Strange asked.

'Whitfield?'

'Who else?'

Two of us could play coy. It was time to stir things a bit.

'He's the man who had Stephanie Myers killed,' I said. 'And Richard Sutton,' I added and hung up.

*

I left the print-outs at Maria's for safe keeping and drove east of town, along the broad flood plain of the River Don. Two centuries ago this was pastureland and you could catch salmon in the river. Now all you'd catch is typhoid.

I drove past the open spaces where the steel mills once stood, the derelict warehouses and factories rotting like huge unwanted carcases. This was once the greatest steel valley in the world. The steel that made the railways, the iron-clad ships, the armaments and the tools to found an empire came from here. When Huntsman invented crucible steel he built his furnace in this valley; when Bessemer invented the converter which was to revolutionize mass steel production he built it here, and it was here that Harry Brearley discovered stainless steel.

The axes and saws, chisels and files that opened up the American continent nearly all came from this valley. The barrels for the Colt .45 were made here and when Jim Bowie died at the Alamo he had a Sheffield knife on his belt.

Now it's practically all gone. All that's left by the Don now is a huge monstrosity of a shopping centre and, further upstream, the Bassett's sweet factory. The great names of the past—Vickers, Cammell, Jessop, Firth, Brown—have gone, replaced by Debenhams and Marks and Spencer and British Home Stores. This was once a city of steel. Now it's a city of Y-fronts and dolly mixtures.

Richard Sutton's Integrated Recycling Plant was just a building site. A row of Portakabins, stacked one on top of the other to save space, a few access roads and holes in the ground, a couple of cranes and about ten acres of thick brown mud. In the distance I could see the M1 viaduct at Tinsley and beyond that the cooling towers beside Blackburn Meadows sewage farm. Rain hung in the air. The atmosphere smelt of smoke and rust.

I walked across to one of the Portakabins. A sign saying 'Site Office' pointed up a flight of wooden steps. The steps, like everything else, were caked in wet mud. I went up them. From the landing at the top there was a view of the canal and a scrapyard next to it full of pulped cars. Along the edge of the canal the council had planted a few trees and a patch of yellowing grass in a futile attempt to prettify the miles of unremitting ugliness. I don't know why the bothered. It was like planting a rose in the middle of a slag heap.

I knocked on the site office door and went in. Two men in wellingtons and yellow hard hats were studying plans on a desk. They ignored me for a couple of minutes while they finished their business. Then one of them went out and the other turned to me.

'Sorry about that. You looking for me?'

'Are you the man in charge?'

'I'm the site manager, if that's what you mean.'

I told him who I was.

'Greg Alexander,' he said and shook hands. His skin was like a scouring pad. 'Grab a chair. How can I help you?'

'I was here the other month,' I said. 'For the laying of the foundation stone.'

'I don't remember. There were a lot of reporters.'

'I thought I'd check how things were progressing.'

'We're on schedule,' Alexander said.

'It doesn't look much different.'

Alexander grinned. His teeth were yellow with nicotine but he looked very fit. Stocky, strong hands, the weather-beaten complexion of the outdoors man.

'Most of it you can't see. We're still doing the founda-tions. We had a small setback. The rock strata weren't exactly what we expected.'

'That mean you could put the price up?' I said.

Alexander chuckled. 'Hey, you know something about building.'

'I bet you had to look hard for that one,' I said. 'When's it going to be ready?'

'Our bit, middle of next year. We're not providing the plant and machinery. That's the complicated part.'

'The recycling technology? Who's doing that?'

'The Germans. No one here can do it.'

'Surprise, surprise.'

'It's a big job. No one has ever attempted it on a scale

like this before. Everything's having to be custom made. You want a tour of the site?'

'I haven't got the clothes for it.'

'We could lend you some boots.'

I shook my head. 'Thanks, but it's only a quick visit.'

I noticed the lettering on the side of his hard hat. 'That the name of your company?'

Alexander glanced up. 'Yep. Fieldsend Construction.'

'Not Fieldsend Consultants?'

'No.'

'You ever heard of a firm called Fieldsend Consultants? A subsidiary maybe.'

'Not that I know of. Could be, though.'

'How much has it cost so far?'

'The whole project? No idea,' he said. 'We're only the builders. I don't know what the architects and all the others have spent.'

'But the building, just your bit of it. What's the total so far? Eight, nine million pounds?'

'Jesus no. Nothing like it.'

'What then?'

'Couple of million at the most and I don't think we've had all of that yet. Most of it's on tick at the moment. You want the exact figure you'll have to ring head office.'

I nodded and got up. 'You've been a great help, thanks.'

'That all you want to know?'

'Yes.'

'I've hardly told you anything.'

'It was more than enough,' I said.

CHAPTER 15

I caught the 10.20 Inter-City to London. The compartment reeked of sour milk and brake fluid. Six seats away a youth in a leather jacket had a personal stereo the whole carriage could hear. We all listened to Bruce Springsteen until

Leicester when the youth got off. An elderly couple sitting opposite him clapped.

I bought a cup of tea from the buffet. The sandwiches looked tempting. Tuna and watercress, roast beef and horseradish, bacon lettuce and tomato. I didn't succumb. They say BR sandwiches have improved recently but I can't tell as I've never yet managed to get one out of the bullet-proof plastic they wrap them in. The tea's changed too. It now comes in round bags with an aluminium tag attached to improve the flavour, and it's called 'Leaf Tea' in case you suspect it's made from some other kind of tea. Like floor sweepings.

We waited for fifteen minutes on an open stretch of track near Wellingborough for no apparent reason and got to St Pancras late. It's good to know some things don't change.

As I walked across the station concourse towards the Underground, two police officers were in the process of arresting a tramp outside W.H. Smith's. The tramp had a bottle in one hand and was shouting drunkenly as the coppers tried to pick him up. They jammed one of his arms behind his back and dragged him to his feet. The tramp was promptly sick all over their polished boots. Welcome to London.

I took the tube to Moorgate. It was way past rush hour but the train was still packed. I stood jammed against one of the doors with the other cattle and inhaled sweat and cheap perfume for what seemed an eternity. After that, even the City smelt clean.

Martin Furness was waiting for me in a wine bar near the Bank of England, an appropriate setting considering the prices they were charging. I let him buy the drinks.

We sat at a table and I ran my eye over the clientele. Smart young women with over-loud, fruity voices, drinking champagne and posing. Men in identical dark suits and white shirts sporting pink and yellow ties to convince themselves they were really mavericks. All the vermin from the financial sewers. Tarted up, but vermin just the same.

I'd rung Martin from Midland Station before I left. I

hadn't seen him for months and we exchanged gossip for a while over a bottle of Burgundy. We'd been close friends once, when we both worked for the *News*. Then he moved to London to do shifts for some of the Nationals and we were no longer so close. He was greyer now, his chin and waistline starting to sag, his face becoming blotchy with booze and business lunches. He'd been a non-practising socialist when I first met him, but he'd long since 'taken his thirty pieces of silver'—his phrase, not mine—and gone to work for a right-wing Sunday. His bank balance was healthy. I had my doubts about his principles.

I said: 'You had time to look at the files since I rang?'

Martin nodded. 'There were a few Charles Whitfields in the cuttings but I checked the picture files. Only one really fitted your description.'

He took a print out of his jacket pocket and passed it to me. I pulled off the rubber band and unrolled it.

'That him?'

I studied the photograph, then turned it over and read the caption.

'Yes.'

He was younger in the picture—it had been taken six years ago—but it was the man I'd seen at the Medico-Legal Centre and on the road near Jacqueline Sutton's house without doubt. The same blond hair, hooked nose and hard eyes.

'You know anything about him?' I asked.

'A bit.'

'What does he do?'

'What you suspected.'

'The City?'

Martin nodded. 'Loosely speaking.'

'Meaning what?'

'He has an office here and is in the same business as everyone else in the City.'

'Making money?'

'And screwing people.' Martin gave a lopsided grin.

'Sometimes screwing your rivals is more important than making money.'

'Everyone needs a hobby,' I said.

'But he's not part of the City. He operates on the fringes.'

'A predator.'

'If you like. I rang around a few people for you. He's not well liked. Not many friends in the Square Mile.'

'Does anyone have friends in the Square Mile?'

'Of course. You've got to have lunch with someone.'

'Is he a crook?'

Martin's lip twisted cynically. 'Crooks are people who get caught.'

Suddenly there was a nasty taste in my mouth and it wasn't the Burgundy. There's something ineffably dirty about London and it's not only the air and streets. You feel it as soon as you get off the train at St Pancras. It's like an enormous cow pat. From a distance it's just an indistinct brown heap whose odour you can barely smell. But close to you see the flies and beetles crawling all over it and the foul steaming vapours practically knock you out. I wondered how Martin could work as a City journalist. You can't spend your days wading through shit without some of it rubbing off.

'What's his main business?' I asked.

'Difficult to say. He's a secretive man. Shady, some would say. He's a gambler.'

'Isn't everyone in the City?'

'Not the way he is. Businessmen love that glamorous image of the entrepreneur but most of the people here are very dull bankers and accountants. They think they're risk-takers but the only gamble most of them ever take is on how much they can fiddle their expenses.'

'They sound like journalists,' I said.

'They're pen-pushers. Grey men who make sensible investment decisions and wait for their pensions.'

'But not Whitfield.'

'No. He's an outsider, that's partly why he's not trusted.

He's the guy in the black hat who comes into the saloon and cheats at poker.'

'Successfully?'

Martin shrugged and poured himself some more wine. He was on his third glass already.

'Not always. He's made a few bob in his time but he's spent a few too. He favours the flamboyant lifestyle, but he's not as rich as he'd like people to think.'

'Is he in trouble?'

'Impossible to say with any certainty. In this business you're not in trouble until you're in the bankruptcy court.'

'Does he own any companies?'

'He's the kind of person whose name gets linked with various companies from time to time. A stockbroker friend I rang said he had a controlling interest in an engineering firm in the Midlands.'

'Know the name?'

'Harman Engineering.'

It meant nothing to me.

'Another bottle?' Martin asked, finishing the one we had. I shook my head.

'Still as abstemious as ever, I see.'

'It puts me to sleep at lunch-time.'

'Me too. But I've got to do something in the afternoons.'

He smirked and waved a waitress over. He ordered another bottle of Burgundy.

'I know,' he said. 'It's bad for me. Sometimes I get a pain, just here.' He rubbed his belly below the ribcage. 'I think it's my liver.' He didn't sound very worried.

'Why don't you cut down, then?'

'I will. I'm planning to give it up altogether for Lent.'

'Lent's four months away,' I said.

'I know. Cheering thought, isn't it?'

He had always been gregarious, first into the pub after work and last out. Like most journalists, he claimed he picked up stories in bars. But all journalists do in bars is drink.

'You staying down?' he asked.

'No. I have to go back this evening.'

'You still living in that dive in Burngreave?'

'Yes.'

'Jesus, Michael, how do you stand it? How many years have you been there now?'

'Enough.'

'Why don't you move down here? I know a few people. I could fix you up with something.'

'It costs too much,' I said.

'You'd get a good salary.'

'It still costs too much.'

He looked at me, then shrugged dismissively. 'You can't live on principles, Michael.'

'Maybe it's good to try now and again,' I said.

He took a gulp of wine and didn't reply. It saddened me. We'd had the same outlook once. We'd started together with the same ideals and shared the same disillusionment as the reality of journalism failed to live up to our expectations. We'd done our shorthand and law exams together, studied the codes of conduct and ethics of journalism and then gone to work for a newspaper where most of the reporters didn't even know how to spell ethics. We'd sweated on stories together, endured the mindless autocracy of the Newsdesk and consoled each other over a pint when everything we wrote was hacked up and reduced to the lowest common denominator of crap.

It still counted for something, but less and less as the years went by. He'd taken a different path from me. We were both prostitutes, only I now worked the streets while he'd moved to a larger brothel where the pay was better, the beds more comfortable. I didn't envy him. I had independence and choice and no pimp to push me around. Yet sometimes, staring at the damp, mouldy wallpaper in my flat, I wondered what it would be like to be back in the bordello. Maybe I'd like to sell out too, but the price is always too high.

Martin said: 'You didn't just come down for that, did you? I could have told you most of it on the 'phone.'

'I'm going to Companies House.'

'To do what?'

'Check a few things.'

'On Whitfield?'

'Maybe.'

Martin half smiled. 'You always were a cagey bastard when you were working on something. Don't you trust me?'

I grinned. 'No.'

He pushed back his chair and stood up. The wine didn't seem to affect him.

'I'll run you over there. The old banger's outside.'

Martin's 'old banger' turned out to be a J-reg Lotus, so sleek and close to the ground it looked as if it had been run over by a steamroller. I got down on my knees and crawled into the passenger seat.

'Is this yours?' I asked.

'Of course. One of the perks of the job.'

'The paper gives you a Lotus?'

'Christ, no. It's not a company car. I got it myself.'

'They're paying you too much,' I said.

'I made the money on the side.'

'Doing what? Buying shares and then tipping them in your column?'

'Far too obvious. No one does that nowadays. There are more subtle ways of supplementing your income.'

I didn't ask him what they were. There are some things about your friends it's better not to know.

'Does nought to sixty in four seconds,' Martin said.

I looked out of the window at the traffic. 'In these conditions it'd take you three hours to get to sixty.'

A black cab cut in front of us and Martin banged on the horn. 'You coming down again soon?'

'I don't know.'

'Make it a weekend. You could stay at my flat. You know I've got a new one.' He told me what it had cost. I thought he was giving me the long distance 'phone number for Rio de Janeiro.

'It's in Maida Vale,' he said.

'Is that good?'

'Excellent location. Good investment.'

In London no one buys a flat to live in. They buy it to make money.

'I'll see what I can do,' I said. I wanted to spend a weekend in London the way I wanted to spend a weekend in a septic tank.

'Drop me off, Martin, it's not far to walk. You'll be stuck here all day.'

The traffic was nose to tail for as far as I could see, which, admittedly, given the lowness of the Lotus, wasn't all that far. But a lorry three cars in front of us was farting clouds of oily exhaust and the stench was making me nauseous.

Martin twisted the wheel to the left and cut down a side street. Rubbish blew along the pavements like tumbleweed on a Wild West film set. He pulled in by the kerb.

'Thanks, Martin, I'll be in touch.'

'You got a good story, we'll be happy to run it.'

'I'll remember that.'

'But if you're messing with a man like Whitfield, Michael, watch your back. You know what I'm saying?' I nodded. 'He's not a very big fish by City standards, but then piranha aren't very big, either.'

I swung my legs out on to the pavement. My feet were almost above me. 'You got a winch to help me out?' I said.

I struggled upright and bent double to peer back in.

'You mind if I hang on to that photograph?'

'Keep it. There were plenty more in the files.'

I lifted a hand in farewell and watched him drive away. The photograph was an interesting revelation. It was a flash shot, taken at night outside a nightclub. A gossip column picture. It showed Whitfield in a DJ and black tie walking across the pavement from a chauffeur-driven Rolls. On his arm was the obligatory blonde, all smiles and slit skirt. The caption on the back read: 'Millionaire financier Charles Whitfield and a friend attend the charity night at Club 467.'

The friend was Jacqueline Sutton.

Companies House was an ugly concrete building set in one of those soulless fringes of the Square Mile which seem to be nothing but graffitied subways and dreary office blocks. There were no shops, no houses, no real inhabitants to give it any character: just zombies in charcoal suits with their personalities locked away in their black attaché cases.

I went through the glass doors into the long, empty foyer. The security men were searching people's bags. I went into the Index Room. Computer terminals and microfiche machines were lined up in chest-high rows. I followed the instructions on one of the computer screens and typed in the name Fieldsend Consultants.

The entry came up on the screen. I noted down the company number and went to the counter near the door. I paid £2.75 for a search ticket.

'What do I do with it now?' I asked the woman behind the glass window.

'Just follow the green line.' She pointed at a green stripe painted on the shiny chessboard lino.

I followed the line out of the room, down the foyer, round a couple of corners and into the Search Room. I wondered why they had a line on the floor instead of signs. Maybe the City types couldn't read.

The Search Room was even more bare and impersonal than the Index Room. There was a plain wooden counter with a stack of numbered pigeon holes next to it. I handed in my search ticket, then sat in a line for an hour while they dug out the microfiched record on Fieldsend Consultants.

I took the small manilla envelope into an adjoining room which contained nothing but microfiche viewers and chairs covered in a gaudy orange and yellow fabric, now faded and worn by thousands of anonymous bums.

Inserting the microfiche into a machine, I went through the registration documents for Fieldsend Consultants. Several pages were devoted to the objects of the company, a list covering every possible business activity. It looked like an off-the-shelf company to me, bought ready formed with articles of association to suit all requirements.

There were only two directors, the minimum required by law. Both had signed the Memorandum of Association and listed their respective shareholdings. One of the directors was Charles Whitfield. That didn't surprise me. But the other one took my breath away like a punch to the guts. I stared at the name for half a minute or more. Then the pieces started to fit together.

I flicked through the rest of the record. No accounts had been filed, but then the date of incorporation was only March of that year, eight months earlier. About the time the payments from RPS Trading had started being made.

I handed in the microfiche and went back to the Index Room. I checked a few things on the computer terminal and made two more searches before I left.

Outside in the street, I found a call-box and rang directory inquiries. There was no listing for any firm called Fieldsend Consultants. I asked for the numbers of all the C. Whitfields in London. It didn't make me popular with the switchboard but I eventually got them. There were fourteen in all. I rang every one. Only six answered and none was the Whitfield I was looking for.

I wandered around and found a newsagents where I bought an A–Z. The registered office of Fieldsend Consultants was recorded at Companies House as in Finsbury Square. I looked it up in the A–Z and discovered it was just down the road.

The address turned out to be a solicitor's office. I went in and asked how I got in touch with the directors of Fieldsend Consultants and was told to write a letter to that address and it would be forwarded. There was no telephone number or trading address for the company. I hadn't really expected there to be: I already knew it was just a shell company, as insubstantial as candy floss and nothing like as wholesome.

I caught the six o'clock train back to Sheffield. It left St Pancras at ten to seven 'due to operating difficulties', i.e. the driver hadn't shown up.

I reached Sheffield Midland at nine-twenty, relieved to be back in a clean city, and rang Maria from one of the concourse 'phones. I wanted to go round and pick up the photocopies I'd left there and perhaps broach the subject of sleeping on her settee for another night.

Her voice sounded odd when she answered.

'It's me, Michael,' I said. 'You all right?'

'Michael, go to the—' she began hurriedly then broke off with a cry of pain. I heard movements at the other end, a low whimper, footsteps, a confusion of sounds.

'Maria? Maria, what's—?'

A man's voice interrupted me. 'Shut your mouf, McLean, and listen.' He had a cockney accent, a rasping whine I recognized even before he said: 'Remember me, McLean? How's your nose?'

I felt an icy, gut-freezing sickness in my belly. The thugs with the pliers had found Maria.

CHAPTER 16

I swayed against the side of the 'phone booth. It smelt of stale cigarette smoke. I tried to keep my voice steady.

'What do you want?'

'A word wiv you, McLean.'

'I'll come to the house.'

'No, you won't. And dahn't get ideas abaht sending the police either. We won't be here. Nor will your lady friend.'

'Leave her out of this. She isn't involved.'

'She is nah, sonny boy. Here's what you do. You drive up on to the moors.'

'Which moors?'

'You take the same road Sutton took, understand? You park by the side of the road wiv your lights on.'

'Park where?'

'Anywhere. We'll find you. A nice clear open stretch of road so we can see you're alone. You go there nah.'

The 'phone went dead in my hand. I held the receiver clenched to my ear while I tried to control the anger which threatened to overwhelm my reason. I knew I had to stay calm.

They'd thought it all out carefully, chosen an exposed, isolated rendezvous where they could approach me without fear of being ambushed. I had to go alone. Any kind of overt police presence would be too obvious and there was no time for anything more subtle. Besides, it was my problem. I'd caused it all; now it was up to me to find a solution.

I retrieved my car from the station car park and drove out of the city. The roads were clear and I was out of the built-up area in under fifteen minutes. I drove automatically, two thoughts obsessing me: how had they found out where Maria lived and what had they done to her?

I stopped on the flat plateau top of Burbage Moor and half pulled off the road on to the grass verge. I switched off my headlights and sat in the semi-darkness. Outside, the heather was a seemingly endless ocean, dark, undulating, closing in oppressively from all sides.

It was a cold night so I left the engine running and the heater on. I waited, tense, watching the inside of the windscreen steam up. Occasionally headlights appeared behind me and I watched them approach in the rear-view mirror. But the cars always drove straight past and on across the moors.

Then another set of lights pierced the darkness. They came up and stopped a few hundred yards back. I could just make out the shadowy outline of a car. It waited for a short time then came past me very slowly. It was the black BMW. One of the thugs was driving, the other in the back seat with Maria next to him. I saw the paleness of her face in the diffused aura of the headlights, but not her expression.

The car stopped in front of me and the driver got out. He had sticking plaster on his forehead from our encounter in the timber yard. I switched off my engine and watched him. The jacket of his black suit was undone and one of his hands rested on his belt just inside the jacket flaps. I guessed he had a gun stuck in the top of his trousers.

'Get aht and put your hands on the top of the car, McLean,' he shouted. Maybe he was being cautious, maybe he'd just seen too many American cop shows. I did what he said.

He came over and frisked me, superficially, but enough to find the rolled photograph I still had in my inside pocket. He put it in his own pocket without looking at it.

'Where are the keys?'

'In the ignition.'

'OK, walk to the car.'

I walked to the BMW.

'Get in the driver's seat.'

I got in. The second man said to me from the back seat: 'Start up and drive straight on.'

I turned the key and looked in the mirror, trying to see Maria's face. The first thug was walking back to my car.

'You all right, Maria?'

'Shut it, McLean,' the thug said.

'Did they hurt you?'

'I said shut it.' A pistol barrel jammed into the back of my neck.

'I'm all right,' Maria said. Her voice was soft but steady. An undertone of anger, probably with me. This was going to take some explaining.

I drove across the moors. The road dipped down to the two bridges across Burbage Brook and the gravel car park where in summer you could buy ice-cream and cups of tea from a van. It was deserted now, as bleak and empty as the wilderness that surrounded it. The first thug followed in my car. The road went uphill then divided into two, the right fork heading towards Stanage Edge, the left to Hathersage. We took the left fork, the route Richard Sutton had taken just before he died.

We descended the hill in silence, but when we reached the point where Sutton had crashed, the man in the back couldn't resist saying: 'Careful here, McLean. Accidents have been known to happen.'

I said nothing. It confirmed what I'd already worked out: the two of them had murdered Sutton.

We went down into Hathersage and the thug told me to turn off through a wide gateway. It was the Suttons' house.

The thug got out first with Maria. The second one had arrived in my car. He ordered me out and we all went into the house. They took us through to the back, into the sitting-room where I had interviewed Jacqueline Sutton. They put us on the flowery sofa next to each other. Maria looked at me reproachfully. Her eyes were frightened.

'I'm sorry, Maria,' I said. 'I really am.'

'It doesn't matter,' she said quietly.

I put my arms around her and held her. She didn't resist. Her body was trembling.

'No more of that.' The first thug broke us apart and threw me across the room into an armchair. He grinned.

'The bit of skirt's for us. Me and Ronnie. We're saving her till later. I'n't that right?'

Ronnie grinned too, like a Rottweiler in a dentist's chair. 'We're going to have a bit of fun wiv 'er. Like we did wiv the other one, the Myers bird.'

He strolled across to Maria and casually jammed his hand down the front of her blouse. She lashed out with a foot and Ronnie laughed, avoiding it easily.

I sprang up out of my chair and tackled him around the waist, butting him hard in the solar plexus with my head. He hardly seemed to feel it for he swung one of his fists in an arc and clouted me on the side of the head. A single sharp pain jarred through my skull and I tumbled on to the carpet.

I saw a foot swinging round, heard a door opening behind me, a man's voice saying, 'That's enough' and Maria crying out, 'Michael, oh Jesus!' before everything went suddenly blank.

My head was burning hot. The pain was everywhere, penetrating my cranium like clusters of misplaced acupuncture needles. Something cool touched my forehead and I opened my eyes. Maria was holding an ice compress to my face, moving it gently over the skin.

I turned my head sideways. Ronnie and his mate were standing against the wall near the door and in chairs facing me were Nigel Sinclair and Charles Whitfield.

Whitfield was smoking a small cheroot and toying idly with a glass of wine on the arm of his chair. He looked as if he'd just finished an excellent dinner and was waiting for the floorshow to begin. I had a feeling we were going to be the star turn.

'Ah, so you are back with us, McLean,' Whitfield said. 'How nice.' He had a purring voice but his politeness was more menacing than the most open threat.

He leaned forward and picked up some papers from the coffee table.

'It was most kind of you to obtain these photocopies for us. We really do appreciate it.'

I glanced sharply at Maria. She shrugged apologetically.

'That's how they caught me. I came home from work and found the papers in the house. I thought you must have forgotten them so I took them round to your flat. Those two gorillas were there. I'm sorry.'

I squeezed her hand. 'It's all my fault, not yours.'

'It was quite fortuitous,' Whitfield said. 'They're very valuable to us. I wonder what else you have that might be of interest. Dave.' He raised a finger at the two thugs. 'You searched him?'

'Yes, sir. No weapons. Just this.'

Dave came forward and handed the rolled-up photo-graph to Whitfield. Whitfield snapped off the rubber band and looked at it. His expression didn't change.

'You find that interesting?' I said hoarsely.

Whitfield levelled his cold blue eyes at me. 'An old snap? Why should I?'

'What about her? She not putting in an appearance, or does she leave all the dirty work to you and your two chums?'

Whitfield chuckled. There was no humour in it, just contempt.

'Mrs Sutton has nothing to do with this.'

'You're in her house.'

'She has gone out for the evening. It just happened to be convenient for us to use it, particularly as I'm a house guest here. As you can see, we are old friends.'

'She know she's giving hospitality to the man who murdered her husband?'

Whitfield's face remained implacable. Beside him, in the other armchair, Nigel Sinclair licked his lips and shifted uneasily. I looked at him. His eyes were frightened; a man out of his depth.

'He knows, Charles.' His voice was unsteady.

'Calm yourself, Nigel. He can do nothing.'

'The police know too,' I said.

Sinclair's mouth twitched. 'The police! Charles, I . . .'

'Be quiet, Nigel,' Whitfield interrupted smoothly.

'Yes, shut up, Nigel,' I said. 'The office boy should do as he's told.'

'I'd advise you to shut your mouth, McLean,' Whitfield said.

I've never taken advice like that. 'It's not like you to step out of line, Nigel,' I continued, trying to divide the opposition. 'You fiddle the books for Charlie boy here, steal all that money, do as you're told all the way along the line, and for what? You sure he isn't going to cut you out and run off with all the dosh himself?'

Whitfield gave a tiny nod and Dave stepped quickly over and slapped me across the mouth with the back of his hand. Maria tried to punch him. I admired her for that. Dave raised his hand to hit her too but Whitfield shook his head. Dave backed off. I could taste the salt of blood on my lips.

'Losing your nerve, Charlie? Or did I get too close to the truth?'

'You sure he hasn't told the police?' Sinclair said agitatedly. A nerve in his cheek started to twitch.

'He's trying to rattle you, Nigel. If the police knew, they'd have been asking questions by now.'

Somewhere in the depths of the house a bell rang. The front door. Sinclair's eyes darted towards the door. I felt Maria go tense. I didn't look at her. She probably thought it was help arriving, but I knew differently. I could guess who it was.

Whitfield nodded at Dave who left the room. Half a minute elapsed before he returned. Behind him, in a black coat and homburg, was Stuart Sutherland.

I swung my legs off the settee. My head ached but my mind was clear.

'Hello, Stuart. I wondered when you'd show up.'

Stuart took his coat and hat off very deliberately before sitting down in an armchair. He pulled his trousers up at the knee to protect their knife-edge crease as he did so. His composure was impressive.

'So you knew,' he said.

There was no point in pretending otherwise. They weren't going to let us go whatever happened.

'I went to Companies House, saw the registration documents for Fieldsend Consultants.'

Stuart glanced at Whitfield. 'I told you he was dangerous. We were too soft the first time.'

'That's right, Charlie,' I said. 'You should have had your boys dump me in the canal instead of just roughing me up. You weren't so squeamish about Debbie Nolan, were you?'

Whitfield handed Stuart the photocopies from the coffee table. 'The woman had them.'

Stuart stared briefly at Maria. 'I suppose you know what these are?' he said to me.

'Of course. Who told you I'd got them? Jacqueline Sutton?'

'She isn't involved,' Stuart said. I believed him. I was glad. I didn't like to think I'd been wrong all along about Jacqueline.

'So who did?'

'We guessed. Stephanie Myers said you'd asked her

about the briefcase. When we found she didn't have it, it was reasonable to assume you might.'

'So you sent Pinky and Perky round to wait for me in my flat. You were slow there, Stuart. Didn't you know Sutton had left the photocopies at Stephanie's?'

'We didn't know they existed until Debbie Nolan mentioned them to Nigel.'

'Ah, that must have been a blow. To have killed Sutton and burnt the records and then discovered there were copies of the key accounts floating around. Poor Debbie. Did she know what they meant?'

'No.'

'So why kill her?'

'Because she was going to tell you. I was waiting by the reception desk at the Medico-Legal Centre after Sutton's inquest. I overheard her giving the receptionist a note for you. We couldn't take that chance.'

'And Stephanie?'

'She tried to blackmail us. She got too greedy.'

'Wanted too much for the photocopies? No one deserved what you did to her.'

Stuart shrugged. 'She was a foolish woman. She threatened to go to the police. We had no choice.'

'Why didn't you just run, Stuart? When Sutton found out what had been going on. You had six million in the bag already. Wasn't that enough?'

He took off his spectacles and rubbed them on his silk tie.

'The next instalment of the loan was due on December 1st.'

'How much? Another three million? I get it. You wanted to hang on for it. So you killed three people. A million quid for each corpse, cheap at the price.'

Whitfield waved his cheroot impatiently. 'I think we've talked enough, Stuart.'

Stuart put his spectacles back on and blinked. He looked so harmless, so ordinary, yet underneath there was pure ice. I'd always known he was ruthless, but I never thought he'd kill for gain.

'Tell me, Stuart,' I said. 'Out of curiosity, why did you set fire to Sutton's offices? It *was* you, wasn't it? Sinclair gave you his keys before going to his dinner to establish his alibi.'

'Let's end it here, Stuart,' Whitfield said.

'It won't make any difference,' Stuart replied. 'Not now.'

He looked directly into my eyes. I shivered. I knew what he meant. He'd had three people killed to cover up what he'd been doing. He wouldn't balk at two more. Next to me on the settee, Maria turned to watch me. She knew, too. I gripped her hand hard.

'To destroy the accounts, of course,' Stuart said.

I shook my head. 'You didn't need to. Sutton was the only one who knew you'd been stealing the money. By killing him you removed the threat. There was nothing to stop Sinclair continuing to cook the books. Yet you burnt the records all the same. That was stupid. You went to all that trouble to fake an accident so the police wouldn't ask questions about Sutton's death, and then you set fire to his company accounts, an action which was bound to arouse police suspicions. And maybe make them look more closely at Sutton's business, which was the last thing you wanted. Why?'

Stuart stole a brief glance at Whitfield and in it I saw defiance, resignation but also apology. I knew what had happened then and almost laughed out loud.

'Jesus, it's so simple. That old rule of journalism. Look everywhere for a conspiracy and nine times out of ten you'll find it's really nothing more than a cock-up. That's what happened isn't it? You panicked.

'Sutton discovered the doctored accounts and said something to Sinclair. Sinclair rang you and Whitfield and you over-reacted. Whitfield got his goons to follow Sutton and knock him off in a faked accident, but none of them knew he was teetotal.

'In the meantime, you got the office keys from Sinclair

and destroyed the records without thinking it through. The right hand not knowing what the left hand was doing. You ballsed it up, didn't you, Stuart?'

He flushed. He was too vain to admit it, but he'd lost his cool in those crucial hours after Sutton discovered his company's money was being embezzled. He wasn't going to lose it now, though.

'You're right, Charles,' he said calmly. 'We've done enough talking.'

Whitfield nodded at Dave and Ronnie. They didn't need to be given instructions. They came over to the settee and hauled me and Maria up. There was no point in resisting.

'Don't do it, Stuart,' I said. 'I've told the police everything I know. You won't gain anything from this.'

'He's lying,' Whitfield said. 'He's tried that line already.'

Stuart stood in front of me and raised his eyes to mine.

'I married your wife, Michael. She sometimes talks about you. She says there was one characteristic she always admired in you.'

'Only one?' I said, hurt.

'You always did everything on your own. No passing the buck, no relying on others, no sharing of stories. You wouldn't give information to the police if you were on your last gasp.'

'I've got softer since I was with Alison.'

'You're bluffing, Michael. I'm going to call it.'

He stepped out of the way as Ronnie and Dave pushed us out of the room.

We were taken outside. Maria whispered to me: '*Did* you go to the police today?' I shook my head and looked the other way. I knew her expression would hurt too much.

They put us in the cars again, the same arrangement as before. Ronnie sat in the back of the BMW with Maria while I drove. Dave came behind in my Cortina. They had obviously been briefed in advance.

We took the back road out of the village, past the church and the Scotsman's Pack pub, and drove up on to the moors.

'You guys could help yourselves by letting us go now,' I said.

'You talk too much, McLean.'

'It might do you some good with the police.'

'The police have got nothing on us.'

'You don't really think you can get away with this, do you?'

Ronnie chuckled. 'Why not? We got away with the others.'

He ordered me to pull over when we got to the crest of the hill. Then he waited for Dave to park behind us and come round to the driver's door.

'Out.'

Dave yanked open the door and beckoned me out with his pistol. I stepped out on to the road.

'On to the verge.'

Ronnie pushed Maria towards me. She stumbled on the tufts of grass and I caught her before she fell. I didn't let go.

'Easy now, we're all right.'

'Move along the path,' Dave said. He'd taken a bottle from the glove compartment of the BMW and was taking a swig. He passed it on to Ronnie. It was Bell's whisky.

'Is this going to be a repeat of Sutton's accident?' I said.

'We never repeat ourselves,' Dave replied, wiping his mouth on his sleeve. 'Now move off.'

They herded us along the path. It was a cloudy night but the moon occasionally broke through to illuminate the track. I knew where it was in any case. I'd been along it a thousand times. It was the path that led up on to the top of Stanage Edge. I could see the massive gritstone cliffs looming up before us, black and uneven against the paler sky.

They took us up on to the top. The wind screamed into our faces. I leaned forwards to keep my balance. Maria grabbed hold of my arm to support herself.

We walked a short distance along the path at the top of the Edge, far enough away from the precipice to avoid any danger of being blown over. Once I looked back and saw Ronnie peering over the cliffs and shaking his head at Dave. They were going to push us over. Smash our bodies on the rocks fifty feet below but they were trying to find the best spot.

It was then that a wild, outrageous idea came to me. I felt a small surge of hope. But it all depended on how far along the Edge we went. I looked around, trying to recognize the landmarks. To our right there was nothing but moorland stretching away to Stanage Pole and Redmires Reservoir. The only indicators were the boulders by the path and the slight undulations in the terrain. I tried desperately to remember exactly how far we had to go. We were close, I knew that much, but all the rocks looked the same in the dark and it was a long time since I had been this way.

'That's far enough,' Dave said. He was only a few yards behind us but he had to shout to make himself heard above the wind. Maria and I stopped and turned.

'Walk to the edge.'

'Is this it?' I said. 'Another unfortunate accident.'

'Couple out walking at night, miss the path in the dark and fall over the cliff. Tragic waste of life.' Dave grinned. 'Further.'

I took two more paces. The wind gusted up the face of the Edge, sandblasting my skin with grit. I stared around madly, running out of time and feeling the spectre of death creeping closer. It was somewhere around here. Jesus, I knew it was. I used to come here as a kid, I knew exactly where it was. Look for the outcrop with the incision on the western side. The different levels of rock that resembled huge steps. We hadn't passed them, they had to be nearby. But where? Then I realized. We were standing on them. I felt a sudden, gasping sensation of relief, as if my lungs had been sucked out of my body. I took Maria's arm.

'Right to the edge,' Dave shouted, waving his gun at us.

I pulled Maria towards me, putting both arms around

her waist. I moved backwards, looking sideways over the sheer precipice until I saw what I was looking for.

Ronnie was moving nearer, his lips pulled back from his mouth in a wolfish grin. I realized he was enjoying himself. He was going to push us over.

I put my lips close to Maria's ear. 'Hang on to me tight. Don't panic. Brace yourself.'

Then I did what I knew they least expected. I jumped.

CHAPTER 17

I felt the wind, the blackness of the night rush past. Maria cried out in alarm, clutching at me as the void opened up beneath us. But we touched rock a bare instant later. My knees were already half bent, ready to absorb the shock as we landed on the ledge I knew was there some twelve feet below the top. I rolled over towards the rock face, cushioning Maria with my body. She was winded, choking impotently for breath. My side burned with pain but it was bruising only, nothing worse.

I pulled Maria under the overhang. Ronnie was yelling up above us and I knew he'd be peering over the edge, trying to see where we'd gone. We had perhaps just a few seconds grace, no more. I crawled further inside.

We were in Robin Hood's Cave, an aperture worn in the face of the cliff by the scouring action of wind and grit. It had a narrow ledge outside, deeply eroded into a rounded basin with a raised side protecting the outermost edge. It was that which had stopped us rolling off and tumbling on to the jagged boulders far below.

Maria was on her hands and knees, struggling for air. I gave her no chance to recover but forced her deeper into the cleft. The roof was low and we had to crouch like apes to pass through. There was rainwater in the hollow inside and one of my feet kicked something metallic. A tin can most likely. When I was a kid I used to come out here with my mates for picnics and it was still used as a shelter by fellwalkers. In daylight the scorch marks of fires could be seen on the roof.

'Don't stop,' I whispered to Maria. 'And keep your head down.'

At the back of the cave the walls curved round almost parallel to the line of the Edge. Where they met was a horizontal slit less than eighteen inches high through which the pale light of the moon glimmered. I slithered through it on my belly and turned to drag Maria after me. Her skirt ripped on one of the sharp outcrops.

'I'll buy you another,' I said softly.

'For Chrissake, you think I care?' she replied, teeth gritted. 'I thought that was the end, when you did that.'

'I warned you.'

'Not that you were going to jump. Jesus, I've never been so scared.' She was recovering her breath fast. 'Those two are going to find us here.'

'I know.'

'So what the bloody hell are we lying here for?'

She was angry. I wanted her to stay that way. Anger inspired action, overcame the fear and panic which was only just below the surface in both of us. We'd given ourselves a temporary reprieve but it would be shortlived if we didn't get down off the Edge. Ronnie and Dave must have worked out by now that we hadn't jumped very far and would be looking for a way down to find us.

I stretched out my neck and peered upwards. Ronnie and Dave were four or five yards away to my left, directly over the cave which was not visible from above. They were close to the ground, bracing themselves against the wind, looking over cautiously. Moonlight gleamed for a second on Dave's gun. I didn't want to be anywhere near that cave if they started shooting.

I turned my gaze downwards. We had come out of a side entrance to the cave but were still sheltered by the overhang. Below us the rocks fell away in what appeared to be a sheer cliff. But I knew it wasn't sheer. The gritstone edge was made up of different sized blocks, slashed with fissures and crevasses. In the darkness they looked smooth and unclimbable but there were hand and footholds everywhere.

'We've got to go down,' I whispered in Maria's ear.

She turned and I sensed rather than saw the incredulity on her face.

'You mad? It's a precipice.'

'There's no other way. We can't go up and I'm not hanging around for them to come down.'

'They'll see us.'

'That's a chance we have to take.'

'Or we'll kill ourselves.'

'I'm an experienced climber, trust me,' I said.

'That's news to me.'

It was news to me too but I didn't say anything. It was not a moment for telling the truth.

I pulled myself along the rock, feeling over the front edge with my hand and looking for the best place to go down. There were only a few possible routes. The easiest descended just to the side of the cave mouth but it was also the most exposed. We would be seen for certain if we attempted it. Others were so steep they would have been suicidal in the dark, which left only one realistic route—a vertical crack to our right. It was a deep gash in the cliff, big enough to climb down without being seen from either the side or above. There was only one problem: to reach it entailed traversing a sloping boulder and leaping across a yard or more of open air. One slip and we would save Ronnie and Dave the bother of finishing us off.

'I've found a way,' I said, drawing back in under the overhang. I pointed across at the fissure. 'It goes almost to the bottom.'

'I'm not going down that,' Maria hissed.

'There'll be handholds. Look, the rocks on either side are out of line. There are ledges every few feet. It'll be like going down stairs.'

'You must have funny stairs.'

'It's the only way, Maria. They know we're under here somewhere. Getting down to the cave is easy. All they have to do is find the route and we're sitting targets.'

She glanced upwards anxiously, then across at the crevasse. She shuddered.

'I'm going to kill you for this, McLean.'

'You'll have to join the queue,' I said.

I spun my legs round on the ledge and dropped them over the side, feeling for purchase with my toes. I edged sideways, lowering my body at the same time. I was still covered by the overhang but a few feet further down I would be out in the open, clearly visible to anyone looking over the top. I craned my head upwards. I could see no sign of either Ronnie or Dave. I let my body slip down the face of the rock. It was steep, but nothing like vertical, and very coarse. I used the friction between my clothes and the sandstone to control my descent until I found another foothold.

There were voices above. I pressed my face to the boulder and risked a glance. Two silhouettes moved against the skyline. They were further away than before, exploring the rocks beyond the cave entrance. I let out a small breath of relief. They were looking in the wrong place: there was no way down there. Yet they only had to look my way and they would see me spread-eagled on the cliff. I moved quickly. I dropped lower until my feet found a horizontal crack, then I edged sideways along it until I could go no further. Beside me the chasm was a deep tube of stygian black.

I reached out to the buttress on the other side. By stretching I could just get a grip on one of the spurs. I shuffled my feet along the crack and then stuck my right leg out over the chasm. It found a narrow ledge on the other side and in one movement I pulled myself across and into the shelter of the buttress. I'd been right. The rocks behind were out of alignment, providing a relatively easy stepped descent to the bottom.

Recovering my breath, I looked back up at Maria. She was still flat on the ledge, just a motionless shadow against the rock. I waved an arm. She didn't move. I waved again, more urgently.

'Come on, for God's sake.' I kept my voice low, knowing it would carry to her but no further. The wind was howling up the Edge, drowning all sound except within a narrow radius.

Maria was terrified, too frightened to move, that was the only explanation. She was only three yards away from me but one of those yards was over a sixty-foot ravine. I had to persuade her to try. Swiftly I took off my jacket and pullover and tied them together into a makeshift rope. Then I climbed a few feet up the buttress and threw one end to Maria. She caught it in one hand and pulled it tight. It was a flimsy lifeline, it would never take her weight if she fell, but it was a psychological reassurance. I urged her across again.

She copied what I'd done, sliding out over the edge and clinging to the rock. Her feet scrabbled for a hold and she looked across at me for help. Further down I signalled, a few inches more. She slipped lower. I could see panic in her face. Then one of her toes found the crack and she stopped sliding. Thank God she was wearing sensible flat shoes and not heels.

'Hold on, you're nearly there,' I said.

She was almost within touching distance. I leaned out, encouraging her to move towards me. Her eyes flickered.

'Don't look down! Edge along the crack.'

She started to shuffle sideways, one hand clutching the boulder, the other the arm of my pullover. Out of the corner of my eye I saw the two silhouettes move on top of the Edge. Dave and Ronnie were coming back our way. I tried not to look. Maria mustn't know. I tugged on the jacket and pullover.

'Further. Right to the edge.'

The silhouettes had disappeared.

'Quickly, Maria. Just a few inches more.'

A stone tumbled down from above. Maria froze. Then

Ronnie and Dave appeared, looking over on hands and knees. Ronnie gave a shout. He'd seen us.

'Move, Maria,' I yelled. It made no difference now if they heard me. It jarred her into action. She dragged herself hurriedly over the rock and stretched her arm towards me. I pulled in the jacket then caught her wrist with my left hand, my right arm hooked around the buttress to prevent us both falling off.

Dave was taking aim with his pistol. I knew there was no time to do anything gently. I wrenched Maria sideways, pulling her into space. For a moment she dangled over the chasm. She screamed. There was a pistol shot, a whine of bullet on rock, then I had Maria on to the buttress and round into the safety of the gulley.

I pulled her to me, moving back along the ledge. Above us a slab of rock offered complete protection from Ronnie and Dave. Maria was sobbing. Not weeping, just catching her breath in great spasms. I murmured meaningless words of comfort to her. Then I pushed her away gently.

'You OK?'

'No, I'm bloody well not OK,' she said vehemently.

'Good,' I said.

I untied my pullover and jacket and put them back on. I was shivering already with the cold.

'It's easy from now on,' I said. 'We have to hurry. They'll come down after us.'

Maria nodded. She was too breathless to speak. I climbed on to the boulder below us and reached up to help her. it would be only minutes before Ronnie and Dave found a way down and now they knew for certain where we were.

We scrambled down the gulley. Once, looking round the buttress, I saw a figure crossing the slab higher up. Just one. I wondered where the other was.

At the bottom of the gulley we followed the foot of the cliffs, clambering over the rocks and keeping to the shadows. It was too dangerous to venture into the open, we would be spotted almost at once, even when the moon was hidden behind clouds.

Maria was desperately tired, stress adding to her weariness, and I had to pull her forcibly over some of the obstacles. Her hands and legs were smeared with blood where the sharp rocks had grazed her. Periodically we stopped to listen. One of the thugs was behind us, but some way distant. On an open stretch I caught a glimpse of him, it was Ronnie. He was moving carefully, checking all the nooks and crannies in the base of the cliff in case we'd gone into hiding. In his right hand was a pistol.

But where was Dave? Still on top of the Edge? Returning to the car to summon reinforcements? I tried to guess what I might do in his place. Our escape must have momentarily confused them, but they were arrogant bastards, confident of their abilities as killers. They'd be pretty sure that between them they could finish us off.

Then it came to me. Shit! I stopped dead and pulled Maria to the ground.

'What is it?' she whispered.

'Stay still.'

'He'll catch us. We have to get to the road.'

'Sssh.'

I put a hand over her mouth and listened. Nothing, except the buffeting of the wind and the steam piston beat of my own heart. But I knew I was right. I knew what I'd have done in Dave's place. I'd have run along the top of the Edge and descended to the east where it was lower and less dangerous. I'd have cut off the escape route to the road. Jesus, and we'd nearly walked straight into him.

I put my lips to Maria's ear. 'Don't make a sound. The other one's up ahead somewhere, waiting for us.'

She pulled my hand away. 'Then we're trapped.' There was an undertone of despair in her voice.

'Move back towards the cliff.'

'Michael . . .'

'Do as I say.'

We crept into the shadows at the base of the Edge. I felt around for a rock to use as a weapon.

'What are you doing?'

'Stay here, I won't be long.'

Maria clutched at my arm. 'If you think I'm staying here on my own, McLean, I've got news for you.'

'I'm going to tackle Ronnie.' I weighed the rock in my hand.

'Two's better than one,' Maria said. She picked up a loose stone.

She had guts all right. She was coping better than I'd thought.

'I'll try to get behind him,' I said. 'When he gets nearer try to draw his attention.'

Maria shook her head. 'Uh-uh. You think I'm setting myself up as a target? I'm coming too.'

'And you called me a stubborn bastard.'

I dropped to a crouch and moved out into the chaotic jumble of boulders which followed the line of the Edge. Maria stayed at the foot of the cliff, moving parallel to me. I pulled myself up one of the huge slabs of sandstone and risked a look. Ronnie was less than thirty yards away, still moving cautiously. I went round the side, keeping my head well down. Maria disappeared from sight.

Ten yards further on I took another look. Ronnie was nowhere to be seen. I slid into cover to consider where he might have gone. Maybe behind a boulder, maybe into one of the cavities in the cliff. He couldn't have been far away.

I sat very still and listened. Nothing. I turned my head to look behind me and something hard pressed into the side of my neck. A voice whispered in my ear: 'Bang.'

I turned very slowly. Ronnie was tucked into a cleft between two rocks, a grin slitting the lower half of his ugly face.

'Got you,' he said genially, digging the pistol harder into my neck.

I swallowed and tried to turn further.

'That's far enough,' Ronnie said. 'Now where's your little lady friend?'

A rock thudded down suddenly on to the back of Ronnie's

skull. He collapsed forward against me, his pistol clattering into the rocks beneath us. Maria came into view.

'Right behind you,' she said softly.

I pushed the unconscious Ronnie away from me and looked at her.

'Don't say anything,' she said. 'Just find the gun.'

We bent down and started searching the ground around out feet. Unfortunately, there was no real ground to speak of. We were on a mound of boulders, rocks tossed in a jagged heap with dozens of cracks and crevasses down which the gun could have fallen. I felt around, probing all the clefts as far as my arms and fingers could reach.

'You see it?' Maria asked urgently.

'It's too dark. It's gone.'

'It must be here.'

I took her arm. 'It's gone, Maria.' I shut off the feeling of despondency which welled up inside me. Our one chance of evening the odds against us had gone.

She leaned back against a boulder. She looked all in. 'What are we going to do? Stay here until daylight?'

'The other one will come for us long before that.'

'Then what?'

'There's the hill.'

Below the base of the cliff the ground sloped away in a steep embankment. In summer it was covered in dense vegetation but now it was just a scrubland of dead bracken and heather. It offered no cover whatsoever.

'We can't go out there,' Maria said. 'He'd shoot us for certain.'

'You're not coming,' I said.

It took her a moment to understand. 'No, I won't let you,' she whispered fiercely. 'We'll stay here and fight.'

'He's got a gun, Maria.'

'So had this one.'

'We were lucky this time.'

She started to say something but I clamped my hand over her mouth again. 'Listen to me. You stay here when I make a break for it. When Dave comes after me you go back to the car. I'll take him well away from the road. You understand?'

She twisted her mouth out from under my hand. 'Damn you, McLean. Don't do that to me. What if he doesn't come after you?'

'He will. He has to. He can't let me escape.'

Maria shuddered. 'We don't have the car keys.'

I rummaged in my jacket and took out my wallet. There was a spare ignition key in one of the pockets, a key Dave had missed in his sloppy search. I gave it to her.

'Get to a phone-box. Ring South Yorkshire CID, a detective-sergeant called Strange. Tell him what happened.'

'But Michael, you . . .'

'Sssh. Did you hear something? Get back into that slit.' I stuck an eye over the boulder. I could see nothing, but I sensed that Dave was closing in. If I was going, it had to be now.

'Wait for him to come after me,' I said. 'Don't do anything until then.'

She said nothing. She put an arm around my neck and kissed me once. Hard. I'd think about that one later. If later ever came.

I got down on my belly and snaked across the ground, away from the cliff. The withered bracken stalks crackled under my weight but noise was irrelevant now. I *wanted* to be spotted. The first few yards were in the shadow of the Edge but then I was in the full moonlight, about as inconspicuous as a fox at a hunt ball.

Dave saw me immediately. He started yelling. I didn't hang around. I scrambled to my feet and sprinted down the hill, crouching low, swerving, doing everything I'd read you should do when someone's about to take pot shots at you. I heard two gun reports but neither bullet hit me. I hoped it was a good omen.

I stumbled over a tussock of grass and rolled into a ditch as a third shot echoed across the valley. That bullet I heard, a hiss in the air above me like a viper's sigh. He was getting better. I pulled myself up and risked a look back. Thank

Christ. Dave was coming after me, lumbering down the hill to my right. He moved awkwardly over the rough terrain, watching his feet more than me.

I ran on, oblivious of the dangers. I knew I could easily snap an ankle in a hidden hollow but that was the least of my worries. There was a narrow metalled road at the bottom which followed the incline to join the main road where we'd left the cars. It was tempting to run along it and gain some ground but Dave was already moving sideways to cut off that possibility. He knew what he was doing all right.

Instead I ran across the road and leaped over the dry-stone wall into a field at the far side. I peeked back over it, straining my eyes to see if there was any movement under the Edge, but it was too dark to see. Maria could have been anywhere. Dave had lost a bit of ground but the odds were still heavily against me. I was probably fitter than he was and I knew the terrain, but Dave had a gun.

I ducked down and ran across the field, the wall covering my back. My lungs were aching already, my guts churning with a sickly fear. If I didn't use my wits, I knew for certain I would die on that godforsaken moor.

I lay in a shallow gulley between two clumps of heather, gasping for breath and watching the hillside above me. It had started to drizzle and my face was bathed in a fine spray of rain and sweat.

I watched the skyline, partly for Dave, partly for the flicker of headlights which might indicate Maria had reached the car. There was nothing. The sky was bruised in shades of blue and black but there was no trace of artificial light. I prayed Maria had made her move at the right time and had been sensible enough not to switch on the lights. I hadn't heard an engine start but by now I was too far away.

I wiped the moisture from my eyes and twisted round. I could see right across Hope Valley. There were scattered farmhouses on the far slopes but not a single light showed.

I checked my watch. It was half-past one. Far below me, behind the bulge of the spur, was Hathersage. It was the logical place to head for, the nearest settlement of any kind. Yet for that very reason I was reluctant to go there. Dave would know that was the most obvious choice for me and if I was to escape I had to do the unexpected.

I scuttled sideways, moving along the contours close to the ground. Where the hell was he? If he'd followed directly behind me, he should have appeared by now. He was giving me too much time and he wasn't the type to give anyone time. Why?

I threw myself suddenly into the heather and slithered round. Jesus, I knew why he hadn't appeared. He'd done it to me again. He was a professional and the last thing a professional would do would be to expose himself on the brow of a hill with the sky behind. He knew I wasn't armed so there was no danger of being shot, but it was nevertheless something he would instinctively not do.

So if he wasn't behind me, he was either round to the sides or, just possibly, in front of me. I calculated how long I'd waited in the gulley. Was it long enough for him to have circled round? The sweat went cold on my forehead. There was just a chance he was below me on the hill waiting to catch a glimpse of my silhouette on the skyline. Waiting to pick me off.

I could see nothing against the charcoal backdrop but that was reassuring. For if I couldn't see him, he probably couldn't see me. I crawled on all fours up the slope. I had to take a gamble. I was a man on the run, a frightened man in a panic. He would not expect me to go straight back the way I'd come. The hunted quarry always keeps running; he does not stop and retrace his tracks into the arms of his pursuers. That was sheer stupidity. So that was what I did.

I ran back the way I'd come, shoulders arched, legs bent to reduce my height. Towards the top of the hill I took to the earth again and wriggled like an eel over the springy heather. The coarse stems ripped the skin on my hands but the pain only made me move faster. Just before the top I stopped and got to my knees. Wherever he was he'd see me now, I had no choice but to show myself. To see if the gamble had paid off.

I moved to a crouch, then straightened my knees and hurled myself upwards over the crest of the hill. The air immediately above me sizzled for an instant like a jet of super-heated steam and the crack of two pistol shots echoed behind me. Two bullets, two misses. I'd chosen the right direction.

I ran across the undulating field and started to scramble over the drystone wall again. A figure loomed up suddenly on the other side and my heart almost leaped out of my chest. It was Ronnie.

He lunged for me. I rolled over sideways and dropped back to the ground on the side I'd started from. Ronnie came over after me but he was slow. Maria had obviously not hit him hard enough to put him out for long, but he was still dazed, his reactions clumsy. I ran for the corner of the field, my legs shaky from the shock of seeing him. I vaulted the wall and hit the road running.

Dave was sixty or seventy yards away. He struck the road at almost the same time, cutting off the descent. He was fitter than I'd expected. Ronnie was behind me, clambering over the wall. He looked more alert now, recovering fast.

I sprinted up the road. They came after me and I realized that if I stayed on the road, there could only be one outcome. I was clearly visible on the ribbon of grey tarmac and well within range. One good pistol shot could bring me down. It didn't need to kill. They just had to wound me and then move in to finish me off.

I swerved sideways and jumped the gritstone wall that bordered the road. The ground fell away steeply on the other side and I tumbled down straight into a patch of bogland. Icy water seeped through my jacket and trousers and the shock took my breath away. I pulled myself to my feet and scrambled across the pools of stagnant water. I was soaked down my left side and the cold was already penetrating my bones. My feet squelched in water-filled shoes.

I stumbled over rounded tussocks of grass which emerged from the bog like dumplings floating on stew. I tried to keep to the grass, avoiding the pools and beds of sodden moss in between, but in my hurry I kept slipping off. By the time I reached dry moorland my trousers were drenched almost to the knees.

Dave had come over the wall behind me but Ronnie was nowhere to be seen. I looked all around. I was terrified enough when I knew where they were, but more so when I didn't. I scanned the hillside in a panic. I'd dropped down into a deep valley: a mistake. I should have stayed higher, kept the two of them below me, or at least on the same level. Now they could easily outflank me if they chose to stay on the valley sides.

There was a farmhouse further down but I didn't give much for my chances of reaching it. There would be people, a telephone, but Dave would almost certainly get there before me, and even if he didn't, I wouldn't have time to ring anyone. Dave wouldn't wait quietly outside because it was someone else's house; he'd come in after me and complete the job.

It was raining heavily now. Even without my immersion in the bog I'd have been soaked through by the downpour. My clothes felt heavy with water, my legs even heavier with exhaustion. But I ran on, pure terror keeping my heart and lungs in overdrive.

Dave tracked me doggedly across the valley for five or ten minutes. It was his persistence that was particularly scary. I knew he would keep going until he collapsed. I saw Ronnie then. He was higher up but much further back than Dave, with a lot of ground to make up. It gave me a tiny grain of comfort. He was flagging.

I recognized suddenly where I was: the slope where Richard Sutton had crashed. I could see the road twisting along the valley edge above me and the sinister outline of the Iron Age fortress Carl Wark behind. The wheel has turned full circle, I thought, with a sudden premonition of death. It was here that Richard Sutton died, here on these stormswept moors beneath that lowering fortress. And perhaps here, too, I would die.

Then I saw something else. Headlights on the road. My first thought was that Maria had found help and come back. Then I realized she wouldn't have had time. But it was still a car. If I could stop it, I had a chance of escaping. The car engine was revving high, coming fast up the hill from Hathersage. I summoned my last reserves of energy and scrambled up the incline. I almost fell to my knees at the top but recovered and ran down the road towards the car, waving my arms like a lunatic.

CHAPTER 18

The car swerved round the final bend and the headlights caught me full in the face. I could see nothing beyond the dazzling glare. I slowed, moving out into the middle of the road. The car turned a fraction and the full beam changed angle. I caught a glimpse of the car's shape, stubby, high off the road. It looked familiar. Something was wrong. I couldn't at first place what. Then in an instant it came to me. The engine note was still the same, the driver hadn't throttled back. Jesus Christ. He was coming for me.

I threw myself across the road and the car's slipstream blew me into the ditch on the far side. It was Jacqueline Sutton's Suzuki. My left shoulder felt as if it had been dislocated. I tried to move my arm. It hurt, but the joint was intact. I got to my knees. The fall had winded me and I could barely breathe. My windpipe seemed to have been rammed down into my lungs. I whooped for air, semi-paralyzed but knowing I had to move or they would end it all there in the ditch.

I forced myself to stand, then looked up the road. The Suzuki had skidded to a halt and a figure was getting out.

It was Charles Whitfield. He was alone. I wondered where Stuart Sutherland was. Whitfield raised his arms out horizontally in front of him, legs splayed. In the dark, with the rain teeming down, it was impossible to make out any detail, but I knew from his stance that he had a gun. His hand jerked before I could react and a streak of fire seared my left arm above the elbow. The force spun me round and into the mud bank behind. It came to me, with a numbing slowness, that I'd been shot.

There was no pain at first. That came a fraction later as I rolled sideways, instinctively moving to make the next shot harder. I clasped my left elbow in tight against my chest and pulled myself up the bank with my right arm.

Whitfield was coming for me. He should have stayed where he was and killed me from a distance but he was shortening the range instead. Perhaps he wanted to make absolutely sure, perhaps he wanted to gloat as he delivered the *coup de grâce*. Whatever it was, those few seconds saved my life.

I was over the top of the bank and out of sight of the road before he could loose off another shot. My left arm burned with an almost unbearable pain, as if the flesh had been branded with an iron. I ran for the top of the escarpment, stumbling over everything in my path. Once I fell and landed on my left side. My vision blacked out in agony and I almost passed out. But something in my subconscious, the instinct for survival, the willpower to overcome physical injury, drove me on.

I'd been unbelievably foolish. Ronnie hadn't dropped back in the pursuit because he was tired. He'd dropped back to go to the BMW. I'd noticed earlier there was a carphone on the dashboard. He'd used it to call Whitfield. I should have realized when I saw the headlights coming up the hill. It was nearly two in the morning. There was no traffic on these moors at that time of night.

I scrambled into the cover of a few boulders and looked back. Dave and Ronnie had reached Whitfield and they appeared to be discussing something in the middle of the road. If Ronnie had been back to the BMW he would have seen that my car was gone, assuming Maria had reached it. They would know that meant she'd gone for help and that before long the police would be out here. I hoped they'd consider it futile to pursue me further, but at the same time I knew they couldn't afford to let me go. For them, it was worth taking a chance, worth taking a gamble they could kill me quickly before anyone else arrived. There were three of them now. And I was wounded. I knew what I'd have done in Whitfield's place.

They broke apart and spread out, three of them in a line. Then they headed for the bank. My heart sank into my guts. They were coming after me.

I slipped my hand inside my jacket and cautiously touched my left arm. My shirt was sticky with blood and the flesh underneath like jelly. I didn't probe very far, it was too painful, but it didn't feel like a serious wound. I knew nothing about gunshot injuries but I suspected the bullet had passed straight through. The injury itself wouldn't be fatal; loss of blood certainly would if I didn't staunch the flow.

There was no time now. I had to find a sanctuary before doing anything about the blood. I scrambled back through the boulders and traversed the hillside below Higger Tor. In front of me, rising steeply from the valley floor was Carl Wark.

I climbed the bank that protected its north western flank. On the top was a flattish plateau, littered with boulders. The Iron Age settlers had taken a natural outcrop and fortified its perimeters with huge rocks. At twelve hundred feet it dominated the broad valley to the east and south, itself overshadowed by the lowering crags of Higger Tor.

In daylight it was a stark, impressive feature on the landscape. At night it was eerie, primeval, almost mystic. The moon was hidden by black clouds, the rain was an impenetrable curtain and Carl Wark seemed to exude the evil spirits of the past.

I crossed the plateau, shielding my face from the driving wind and rain. The droplets were sharp as needles, scouring my exposed skin.

I took shelter in the lee of a boulder and pulled off my jacket. The exertion was taking its toll. My whole body felt leaden and I wanted only to lie down and sleep. I felt slightly faint but knew if I closed my eyes and succumbed to the temptation of rest I would never wake again.

My arm was getting worse. The blood had soaked my shirt to the wrist and dark fluid trickled out on to my hand. I risked a peep out. No sign yet of my pursuers. Taking a handkerchief from my pocket, I attempted to bind it around my upper arm using my good right hand and teeth to tie the knot. It was a general pain down my whole left side now, but when I tightened the handkerchief there was a localized jolt of white-hot heat and I knew I'd found the right spot. It was an ineffective bandage but good enough to cut down my blood loss. I hoped. How long I could last without fainting was another matter.

I put my jacket back on and peeked out again. A silhouette had appeared on the skyline and I recognized it as Ronnie. Then another appeared to his right. Whitfield. I crept away on all fours and silently dropped down into a crevasse on the southern side of the fort.

I had two obvious choices. I could hide somewhere and hope they didn't find me. Or I could run on. Neither appealed much. It was not a very big area to search and they would almost certainly find me if I stayed put. Yet running on was equally hazardous. I would have to climb down the escarpment, dangerous enough in the dark, even more so with only one arm. Then I would have to cross the open land at the base of the fort, presenting an easy target for a moderately good shot. And even if I got away, I was fairly sure they would quickly hunt me down on the exposed hillside. I simply didn't have the energy to keep ahead of them.

There was a third choice, too. I could remain on the fort and fight them. Not openly, that would have been suicidal, but stealthily, one by one. It was extremely risky but my only real hope of survival. I singled out Ronnie. In some ways he was the most dangerous of the three, but he was unarmed and the most reckless. Whitfield and Dave would be careful. Ronnie might just do something foolish.

I eased myself out of the crevasse and started to work round the perimeter towards Ronnie, worming through the boulders with my head kept low. I was shivering with the cold yet my injured arm was burning hot. I had to conserve what was left of my energy. I dropped into a cleft and concealed myself under an overhang. The edge fell away vertically below me. I waited.

They were searching the plateau systematically, Whitfield in the centre, Ronnie and Dave to the sides. I picked up a loose rock and weighed it in my hand. It should do the job, even on a skull as thick as Ronnie's. I stayed out of sight and listened. My ears became accustomed to the background roar of the elements and I waited for an extraneous sound to intrude.

It came faintly, but it was there. A shoe scraping on rock. I poked an eye out, keeping the white of my face well hidden. Ronnie was peering down into the jumble of boulders. I pulled back under the overhang and came out the other side. My head was level with Ronnie's feet. He was looking the other way. I pulled my arm back and hurled the rock. It hit the back of his head with a dull crack and Ronnie toppled forward. Forward into the black vortex where his scream was lost in the shrieking of the wind.

Whitfield and Dave heard it. They came running. Again I did what I thought they would least expect. I stayed where I was under the overhang, my heart pounding with shock. I had just killed a man. I hadn't intended to but it had happened nevertheless. My hands were trembling. Ronnie would have killed me without compunction but that did not justify taking his life. I would have that on my conscience for the rest of my days. If I lasted that long.

Whitfield and Dave were near enough for me to hear their conversation.

'Jesus,' Dave said. 'That was Ronnie.'

'Look over the edge. He may not have fallen far.'

'The bastard must have pushed him over.'

'You see him?'

'No. He's dead, boss. He's dead.' Dave's voice was rising in panic.

'Shut up,' Whitfield said.

'Let's get off this hill, boss. The girl will be back with the Old Bill.'

'I said shut up.'

'We can still get away.'

'McLean's on the edge somewhere. You check that way.' Whitfield's voice was still calm but I could detect an undertone of anxiety.

'Look, boss, let's leave him. We've still got time.'

'We don't leave until we've finished him off.'

'He's a cunning bastard.'

'He's wounded, he won't get far. Now check the edge and shut up.'

They moved away. I leaned back in my hiding place and took several deep breaths. My head felt light. I couldn't seem to get enough oxygen into my lungs. I could remain there but Whitfield was thorough. There were only so many possible places I could be and he'd work his way round all of them until he found me. And they still had two guns. I would have to tackle them, keep my advantage of surprise. I decided to go for Whitfield first. If I got him, Dave might panic and make a run for it.

I gave them time to split up before venturing out and checking their whereabouts. They were about fifty yards apart, probing the labyrinth of boulders which fortified the edge of the plateau. Not for the first time that night I was glad they didn't have torches. They were being careful. I had already killed one of them. They weren't going to let themselves be taken by surprise.

However, they were being just a little too methodical. They'd already searched the inside of the fortress so were assuming I had to be hiding somewhere round the sides.

They were expecting the threat to come from that direction, not from behind. It was a miscalculation I intended to put to good use.

I climbed out from beneath the overhang and lay down on my right side. Then I slithered away from the edge, using my legs and one good arm to drag myself along the ground. It was hard work. The earth was uneven and scattered with sharp gritstone outcrops. I wriggled through narrow gaps, over low boulders and sometimes underneath interlocking slabs. By the time I reached the grassy expanse in the centre of the fort my side felt as if it had been shredded in a cheese grater.

Whitfield was thirty yards away, a fuzzy outline of black against the lighter shade of the clouds. Occasionally he disappeared, dropping out of sight to search one of the ledges just below the top. I crossed the plateau, still on my side so I merged into the earth, and approached Whitfield from behind.

A few yards from the edge I stopped. I'd cut in at a slight angle. Whitfield was to my right, coming towards me. There were no loose stones to hand so I would have to get in close. It made more sense to let him come to me. I was in a crack between two low rocks. I waited, staring upwards at the torrents of rain.

He stepped right over the crack. I reached up with my right arm and pulled his legs away from under him. He fell headlong with a grunt of surprise. I was on my feet before he could recover. I kicked his hand as hard as I could and his gun clattered away across the boulders and out into space. Then I lashed out at Whitfield, but he had rolled sideways and was nearly on his feet.

I kicked out again but my strength had drained away. He dodged the blow and caught my foot in his hands. He twisted and flung me backwards. I took the fall on my right shoulder. The impact still jarred my wounded arm. The pain was like an electric shock. I shook my head to clear the dizziness but my reactions were too slow. Whitfield was on top of me, so close I could feel the heat of his breath.

His hands clamped my neck and squeezed. I choked for air. I took one of his wrists in my hand and tried to force it away. He squeezed tighter. His teeth were gritted, his face a mask of ruthless determination. He was going to kill me with his bare hands.

I reached up and suddenly jabbed my thumb and forefinger into his eye sockets. He cried out and released my neck. I hit him in the jaw with my elbow and twisted out from under him. I no longer felt the pain in my arm. Staying alive was my only concern.

Whitfield came for me again. He had every advantage. Not just because I was injured. It was a mental advantage too. He was a violent man. The aggression I found repugnant was a natural part of his make-up. He would have no moral qualms about killing me.

I retreated to the next boulder as Whitfield rushed forwards. He feinted to my right, then hit me hard on the left arm, directly on the gunshot wound. I yelled and clutched the arm. Whitfield grinned and hit me again, the same place only harder. I tried in vain to protect myself, stumbling away backwards, but prevented from retreating too far by the sheer drop behind me.

He was almost enjoying himself. I could see it in his face. He rushed me. I dived sideways and fell into a cleft. A jagged outcrop slashed my jacket and grazed my back. Whitfield kicked down at me, aiming for my head but I was still rolling. His shoe caught the edge of my ear and he overbalanced and fell in on top of me. I pushed him away with my knees and stumbled to my feet.

Dave was running towards us, shouting. Somewhere in the distance I could hear a high-pitched siren but it barely registered before Whitfield was moving in again. There was blood in my mouth, my left arm was a soggy pulp and my whole body sagged like a collapsed marionette. Dave was going to shoot me. If Whitfield didn't throw me over the edge first.

I fended off another punch but Whitfield got a grip on my waist. He pushed and I started to tumble backwards.

It was the final moment. I was going over the edge. I flung my arm around Whitfield's neck and pulled him with me. His body flailed over as we fell and I landed on top of him on a projecting slab some ten feet below the top. His head cracked on the rock and he went limp against me. I lay in a heap sobbing for breath. I waited for the bullet to come from above.

A minute passed, perhaps two or three. Nothing happened. I extricated myself from Whitfield. He was unconscious but still breathing. Slowly I climbed back into the fortress. Dave had gone. Lights were coming across the moorland. Beyond them, above the road, blue lights revolved in the sky.

I stumbled across the plateau and down the low north slope of the fort. The lights seemed to take an eternity to reach me. There were several figures. Something was wrong with my eyes, everything was blurred. Then two figures came into focus. Maria and Chris Strange.

I staggered towards them. 'Oh Michael, Michael.' Maria came running. But before she could reach me the ground disappeared beneath my feet. I fell forward into the heather and my world was obliterated in a black shroud.

CHAPTER 19

A young staff nurse in a pink uniform and white cap came in and started to clear away the plates on the table in front of me.

'Did you enjoy your lasagne, Mr McLean?'

'Is that what it was?' I looked at the congealing yellow and brown remains on the plate. 'Give it a decent burial, will you?'

The nurse smiled thinly, the way hospital staff do when they're trying to humour a dangerous psychopath.

'You've a visitor outside. If you're up to it.'

'Who is it?'

'The police.'

'I'm not up to it,' I said.

The door opened and Chris Strange came in. His face was drawn, his eyes bloodshot. Even his moustache seemed to droop with fatigue. He pulled out the chair from behind the door and brought it to the bedside. He waited for the nurse to plump up the pillows behind me, then sat down.

'Not too long, Sergeant,' the nurse said. 'He's lost a lot of blood.'

'I'll be especially nice to him,' Strange said, looking at me like a wolf contemplating a consignment of lamb chops.

He turned to watch the nurse leave the room, then studied me without saying anything. My left arm was bandaged and in a sling. My whole body ached as if it had been pummelled by an over-enthusiastic masseur.

'You look the way I feel,' Strange said. 'You OK?'

He was being nice to me. I didn't believe it.

'Not bad. The bullet went straight through the muscle.'

'Pity he didn't aim a few inches further in.'

I knew it couldn't last.

'How's Maria?' I said.

'OK. She's got a lot of guts, that girl.'

'I know. Where is she?'

'Home. We wanted her to have a check-up but she said she was OK.' He glanced around. 'You got anything to eat in here? Grapes or something.'

'You missed lunch?'

'And breakfast.'

'It's usually the visitors who bring the grapes.'

'You're lucky I didn't bring a warrant.'

'What happened?'

Strange removed his coat and dumped it across the foot of the bed. His suit underneath was damp and crumpled like used Kleenex.

'I just spent half the night on Carl Wark in the pissing rain. Me, couple of DCs, the ambulance boys and a few sheep. I'm telling you, the sheep can keep it,' he said with feeling.

'You get Whitfield?'

'He wasn't going anywhere the state he was in. What happened to him?'

'I don't remember too clearly. I think he tripped and banged his head.'

'Oh yeah? And the guy at the bottom of the cliff? I suppose he tripped too.'

'Events are a little hazy.'

'Well, you'd better start remembering, McLean, because you're in deep shit.'

'Was he dead?'

'Who? The guy at the bottom? Two broken legs, a lot of bust ribs, fractured skull. A lucky bloke. He's down the corridor, Whitfield too, with a police guard on each door. When you're all up and about you'll be able to have after-noon tea together.'

'I'll look forward to that. There was a third man.'

'We picked him up near Fox House.'

'And Sutherland? You get to him?'

'He'd already gone when we got to his house.'

'He'll be out of the country by now.'

'The airport police pulled him in at Manchester. He was booked on the first flight to Geneva.'

'Was he alone?'

'Yes.'

I wondered if Alison knew what he'd been doing. 'A good night's work.'

'I'm only just starting.'

'Anyone charged yet?'

Strange grinned maliciously. He knew exactly what I meant.

'Yes. Which makes it all *sub judice*. Too bad, McLean. No story. Not unless you want a contempt charge added to the list.'

'List?'

'Of charges against you. It's pretty long already. With-holding evidence, obstructing the course of justice, assault . . .'

'Assault? Who did I assault?'

'Well, there's a couple of blokes down the corridor who don't look too well to me.'

'They were trying to kill me. You can't seriously be going to charge me?'

'Depends how much you cooperate.'

'I always cooperate, you know that.'

'You never cooperate, McLean. Now, I want some answers so don't piss me about.'

'What do you want to know? Maria must have told you all about last night.'

'She made a statement, yes. But there are one hell of a lot of gaps she can't fill in.'

'You pulled in Nigel Sinclair?'

'Down at headquarters.'

'Getting anywhere?'

'He's proving pretty talkative.'

'Is he now? And Sutherland?'

Strange screwed up his face in distaste, as if he'd taken a mouthful of salt. 'Sutherland,' he said, 'has a very good solicitor.'

'I thought he might. He going to slip away?'

'Not if I can help it. And nor are you. I'm supposed to be asking you questions, not the other way round. And no bullshit, McLean, or I'll hang you out the window by your bad arm.'

'I love your bedside manner. You must practise a lot.'

'Start at the beginning.'

'Seems as good a place as any. How much do you know already?'

'Never mind how much I know. Just give me what you know.'

'OK. Let's take Charles Whitfield first, a gambler, specu- lator in shares, an asset stripper. He takes risks, buys and sells companies in a small way, takes his profits where he can, sometimes not very much, sometimes a lot. He lives flamboyantly, spends freely, stretches his resources to the limit.'

'I get the picture,' Strange said.

'A couple of years ago a company he owns, Wheatfields plc, acquired a business in the Midlands called Harman Engineering. Metal bashers in Wolverhampton. I don't know the details but the bare facts are on file at Companies House. His partner in the acquisition was Stuart Sutherland's family business, Sutherland Cutlery.'

'They knew each other?'

'Sure. Don't ask me exactly how, but there were common links. Sutherland's wife, Alison, was a close friend of Jacqueline Sutton's and Jacqueline was one of Whitfield's old flames. There was also Nigel Sinclair. At the time of the acquisition he was finance director of RPS Trading, but a few years earlier he'd been finance director of Wheatfields. There were all sorts of ways Sutherland and Whitfield could have met.'

'This is all a long time ago. What's it got to do with now?'

I adjusted my bandaged arm on the top of the blankets. The painkillers couldn't quite remove the dull throb of pain from the bullet wound.

'The merger turned out to be a disaster. The engineering firm was a complete turkey. Sutherland and Whitfield couldn't sell it, couldn't recoup what they'd paid for it. Sutherland's firm, in any case, was struggling to survive. They were both close to going bust. So they came up with a plan to bail themselves out with Richard Sutton's money.'

'To put into the company?'

I shook my head. 'I doubt it. I reckon their businesses were beyond saving. It was simple embezzlement. They were going to disappear with the money, probably abroad.'

'And that's where Sinclair came in.'

'Yes, Whitfield's old pal. He was persuaded to join them. He was perfectly placed to fiddle the accounts. And the recycling plant made it easier.'

'Why?'

'You ever tried to embezzle money?'

Strange said drily: 'Don't get much chance in my job. More's the pity.'

'I don't think it's all that easy. If you're at the top of the company it must help, but even then the web of deception you have to spin could ensnare you. In a company like RPS you'd have to change so many figures, doctor so many accounts, it would be easy to overlook something and get caught.

'But the recycling plant was a one-off major project with specific accounts and fewer figures to alter. It was also being partially funded by the European Coal and Steel Community, which meant large sums were coming in over a relatively short time, but not necessarily going out for several months.'

'They decided to steal it.'

'Register a shell company with a name almost identical to the legitimate contractors on the recycling plant and siphon off the funds.'

'Registered where?'

'London.'

'Why not some offshore company through nominees, all untraceable?'

'You think Sutton wouldn't have noticed payments being made to Jersey or Liechtenstein or wherever? They got away with it for eight months because he thought it was all above board. They wouldn't have lasted two weeks with an off-shore operation.'

'But Sutton did rumble them.'

'The day he died. He confronted Sinclair. Sinclair contacted Whitfield and Sutherland and Whitfield got his two goons . . .'

'Sellars and Hampsten?'

'Is that what they're called? Ronnie and Dave. They knocked him off the same day, before he could tell anyone else.'

'How?'

'I don't know for sure, but I've a theory which fits the

facts.' I told him what I'd told Maria in the Chinese restaurant.'

When I'd finished, Strange said: 'Any proof?'

I gave a sardonic smile. 'They're pros. Everything's circumstantial. But they did it, all right. They as good as admitted it to me.'

Strange took off his jacket and went to the radiator under the window. He felt the pipes, then draped the jacket over them.

'Still damp from the moors,' he said. 'Thanks to you, I've ruined my best suit.'

'I'd hate to see the others,' I said.

'We got a warrant last night. Woke a magistrate at one-thirty after your friend Miss Wells phoned me. Searched Sutton's house for some photocopied accounts she said were there.'

'You find them?'

'Just a few ashes in the kitchen sink. Miss Wells said you had the photocopies to start with.'

I could see what was coming.

'You asked Sutherland and Sinclair about them?' I asked.

'Uh-uh.' Strange shook his head. 'Let's stay where we were. Where did *you* get those photocopies?'

'I don't think that's important, Chris.'

'I'll decide what's important. Where did you get them?'

I conceded. 'From Stephanie Myers.'

'Ah, now we're getting somewhere. How come she had them?'

'Sutton left them with her the night he died. He'd been at her house at Lodge Moor.'

'Why'd he leave them there?'

'Well, he wasn't going to leave that kind of dynamite lying around the office.'

'He could have taken them home.'

'Stephanie's was safer. No one knew about her.'

'And did Myers give them to you?'

'In a manner of speaking.'

'You mean you nicked them.'

I didn't say anything.

'Add burglary to the list,' Strange said. 'You knew they were important evidence.'

'I couldn't be sure.'

'But you didn't come to the police.'

'I don't like to waste your time.'

'You're always wasting my time. It's what you do best, McLean. Stephanie Myers was murdered for those photo-copies, wasn't she?'

I nodded.

'But you already had them. Who did it? Our two friends?'

'Yes. Ronnie and Dave.'

'And did they set fire to the office?'

'Sutherland did that, to cover up the embezzlement by destroying the financial records.'

'But Sutton had already made copies.'

'Debbie Nolan made the copies. That's what secretaries do for their bosses.'

'And that's why she was murdered?'

'It was enough. She certainly knew what was on the photocopies. Whether she knew any more I can't tell. As the chairman's secretary she'd be privy to a lot of confidential financial information. Sutton may even have confided in her to some extent.

'Debbie made the mistake of letting slip something to Sinclair. He told the others. They didn't know the photo-copies existed. They thought they'd burnt everything. It took them a while to work out where they were, that's how I got them first. Sinclair knew they weren't at the office. Whitfield invited himself to stay with Jacqueline and no doubt checked the house. They weren't there. That left Stephanie's.

'They went to see her. She was greedy. She realized the photocopies were valuable, although maybe not why. She tried to put the screws on them so they tortured her to find out where the photocopies were, then killed her.'

'And Nolan? Who killed her, Sellars and Hampsten again?' I nodded. 'You got proof for any of this?'

'No. That's why I didn't come to you.'

'Bollocks. You didn't come to me because you thought you had a nice little exclusive lined up and you didn't want to share it with anyone.'

'What does Sinclair say?'

'He's being helpful.' Strange couldn't stop himself smirking.

'You knew, or had guessed most of that already, hadn't you?' I said.

'Just cross-checking. In case Sinclair left out any salient details.'

'Or I did.'

'You have a habit of leaving out salient details, remember? Like when you rang me yesterday.'

'I wanted to be sure of my facts first.'

Strange gave a snort, part disgust, part disbelief. 'Spare me all that journalistic crap. We both know what you were doing.'

Strange looked around the hospital room. It had grey walls and brown lino on the floor. There was a chipped washbasin in one corner. It had the uniform drabness of an army barracks; institutionalized, impersonal, sterile.

I studied his lined face. His moustache was still damp from the rain. He was no intellectual, but he must have seen most things in his twenty-odd years on the force. Policemen get good at guessing and not much ever surprises them.

'What did they have, six, seven million already?' Strange said. 'Yet they killed three people to get more.' He turned his eyes back to mine. 'Why?'

'You know many rich people? Really rich,' I said.

'You don't get too many down Snig Hill,' Strange said drily.

'They've got a mentality. A sort of pathological greed. And they live expensively. Six million wasn't enough for them to sacrifice everything they had, to assume new identities and disappear. They wanted more.

'Sutton had to go because he found out what was happening. It was risky, but they made it look enough like an accident to fool nearly everyone. It was even quite a good move. With Sutton out of the way it was easier getting the rest of the money. They might well have got away with it; it was worth the risk.'

'What about the others? Nolan and Myers.'

'Unforseeable consequences. But they'd gone beyond the point of turning back. If you kill one person to protect yourself it's only a short step to kill a couple of others. Especially when you've hired two professionals to do the dirty work. Are Ronnie and Dave going to squawk?'

'We're working on them. If they see they're going to carry the can for the others, they might loosen up a bit.'

Strange went to the window and stared out. He looked very tired. The glass pane was smeared with trickles of rain.

'It's a shitty world, isn't it?' he said quietly. 'Full of shitty little people doing dirty things for dirty motives. Everything becomes corrupted. Even the good things get drowned in the never ending swirl of sewage. Then someone like me has to shovel up the filth and pretend the world's a cleaner place for it, when we all know I'll have to start right over again the next day. And I carry on doing it because each morning I hope it's going to be different. I keep hoping that just once in my life I'll be surprised.'

'You're getting sentimental,' I said.

'All cops are sentimental. How do you think we stick it?'

Strange picked his jacket off the radiator and put it on.

'You going to recover the money?' I asked.

'Do you care?' Strange said.

'No.'

'Nor do I.' He straightened his tie.

'And the charges against me? You going to make them stick?'

'Hell, yes. It's time someone stamped on you, McLean.

Just because you're a reporter doesn't mean you've the God-given right to interfere in police business. You overstep the mark, you expect to pay the price.'

He lifted up his raincoat and threw it over his arm. 'I'll be back with a stenographer to get a full statement.' He went to the door.

'About last night, Chris,' I said. 'If you hadn't got there when you did, I'd have been dead. Thanks.'

He turned briefly. 'Don't get nice on me all of a sudden, McLean. I prefer you awkward and obnoxious.'

'Feeling's mutual,' I said.

I was trying unsuccessfully to read the newspaper with one hand when there was a knock on the door and Jacqueline Sutton came in. I was surprised. She waited hesitantly in the doorway.

'Do you mind?'

'Come in.' I waved her to the chair by the bed.

'I brought you these.' She put a box of chocolates on the bedside table and sat down. She crossed her legs. She was wearing a grey two-piece suit and pink blouse with a double row of pearl buttons down the front. There were shadows under her eyes.

'I met Sergeant Strange at Reception. He said you were well enough for visitors.'

'I was before he showed up.'

'Oh. Well, look, if . . .'

'I'm fine,' I said. I smiled at her. I was glad she wasn't wearing black any more, it was a good sign. 'It's kind of you to come.'

'It's nothing. They told me you'd been shot. The police, that is.'

'Just a graze.'

'I'm sorry.'

'Nothing to do with you.'

'I feel partly responsible. They said you were at my house last night.'

'That doesn't make it your fault.'

'No, but . . .' She stopped. 'Who did it? Charles?' I nodded. 'He was my guest. He came up after Richard's death. To support me, he said. We were close once. He had me fooled.'

I said gently: 'The police tell you everything?'

'I think so. I was up most of the night, "helping with inquiries", I think they call it.' She looked down at her hands, cupped together in her lap, then back at me. 'I suppose it's all true.'

I wondered which bits she found hard to believe, which bits she didn't want to believe. About Whitfield, about Sinclair, about her husband.

'I'm afraid so.'

'And they did it all for money. Richard, that poor girl Debbie, the other one.'

She couldn't bring herself to say Stephanie Myers's name. I couldn't blame her. It must have been hard to accept that the man she loved went elsewhere to fulfil his sexual needs. In the end, even an exceptional man like Richard Sutton turned out to have feet of clay. Maybe they always do.

'And I thought I knew him. I thought Charles was a friend. Stuart too.'

'It's easy to be wrong about people,' I said. 'At one time I thought you might be part of it.'

She lifted her head sharply. 'Did you? Yes, I suppose that might have been a logical conclusion.'

'You genuinely wanted my help, didn't you? That afternoon I came for tea.'

'I didn't understand what was happening. I had to ask someone. I'm sorry now I got you involved.'

'I was involved already.'

'Where do you think the money is now?'

'Probably in a Swiss bank account. Will it stop the recycling plant.'

'Not if I can help it.' There was determination in her voice. 'We'll make up the shortfall from other sources.'

'You taking over your husband's job?'

'No. But his shareholding passed to me. I think it entitles me to a seat on the board.'

I watched her. She was recovering quickly, making herself do something instead of letting the whole sordid business bowl her over.

'Picking up the pieces,' I said.

'Picking up the pieces,' she echoed.

She stood up. 'I saw Alison Sutherland this morning. You never told me you used to be married to her.'

'It was a long time ago. She OK?'

'The doctor's put her under sedation. It was a bit of a shock for her.'

'I'll go and see her when I'm out of here.'

'She'd like that.'

'Thanks for coming.'

She nodded and smiled briefly as she opened the door. Maria came in behind her, almost bumping into her. They looked at each other.

'I was just going,' Jacqueline said. She slipped out gracefully.

Maria closed the door behind her. 'Who was that?'

'Richard Sutton's widow.'

'Really?' Maria raised an eyebrow. 'She didn't waste much time coming to see you.'

'They're lining up down the corridor to take turns soothing my heated brow. But you get priority,' I said.

'I think I'll pass on that one,' Maria said drily. 'But it's nice to know you're recovering.'

'Must be all the visitors.'

I looked at her. If the previous evening had left any marks I couldn't see them. She was in trousers and a loose Greenpeace sweat top with a dolphin on the chest. No make-up or jewellery. I could have looked at her for a long time.

I held out my good arm and clasped her hand briefly. 'I'm sorry, Maria, I really am. For last night.'

'It wasn't your fault.'

'It was.'

'OK, it was,' she said and smiled. 'How bad's your arm?'

'Clean wound. I should be out in a couple of days.'

She pulled up the chair and sat down. She was holding a plastic Tesco bag which looked familiar to me. She put it on the floor.

'And you?' I said. 'You coping?'

She nodded, but I knew it would take a long time for her to get over what had happened the previous night.

'You ever going to forgive me for getting you involved?'

'I might think about it.'

'If you hadn't got to Strange they'd have shot me.'

'I thought they did.'

'He's just been in. Strange. He's threatening to charge me.'

'With what?'

'A whole list of things.'

'Well, he wasn't very happy last night when I told him what'd happened. I won't tell you what he said about you in case you have a relapse.'

'He wasn't too happy just now, either.'

'Can you blame him?'

'No, perhaps not.'

'Is he serious about the charges?'

'Maybe. But I reckon the Crown Prosecutor will throw them out. Too much of an embarrassment to charge me.'

Maria sat back in the chair. 'Give me the whole story, Michael.'

I told her everything I knew, including all the wild guesses. She listened in silence, occasionally prompting me with a question.

At the end she said: 'Is there enough evidence to prove all that?'

'I don't know. Sinclair seems to have made some kind of confession. They'll get them all for the theft of the money and trying to kill us last night. The other murders I'm not sure about. It depends how incriminating Sinclair's evidence is. Everything against Ronnie and Dave and Whit-field is fairly circumstantial. But it might be enough for a jury.'

'What about Stuart Sutherland?'

'He kept his hands pretty clean. But if it comes to the crunch, the others will shop him. If one goes down, they all will.'

Maria pursed her lips thoughtfully. 'Michael, some-thing's been bothering me. You know the other night, when you slept on my sofa?'

Something in her tone made me wary. 'Ye-es.'

'You said you stayed to reassure me. So I'd know you were safe.'

'Yes.'

'That wasn't quite true, was it? You stayed because you knew those two thugs would be waiting for you at your flat.'

'Ah, I can explain . . .'

'If you'd told me the truth, I wouldn't have gone round to your place yesterday evening, they wouldn't have caught me and last night wouldn't have happened.'

'I'll make it up to you, Maria, I will.'

'You, McLean, are a dirty rotten liar.'

'Not all the time. You have to make allowances. I'm a very sick man.'

'Well, at least that's true.'

'I mean my arm. Look, when I come out of here, why don't I come round for a bit and show you what an honest, trustworthy sort of bloke I am.'

'"Come round for a bit"?'

'I'm going to need some home comforts.'

'Ring your mum, then.'

'She's not the same. I thought maybe I could convalesce at your house. I'd get better much quicker.'

'You seem to be doing fine at the moment.'

I tried to take her hand again. She pulled it away.

'And another thing,' she said. 'I forgot to mention it last night as we were otherwise engaged, but I got a letter at the office yesterday.'

I couldn't see where this was leading. 'And?'

'From the Inland Revenue.'

I groaned. 'Not about my accounts?'

'The Inspector wants to see you on Thursday.'

'Can't you tell them I died in hospital?'

'This is the Inland Revenue we're dealing with here, Michael. For the taxman death is never an excuse.'

I lay back in the pillows. My arm had suddenly started hurting again.

'The injustice of it all. I'm nearly killed by a bunch of psychopaths, I can't use my exclusive story because it's *sub judice*, I'm threatened with half the offences on the statute book by an irate detective-sergeant and now this, the most devastating blow.'

'I'm sure you'll cope. Tax dodgers are usually sent to open prisons.'

'What! They can't possibly send me down, can they?'

'That depends how convincing your explanations to the Inspector are.'

A sudden horrible thought came to me. 'But you'll be there with me, won't you?'

Maria shook her head. 'You're on your own this time, sunshine.'

She stood up.

'Hang on a minute.'

She picked up the Tesco bag and dumped it on the bed.

'What's this?'

'Recognize them? All your receipts and invoices. The ones you dumped on me. I'm afraid I didn't have time to sort through them all. I was too busy being thrown off Stanage Edge. But as you've got all this time in bed, you'll be able to do it yourself, won't you?'

'Maria, look . . .'

''Bye. Enjoy yourself.'

She smiled and gave a little wave, then went out. I was left staring at the back of the door. I tipped the plastic bag up on the bed. Bits of screwed-up paper and wads of invoices cascaded out on to the blanket. I gazed at them bleakly. Boy, do I hate accountants.